Kept Men
and
Other Erotic Stories

By
Jonathan Asche

STARbooks
PRESS
Herndon, VA

Other books by Jonathan Asche available from STARbooks Press:

Moneyshots

Mindjacker

The following stories in this collection have been published previously in a slightly different form:

"The Feast of Monte Villa" previously published by *Mandate*, August 1994.

"Jack's Bounty" previously published by *Torso*, September 1994, as "Undercover Action."

"The Center Ring" previously published by *Indulge*, issue 001, 1994.

"The Vertel Project" previously published by *In Touch for Men*, Issue 214, 1995.

"Forbidden Forest" previously published by *Playguy*, December 1995.

"Cheap Motels" previously published by *In Touch for Men*, Issue 226, 1996

"11:30" previously published by *Mandate*, October 1996

"The Jealousy Game" previously published by *Mandate*, March 1998, as "3-Way Trick."

"The Transformation" previously published by *Inches*, September 1998, as "Ride a Horse Cock"

"Shared Secrets" previously published by *Playguy*, April 2002

"Nocturnal Admissions" previously published by *Playguy*, December 2002

"Reborn in Vinyl" previously published by *Honcho*, January 2005, as "My Life in Vinyl"

"Mr. Sheppard's Son" previously published by *Honcho*, January 2005, as "The Boss's Son"

"The Catch" previously published by *Honcho*, May 2007

"The Go-Between" previously published by *Honcho*, September 2007

"Sex Riot" previously published by *Honcho*, August 2008

"Pagan Moon" first appeared on the Internet, 1996

Contents

Introduction

Harold Robbins once said that next to masturbation, writing was the most fun one could have alone. I agree, though the activities need not be mutually exclusive. Writing porn allows you to combine the two, albeit not simultaneously (I could never type one-handed, and I hate a sticky keyboard besides). Many a story idea has formed from fantasies I've had while jacking off, and there have been plenty of masturbation breaks while writing those stories.

It's fitting, then, that I first realized my desire to write around the same time I'd discovered masturbation – and the works of Harold Robbins. Being what some might term "socially awkward" (or what my classmates termed "a dork"), I had grown accustomed to my own company and consequently learned to enjoy solitary pursuits. I would read, listen to music, and, yes, jerk off. At the time, I was in college studying journalism, a major chosen at the urging of my parents, who thought – ironically, as it now turns out – that working for a newspaper would be a more stable career path than my stated ambition of becoming a bestselling novelist. Realizing my parents might be right after all, I decided to throw myself into reporting.

I was fifteen when I bought my first Harold Robbins novel, from a discount drug store in Petal, Mississippi. It was *Dreams Die First* about the rise and fall of a men's magazine publisher. I remember little about the actual story. What made an impression was *Dreams Die First* had the most explicit sex scenes I'd read outside of the *Penthouse Letters*. The main character, Gareth Brendan, was bisexual. His encounters with men were few but Robbins nevertheless described them in the same unflinching detail as the hetero sex. Those sections of the book were re-read so often that I nearly memorized them.

From that moment on I read every Harold Robbins book I could get my hands on. It was a dream come (or is that cum?) true:

stroking material disguised as real novels. From this dream come true a new dream was born: I wanted to be the next Harold Robbins.

There were more than a few false starts, a couple unpublished novels written before I turned twenty-one, and a stack of rejection letters. In 1986, after receiving a particularly harsh critique from a book agent, to whom I paid an $80 "readers fee" for the privilege, I turned my back on writing fiction. At the time I was in college studying journalism, a major chosen at the urging of my parents, who thought – ironically, as it now turns out – that working for a newspaper would be a more stable career choice than my stated ambition of becoming a bestselling novelist. Thinking my parents might be right after all, I decided to throw myself into reporting.

There was only one problem with this plan: I hated being a reporter. Even as my news stories received praise, getting the information to write them – chasing down sources, convincing them to talk to me, struggling to ask the right questions, struggling harder to write down their answers accurately – was a daily hell. My problem, I realized much too late, was I wanted people to like me, a bad quality to have if you're supposed to be asking a city manager about misappropriation of city funds or a prominent businessman for comments about his son's arrest. I was further hampered by the fact that I was easily intimidated by authority figures, especially those licensed to carry a gun. The county sheriff, the chief of police – even a beat cop – could walk all over me.

Wanting to be liked is also one of the reasons why I refused to admit I was gay until I was twenty-eight years old. The other reason is I'm a chickenshit. That I clung to my denial for so long amazes me now. I was making up movie vehicles for Barbra Streisand while in junior high school – whom was I kidding? Of course, there were other clues: *Playgirl* was always more interesting to me than *Playboy*; I had to force myself not to stare when in a locker room shower; and in my teens, I'd developed a preoccupation with men's packages, so much so that I became distracted during an early driving lesson with my father when I spotted a young, tough looking guy with a particularly large basket walking nearby. Still, I told myself I wasn't gay, employing many of the same excuses that panicked parents use when a son or daughter comes out to them: it's just a phase, I'll grow out of it, I'm just confused. I even convinced myself that my fantasies of gay sex were only that – fantasies. It didn't mean I was gay. I was kidding myself, of course. But, the idea that I was gay terrified me. The verbal cruelty of classmates had drummed it into my head that there was nothing worse than being a "fag" (a more shameful branding than being deemed a "pussy"). Denying who I was seemed the easier, safer path. Only it wasn't.

It was during the early 1990s, one of the bleakest periods in my life, that I started writing gay porn. At the time I was living in Alabama, working as an editor at a small daily paper, trying to keep my secret from my largely homophobic co-workers and terrified they might learn of my weekend trips to gay bars in neighboring cities (where no one knew me). In 1993, I submitted my first story, "The Best Man," about a groom being seduced by his best man on the eve of his wedding, to *Torso* magazine. A few weeks later it came back, rejected. But, the editor had offered me a second chance: revise the ending and show it to him again. In the version rejected by *Torso*, the story ended with the groom going through with his heterosexual nuptials, leaving his best man behind. Changing the ending, so the groom ditches his bride and runs off with his hot best man, got me my first acceptance letter. Instead of becoming the next Harold Robbins, I became Jonathan Asche, erotic writer.

A few years and many published stories later, I moved to Atlanta and, for the first time, began living life as an out gay man. There was the initial letdown of discovering that life amongst my fellow homosexuals wasn't the party I'd imagined; Atlanta's gay community didn't greet me with a free cocktail and a blowjob. In time, though, I was happier ... and was bought a few drinks and got blown a few times, too.

Unlike my sexuality, my writing was easy to keep in the closet. In fact, it made the closet bearable. While I still went searching for sex in neighboring cities, it was on the page that I truly – and safely – explored my sexuality.

Kept Men and Other Erotic Stories is sort of a record of my sexual growth. For instance, while I had no problem explicitly describing blowjobs, rimming and fucking, it was only after coming out of the closet that I felt comfortable writing in the first person. The earlier stories ("The Feast of Monte Villa," "The Transformation,"

"The Center Ring") often have more fantastical storylines. "The Vertel Project," with its hunky mad doctor seeking to turn a fag-basher on to gay sex, is borderline camp. When I met the man who later became my husband, I explored the struggles of long-term, monogamous relationships ("The Jealousy Game," "Shared Secrets").

Just as couples explore new things to keep their sex lives interesting, I tried my hand at writing no-holes-barred raunch ("Reborn in Vinyl," "The Go-Between," "Sex Riot"). Readers will also notice a fondness on my part for detailing certain acts, rimming and cum eating chief among them. The latter actually got me scolded by one editor at *In Touch for Men*, who reminded me that stories had to reflect the safest of safe sex practices. Other magazines weren't so strict about swallowing a load but all insisted on characters wearing condoms unless the story was clearly set pre-AIDS, a policy I don't disagree with. I can certainly testify to the fact that porn is one of the primary places homosexuals get their sexual education. Hence, most of characters in the stories included here don a rubber before fucking.

A few stories are exclusive to this collection. "Crossing the Line" was inspired by a weekend stay with business acquaintances, an older couple, who apparently hoped for more adventurous visitors than my husband and I. Shortly after our arrival, one of them asked, in a voice loaded with innuendo: "So are you two *monogamous?*" Yes we are, but my husband and I did acknowledge to each other that had we been wired differently, we wouldn't have minded playing with these guys who, in their fifties, were quite hot. "Crossing the Line" is what might have happened had my husband and I been "wired differently." "T.M.I." is inspired by this same couple, albeit indirectly. Though neither of the two men was much for self-censorship, one in particular had to share whatever came to his mind. No topic was too personal or too embarrassing to discuss. I'm sure had he hooked up with a twenty-something stud he would regale all who cared to listen – as well as those who didn't – with the intimate details of their sex life, much as the character Tully does in "T.M.I." when a friend visits for the weekend.

Though I've made much ado about Harold Robbins being an early inspiration – some might say a bad influence – only "Swann Dive" and "Kept Men" really embody Robbins' love for the filthy behavior of the filthy rich. ("The Feast of Monte Villa" is sort of

4

Robbins-esque in this regard, but has more in common with a 1970s Italian *giallo*, with characters brandishing cocks instead of knives.) Because I wrote "Swann Dive" specifically for this collection and therefore not held to a magazine's restrictive word counts, I took a little more time in setting up the story, which I think makes the sex so much more erotic and, in the case of this particular narrative, shocking.

"Kept Men" was written over a decade ago but never submitted for publishing because it far exceeded 3,000 words, the preferred story length of most magazines. Now, of course, there are few porn magazines, gay or straight, to submit stories to, so I'm thrilled "Kept Men" finally has a chance to be read. This tawdry tale of young studs conspiring against their sugar daddies probably reads more like a Jackie Collins story than one written by Harold Robbins, and I'm okay with that. But, it was Harold who introduced me to the thrilling world of gay sex, and for that, he will always be in my dirty thoughts.

— Jonathan Asche

The Feast
of Monte Villa

Eric kept swimming, fighting the tide. The waters had turned rough, and he was struggling just to stay above water. He could see the shore, but it still seemed miles off. In spite of his exhaustion, he kept pushing forward.

But, the shoreline seemed to be moving farther and farther away instead of closer. Eric felt as if he were moving in slow motion. Then a wave rose up from behind him, rising so high he saw its shadow fall across him before it came crashing down. The thunderous roar deafened him as he was buried within the tumultuous currents of the sea ...

# # # # #

He felt a familiar, pleasing sensation from between his legs. His eyes opened slowly. He was lying on a bed in a white room. A hospital? He couldn't tell. Everything in his vision was hazy.

Eric looked down toward the foot of the bed. A man was leaning over him. He had Eric's cock in his mouth, sucking it ravenously. Eric couldn't seem to focus on the man. Dark hair, a beard, broad shoulders – this much he could determine, but the finer details escaped him.

He closed his eyes again. The man gulped Eric's cock with lustful abandon. Eric began to moan softly as he felt that hot tongue dance over his rigid shaft, massage his balls and dart into the opening of his ass.

The pleasure was building. Eric thrust his hips upward, trying to feed his nameless cocksucker more of the meat he so obviously craved. The man eagerly swallowed every inch.

A shudder suddenly surged through Eric's body, and he cried out as the climax overtook him. He sent jets of his thick cream into the anonymous mouth, and the man gulped it down happily.

Eric managed one last spurt before sinking back into unconsciousness.

# # # # #

He slowly opened his eyes. Sunlight flooded the white room from a large window above the bed. Eric blinked a couple of times and sat up.

He stretched, his aching muscles seizing in protest. He was naked, with only a crisp white sheet covering him. Able to see clearly now, Eric surveyed his surroundings.

The room was sparingly furnished, but elegant. The bed in which Eric lay had four tall posts at each corner. On either side of the bed were simple antique tables, and on top of those sat delicate glass lamps. The walls were unadorned, except for one large mirror in an elaborate frame hanging on the wall across from the bed.

He had no idea where he was or how he got there. He remembered swimming ... and vaguely recalled getting sucked off (or was that a dream?), but he was lost beyond that.

Eric got out of bed and walked to the mirror. His steps were clumsy, as if he'd only just recently learned how to walk. Whatever had happened to him hadn't done much physical damage, he noted as he studied his naked body in the mirror. A couple bruises – a large one on his arm, a smaller one above his right hip – and a few scrapes. Nothing serious.

Eric ran his fingers through his dark blond hair; it was unruly, but felt clean. Whoever brought him here had taken the trouble to wash it.

And, who brought him here?

Before heading out the bedroom door he looked around for something to cover himself, like a bathrobe or towel, but there was nothing like that, only the sheet on the bed. Hell, Eric thought, whoever else is in this house has already seen all I've got. Let them see it while he was conscious.

He opened the door and peeked out. "Hello?" His voice was hoarse from lack of use.

No answer.

Eric took a couple of tentative steps into a hall. The hall led to a balcony and staircase. The top landing overlooked a large foyer. The rest of the house appeared to be as sparsely furnished as the bedroom. The opposite wall was almost all glass, allowing the sunlight to pour inside.

Standing at the balcony railing, Eric called out again. "Anyone here?"

He had about decided he was alone in the house when a man entered the foyer. He was a young man (Eric guessed in his early twenties, like himself), with a very boyish face and hair so blond it was almost white. Contrasting with his youthful face was a very manly body, all sculpted muscles and tan skin. And it was obvious he knew he was attractive, for although he was not nude, he was dressed for show, wearing only a pair of nearly transparent, loose-fitting lounge pants.

"You're awake," the man said, his sensual mouth widening into a warm smile.

"How long have I been here?" Eric asked, looking down at the man.

"Almost four days. We were afraid you were in a coma, but you woke up the second day you were here. You just slept the rest of the time, so we didn't disturb you," the man explained. "We figured you needed the rest. What's your name?"

"Eric Downing. Yours?"

"Tom." He didn't volunteer a last name. He began to climb the stairs.

"Where am I?"

"Monte Villa."

"Never heard of it," Eric said.

"It's not a town. It's the name of the estate."

"You own this place?"

Tom was at the top of the stairs now. He chuckled at Eric's question. "No, Anthony does. I'm just his assistant."

"And where's Anthony?"

"You ask a lot of questions," Tom said. He was standing in front of Eric now. "Anthony's out now. Do you want something to eat? You must be starving."

"Yeah, and I'm naked, too. What happened to my clothes?"

"You were only wearing a swimsuit," Tom said, stepping closer. "If you'd like I can find you something to wear, though I didn't figure you as the modest type."

"Well, I can't exactly walk around naked," Eric said, suddenly feeling very warm. His heart rate quickened.

"Of course you can," Tom said, smiling. He was very close now, only inches away. Eric felt his blood rush to his crotch, his cock twitching with excitement. "You're very beautiful."

Tom placed a hand on Eric's shoulder, caressing it lightly. "A body like yours, you should show it off as much as possible." Tom's voice was soft and hypnotically seductive. Eric's prick began to swell.

"Relax," Tom continued, taking Eric's dick in his hands and stroking it gently. "I'll take care of you."

Eric closed his eyes and let the waves of pleasure wash over him as Tom massaged his cock. He moved closer, and suddenly Eric felt Tom's moist lips on his own. He responded to Tom's kiss, and soon, their tongues were interlocked in a heated duel. Eric reached up and put his arms around Tom's neck, bringing him closer. He wasn't sure if the earlier episode with the dark-haired, bearded man was a dream or not, but this was real.

Slowly, Eric sank to his knees, his tongue tasting his host's massive chest and rippled torso as he lowered himself onto the hardwood floor. Tom's crotch was before his face. Tom's crotch was before his face, Tom's hard-on fighting against the linen fabric of his loose-fitting pants.

Eric almost gasped as he uncovered that throbbing, uncut cock, rigid and begging for attention. Eric was all too happy to oblige, enveloping Tom's rod in his starving mouth. He teased the foreskin with his tongue and let the length of Tom's shaft glide down his throat. Eric inhaled Tom's musky scent as he took the full thrust of his hard dick.

"That's right, suck it," Tom whispered ecstatically, putting his hands on top of Eric's head. "Suck that hard cock."

Tom thrust his hips forward as Eric continued to gulp his cock. Then Tom pulled away and moved to the stairs, taking a couple steps down. "Sit here," he commanded, "on the top step."

Eric complied. Once Eric was seated, Tom knelt down and placed his hands on Eric's thighs, pulling them apart, so Eric was open to him. Eric's prick was stiff, and the crown was moist with the drool from his cock. Tom smiled and wrapped his hand around Eric's pole, jacking on it a few times before taking it into his mouth. Eric leaned back on his hands and let out a groan as Tom's mouth took him to heaven.

Tom's tongue probed every inch of his shaft. Taking Eric's cock in his hand again, Tom held it while his tongue made little circles down its length. As Tom reached his balls, Eric spread his legs wider. Delicately, Tom kissed and sucked his nuts. He soon moved lower, to Eric's pink little hole. Tom flicked his tongue at the tight opening before he buried his face in his ass and probed deeper.

He stroked his cock and moaned loudly as Tom's tongue dug into his ass. Eric's strokes became faster as his whole body tensed, his balls drawing up within his tightening sac.

Suddenly, jerking his hips upward, Eric released his load. The white, heavy droplets of his cream rained down on his torso and on Tom's head and face.

Giving Eric's spit-slick ass one final caress with his tongue, Tom stood up and began pumping his dick.

11

"I'm gonna give you a shower," he grunted, jacking off so furiously he had to grab the banister with his free hand to steady himself.

Letting out a lusty roar, Tom came. Eric closed his eyes and felt the hot spunk splash onto his chest and abdomen.

After his hunger for sex was satisfied, Tom dealt with Eric's hunger for food. He gave Eric a pair of shorts so tight and skimpy that Eric still felt naked. In the kitchen, he made two turkey sandwiches for Eric. Eric practically inhaled them, chasing them with glasses of iced tea.

"So, what do you do," Tom asked, placing a slice of chocolate cake in front of him.

"As little as possible," Eric joked, taking a huge bite of cake. "Actually, I work at this record store in Santa Cruz – or at least I used to. I'm probably fired now, since I've missed so many days. Not that I really ..."

Eric began to feel very tired. It was as if his whole body had suddenly decided to shut down.

"I think I'm sick," he slurred as the room faded away, and he sank into a sleepy darkness.

# # # # #

Light filled his eyes. Blinking rapidly, he tried to orient himself.

He was in a different room of the house now. It looked like a living room. It was a little more colorful than the rest of the rooms in the house. Above the fireplace was a large abstract painting. Within the swirls of color, Eric could make out three figures entangled in some complicated sexual position.

Eric was on a chaise longue at the room's center, still wearing the shorts Tom had given him earlier. He had an audience of four men.

"Hello, Eric," said a dark-haired, bearded man with intense, blue eyes. "I'm Anthony. I believe Tom has told you a little about me."

Anthony sat in a large chair that almost resembled a throne. He was older, probably his late thirties, early forties, Eric estimated. He wore a black, tailored suit, which, though not revealing, could not conceal the fact that he had a well-built body. Standing behind Anthony's chair was Tom, now wearing a black G-string. He managed a weak smile at Eric, an unspoken apology for having drugged him.

The other two men sat on a black leather sofa. They also were older and wore suits. One had brown, curly hair that brushed the back of his collar. The other had lighter, closely cropped hair. They both had chiseled, masculine faces adorned with vague, knowing smiles.

Eric stammered. "What ... what's going on here?" he stammered.

"Come here, Eric," Anthony said, his voice soft yet firm.

Without protest, Eric stood up and walked over to where Anthony sat. Anthony looked up at him and smiled. Eric recalled the hazy image of the bearded man swallowing his cock, and he realized that it had not been a dream.

Anthony touched Eric's side, his hand gliding over the curve of his hip, around to his back and squeezing his ass. "We're not going to hurt you, Eric," he said in a soothing voice. "Don't be afraid."

His hand moved to Eric's crotch, grabbing him and gently squeezing. "It's almost like fate that I found you," he continued. "I was walking along the beach, and there you were. Wet, bruised, out cold – but beautiful nonetheless."

Eric felt someone behind him and turned slightly. It was Tom, rubbing against him and reaching around to caress his bare chest. Eric turned back to Anthony, who was slowly pulling Eric's shorts to his knees, setting free his stiffening cock.

Anthony took hold of Eric's prick. As he gently fingered it, Tom brushed his hot tongue against Eric's ear and playfully pinched his nipples.

Eric's cock became stone in Anthony's hands. When Anthony took it into his mouth, Eric closed his eyes and leaned back against Tom. Anthony swallowed him whole; Eric could feel the coarse hairs of his beard brushing against his balls. His breathing became faster as

13

Anthony licked and sucked his knob. Tom's mouth traveled down Eric's neck, planting wet kisses down his spine. Then Eric felt Tom's warm breath against the crack of his ass. His tongue worked its way inside. Eric let out a groan.

Anthony pulled away. "I can tell you're feeling better."

Eric opened his eyes. Anthony was smiling and undoing his belt.

"Tom tells me you're quite the cocksucker," Anthony said, unzipping the fly of his suit pants. "Care to demonstrate?"

He pulled out his huge, hard dick. Eric began to salivate upon seeing its unfathomable size – at least nine inches long. Eric dropped to his knees and slowly lowered his mouth onto Anthony's cock, inhaling his musky scent. He took the entire length down his throat, until his nose was resting in Anthony's thick patch of pubic hair.

Anthony moaned appreciatively as Eric feasted on his cock. Eric could feel Tom's tongue at his ass. Occasionally, Tom would let his mouth travel to his balls and play with those sensitive orbs.

As Eric worked on Anthony's prick, he felt more hands and mouths, rubbing his shoulders and kissing his face. Eric lifted his face from Anthony's crotch and turned to see that the two men on the couch had stripped and were now kneeling on either side of him, their cocks quivering.

Anthony chuckled and stood up from his chair. "These are my friends," he said, loosening his tie and removing his jacket. "This is Paul" – he motioned to the one with curly hair – "and this is Mike. I think they like you."

Another chuckle. There was something sinister in Anthony's tone, but Eric was too horny to care. Tom had removed his G-string and was now positioned beneath Eric, gulping his rod. Paul planted a wet kiss on his lips, filling Eric's mouth with his tongue. Mike was now standing, helping Anthony remove the rest of his clothing.

Once undressed, Anthony stood before Eric as a frighteningly powerful being. He had a broad, hairy chest that narrowed down to tight, rippling abs and a firm ass. Muscles in his legs bulged within his skin. Anthony's friends had equally rigid physiques: hard pecs, washboard stomachs and stiff cocks. Eric realized he was the main course of their sexual feast, but he saw it more as a buffet, and he wanted to taste them all.

Anthony and Mike embraced, their lips locked. Their hands were all over one another. Paul now had his dick in Eric's face, and Eric sucked on it hungrily, wrapping his tongue around its pulsing head.

Then Mike moved next to Paul, and Eric had two pricks to sample. His mouth went from one to the other, the pleasure he gave them evident by their sighs and moans. Tom continued to suck Eric's cock.

Anthony's strong hands grasped Eric's shoulders. "Move over to the sofa," he said.

Their next position was carefully choreographed. Anthony had Paul sit on the sofa with Eric kneeling between his legs. Tom resumed his position beneath Eric, enabling Eric to fuck his mouth. Mike stood on the seat of the sofa and Paul immediately took his prick into his waiting mouth.

Anthony had taken a rubber and a tube of lubricant from one of the end tables. He rolled the rubber onto his prick then squirted some lubricant in his hands, greasing his enormous, sheathed cock. He applied a little of the lubricant to Eric's puckered hole, working two fingers inside.

Then Eric felt the head of Anthony's dick force its way inside him, opening his asshole to an almost impossible diameter. Eric, his mouth still full of Paul's meat, let out a muffled groan. Eric felt as if he were being torn in two as he was skewered by Anthony's pole and was amazed when he felt Anthony's balls hit the back of his ass. He had taken the full length of that monster cock and still remained conscious.

Gently, Anthony began to pump Eric's ass. Paul had raised his legs and wrapped them around Eric's neck. Eric toyed with Paul's nuts with his tongue before moving down to his dark hole. Paul was still swallowing Mike's cock, his hands kneading the assistant's shapely ass.

They all changed positions again. Anthony lay down on the floor, and Eric sat on his dick reverse cowboy style. Tom positioned himself over Anthony's face. Mike stood in front of Eric, feeding him his cock. Paul did the same with Tom.

Eric gyrated atop Anthony's rod, squeezing it with his ass muscles. His throat muscles massaged Mike's prick. Tom ground his ass and balls against Anthony's probing tongue while his own tongue traveled up and down the length of Paul's cock.

They were like a massive sex machine, each of them interlocking to tantalize each other with hard dicks, tight assholes, moist tongues and warm, welcoming mouths.

Mike was the first to come. He let out a stifled grunt as he sent his load down Eric's throat. Eric swallowed it greedily.

Paul and Tom came simultaneously. Paul coated Tom's face with his jism, while Tom shot his tangy juice all over Anthony's chest, the drops of cum beading up in his chest hair like morning dew.

Anthony shuddered, overcome by a forceful orgasm. He slammed his cock deep into Eric's ass and released his load.

Only Eric had yet to come. Anthony nudged Eric off his cock and stood up. He then knelt behind Eric, pulling him back against his chest. Anthony pressed his lips against Eric's neck and reached around to stroke his cock. As his strokes became faster, Eric's chest began to heave, and his breathing quickened. Then, in a colossal, ecstatic explosion, he came. His milky cream shot across the floor, forming in small, sticky puddles on the carpet.

Spent, the men collapsed on top of one another.

"Welcome to Monte Villa," Anthony purred in Eric's ear. "I think you'll be a welcome addition to our group."

# # # # #

Tom and Eric were driving along the coastal road leading to Monte Villa. Tom was at the wheel of Anthony's Mercedes, rounding corners at dangerous speeds. They came upon a hitchhiker, and Tom slowed the car. The man was tall and lanky, with well-defined muscles. He looked to be about twenty-five. His brown hair was long and uncombed, and his face was darkened by stubble. What really caught Tom's and Eric's eyes was the bulging crotch of the hitchhiker's tattered jeans.

"What do you think?" Eric asked.

Tom stopped the car. "I think if we clean him up and get rid of those clothes, Anthony would be quite pleased."

As Tom threw the car into reverse Eric readied for their new passenger, removing a cloth and a small vial of chloroform from the glove compartment.

Cheap Motels

Casey peeked out the window, waiting for Ray to arrive. He'd been at this damn fleabag for two hours. He turned away from the window and surveyed his surroundings: the purple crushed-velvet bedspread; the red carpet dotted with cigarette burns; the orange-and-gold patterned wallpaper. Some joker actually named this tacky dump the Palace Inn.

He heard a car pulling up out front. Could that be him? Before he could make it the window to check, there was a knock on the door.

Casey cracked the door, smiled and unhooked the chain. "Thought you'd chickened out."

Ray walked in, and Casey closed the door, careful to hang the 'Do Not Disturb' sign outside before shutting it. Ray held up a briefcase. "It's all right here, five hundred grand in cash."

"Let me see!"

Ray set the briefcase on the bed and opened it, revealing neat stacks of crisp $100 bills.

"Wasn't so hard, was it?" Casey teased.

"Not so hard? You try going to four different banks, hoping no one gets suspicious when you're cashing such large checks," Ray said, his voice becoming shrill.

"I'll tell you what's hard," Casey purred, grabbing his crotch and kneading his dick through his boxers.

Ray's eyes widened, as if for the first time he noticed Casey was only in his underwear. He grinned and shut the briefcase. "Now that you mention it, embezzlement does kinda' make me horny."

Casey watched as Ray hastily shed his suit. Ray was attractive, but in an affected way, with his carefully styled, highlighted hair, tanning-bed tan and cheesy gold jewelry. He looked like a game show host. Even his physique was artificial, his muscles built with steroids.

When Ray stripped down to his socks and underwear – he was wearing a thong – he seized Casey. "I want you so bad," he said, biting Casey's ear and grabbing his round, firm butt.

"You can have me," Casey cooed, running his hands down Ray's back. The two men kissed urgently, their tongues entwining. Casey began to sink to his knees, rubbing his face against Ray's body as he went down, inhaling his Halston-and-sweat scent. On his knees, Casey reached up and grabbed Ray's crotch. Ray was like stone, his dick about to burst from his tiny thong.

Casey pulled Ray's underwear down roughly. His cock popped out, almost hitting Casey in the face. Like him or not, Ray was well hung.

He quickly wrapped his mouth around Ray's throbbing dong, letting it slide all the way to the back of his throat. His tongue circled its shaft and crown. Ray began to grunt and groan and run his fingers through Casey's dark hair. "Oooh, suck my cock, baby," Ray moaned. "Lick my balls."

When Casey thought Ray had taken all he could stand, he stopped and climbed onto the bed. He was careful to close the briefcase and set it on the floor.

Casey's hand slid between his legs. "Your turn, baby."

Ray stepped clumsily out of his underwear and climbed on the bed with Casey. Grinning, he lowered his face to Casey's crotch, nuzzling his cock through the fabric of his boxers while tugging at the waistband. Once he had stripped off Casey's underwear, Ray gasped as if he'd never seen his cock before. He took the thick rod in his hand and guided it into his mouth. Ray slurped and sucked his dick lustily as Casey lay back on the pillows and let the pleasure overtake him. Ray nibbled at the base of his cock and tongued his balls. Soon, his mouth was at Casey's ass. Casey spread his legs wider, and Ray's tongue dove deeper.

Ray's oral probing of Casey's asshole came to an abrupt halt. "I wanna fuck you," he growled, hopping off the bed and picking his pants off the floor.

Fumbling around in his pants pockets, Ray withdrew his billfold, in which he always carried a rubber and a small packet of lube. Finding the plastic packets, he tossed the wallet on the bedside table and tore open the condom wrapper.

Breathing hard, Ray rolled the condom over his firm cock and greased it up. Prying Casey's legs even further apart, he forced his dick into his tight hole. Casey grimaced in pain, but soon, the initial shock subsided, and he felt nothing but ecstasy.

Ray began to pump his ass forcefully while jacking off Casey. Casey grabbed Ray's butt and pulled, as if trying to drive him deeper into his warm ass.

"You love me, don't you baby? You love me?" Ray pleaded through shallow breaths.

Christ, Casey winced. *Can't the guy just fuck without having to hear a goddamned marriage proposal?* "Yeah," Casey grunted.

"Let me hear you say it!" Ray begged.

"I ..." Casey began, but suddenly let out a raspy howl as his dick exploded. Hot jets of cum splattered his torso.

"Oh, baby," Ray practically sobbed. His body shuddered then tensed. With one final groan, he shot his load.

"That was soooo good," Ray panted, falling on the bed beside Casey. He rested an arm across Casey's chest and kissed him. "I can't wait to leave L.A. We'll fuck like this every day in Cancun."

Just be patient, Casey told himself. *Be patient, and you'll have your chance.*

His chance came minutes later. As he always did after getting off, Ray was soon fast asleep.

Casey slid out of bed and got dressed, quickly and quietly. He pondered taking the keys to Ray's Cadillac but decided against it. The police would be looking for Ray, not him. Best to take his own car.

Taking one last look at Ray, Casey snatched up the briefcase and disappeared out the door.

An hour later, Casey was speeding across the California desert. Periodically, he would burst out laughing at what he had done. It had been so easy; so easy that he almost forgot that it was a plan that took nearly six months to bring off.

He was a messenger when he met Ray, an accountant at an indie movie studio. Casey had his idea for acquiring easy riches for some time. It was simple: Find someone who had access to large sums of money, win him over with his body, convince him to steal, and then take the loot himself.

The hard part was finding the right person. He encountered several people who had access to money, but most of them were too sharp and would have caught on to his scheme. When he saw Ray ogling his crotch while they were on the elevator, Casey knew he had found his man. Ray may have had a head for figures, but he was an imbecile the moment you grabbed his dick.

But Ray was past tense now. *Another hour and I'll be in Arizona*, Casey figured. He was headed for Phoenix, and hoped to get a flight from there to Miami. Of course, getting the money through airport security might be a problem ...

Shit, getting to the airport might be a problem, Casey realized when he looked at the gas gauge. The red needle was hovering above E.

His car was running on fumes by the time he found a station, 10 miles later. Earl's Pump 'N Pay read a rusted sign out front. Were it not for the presence of two other cars at the station Casey would've sworn the place was out of business. But for now, it was an oasis.

As Casey pulled off the road, he noticed a Jeep parked several yards away from the station, its hood up and steam wafting up from the engine. What held his attention was what was standing near the broken down Jeep: a beautiful, sun-bronzed stud, talking on a cell phone, his clothes fitting him like a second skin. Even from a distance, Casey could see the fair sized bulge in the man's faded Levi's. This guy was packing.

Casey pulled up to one of the pumps and cut the engine. He checked the rearview mirror, getting another glimpse of the hunk by the Jeep. He was punching numbers on the phone, obviously pissed. Then he turned, and Casey got to see his hot ass. With that gorgeous vision burned into his mind, he stepped out of his car.

He was about to grab a nozzle from the pump when an old man with a slight hump on his back approached him. "Fill 'er up?" he asked in a voice cured by Pall Malls and whiskey.

"Uh, sure," he told the elderly man. "Ya' got a restroom?"

The old man nodded and pointed to the side of the dilapidated building.

The men's room was filthy but not quite the horror Casey expected. He hurriedly took a leak, flushed the rust-stained urinal and moved to the sink.

As he was washing his hands the door opened. He looked up and saw the Jeep's owner in the cracked mirror. "Hey," the guy said, nodding at Casey. Casey nodded back and quickly returned to washing his hands.

The man walked up to the urinal and unzipped his pants. Casey sneaked a look. The guy was huge! He wet his lips and turned away before his staring became obvious.

He reached for the paper towel dispenser. It was empty, of course. "Damn," he muttered, trying to shake his hands dry.

"Real class place, huh," said the man, zipping himself up. "Probably better off pissing outside."

Casey smiled in agreement. The man had short, brown hair and pale blue eyes that shimmered beneath his heavy brow. His gorgeous face was covered in stubble, making him look rugged and tough.

The man stepped up to the sink, held his hands under the water for no more than 10 seconds and followed Casey out of the men's room, wiping his wet hands on his jeans.

"Say, I was wondering if I could ask a favor?" he said as they stepped into the hot afternoon sun.

"Maybe," Casey said. "Depends on the favor."

"Well, my fuckin' Jeep decided to bust a radiator hose, and the geezer who runs this place says he can't get a replacement 'til tomorrow. I tried calling a garage in the next town, but I can't get a goddamned signal out here …"

"You need a ride?"

"Yeah. Just to the next town. I can spend the night there and get my Jeep in the morning."

"No prob'," Casey said, happy to have this beautiful example of manhood in his life a little while longer.

"Thanks," the man smiled. "By the way, the name's Trent."

Trent. Even his name is rugged.

"I'm Casey."

After Trent grabbed a duffel bag from his Jeep and Casey paid for the gas, the two men hit the highway.

"So, where you headed?" Trent asked, stretching out in the passenger seat.

"Phoenix," Casey said, refusing to elaborate. Fortunately, Trent didn't push it.

"I live near there, in Buckeye. On my way back from vacation," he said. "Went to San Diego, saw some friends, y'know."

Casey wasn't listening. He kept trying to imagine Trent naked, trying to get a mental image of Trent's cock, hard and waiting for him. He'd glance over at the inviting bulge in Trent's crotch, and wished he could reach over and grab it. The idea was making Casey hot and causing his own dick to swell uncomfortably in his jeans.

The sun was beginning to set by the time they reached the next town, a place called Borack. "There's a motel," Trent pointed. "That'll be fine."

It was called the Covered Wagon Lodge and had a flickering neon wagon wheel out front. Another neon sign flashed 'Vacancy,' as if there would be any doubt.

Casey pulled up to the office, and Trent hopped out to get a room. He returned to the car a few minutes later, room key in hand.

"You don't have to be in Phoenix right away, do you?" Trent asked when the car came to a stop in front of his room.

"My plans are flexible." Casey's heart was racing.

"Well, why don't you stop for a bit," he said, putting a hand on Casey's thigh. "That's a long drive. You don't want to fall asleep at the wheel."

Casey needed no more persuading. While Trent unlocked the room door, he got his things out of the trunk. He grabbed his gym bag then looked at the briefcase. If he brought it in, Trent might question it, but Casey wasn't too crazy about leaving the money out of his sight for very long. He decided to take his chances with Trent's questions.

The room had a western theme, in keeping with the name of the motel. The faded bedspread had a pattern of galloping horses on it, and on the wall opposite the bed hung a bad painting of a lone cowboy riding into the sunset.

"Wonder if this is the honeymoon suite?" Casey joked, setting his gym bag on a chair by the front door. He put the briefcase underneath the chair. Trent was sitting on the bed with his back to Casey, taking off his boots.

"No, but it can be," he said, turning to leer at Casey.

Casey returned his gaze. The two men didn't move or speak, hypnotized by each other's sexuality. Trent was the first to break the spell, standing and unbuttoning his shirt. His chest was broad and covered with hair. Casey stopped him when he began to unzip his pants.

"No, let me," he said.

He walked toward Trent, stripping off his shirt as he went. Casey had a tight, muscular body that was almost like that of a high school boy's – manly, but not quite fully developed. Judging by the smile on his face, Trent liked what he saw.

Casey sat on the bed in front of Trent. At first, he just ran his hands down Trent's torso, feeling his firm muscles. Leaning forward,

Casey pressed his face against Trent's abdomen, letting the silky hairs caress his face. Trent's skin smelled clean and natural. Casey began to kiss his stomach while his hands moved to Trent's crotch.

Trent was breathing heavy as Casey unzipped his fly. Casey pulled Trent's jeans down past his thighs. He was wearing a pair of simple white briefs. They bulged enticingly.

"I don't know if I can handle it," Casey said, smiling up at Trent while rubbing his crotch.

"You knew what you were getting yourself into," Trent replied. "I saw you looking at me when I was taking a piss."

Casey blushed and turned his attention to what Trent was hiding in his Jockeys. Slowly, he pulled the underwear down. Trent's hard cock fell forward. It was almost two inches in diameter and about eight inches long. The head practically came to a point, making Trent's dick resemble a stake.

Wetting his lips, Casey took Trent's rod into his mouth, letting his meat press against his tongue. Trent let out a satisfied sigh as Casey went to work, licking and sucking his fat pole. Casey flicked the corona of Trent's cock with his tongue then took the whole thing down his throat until he felt Trent's balls at his chin.

Trent pulled away. "Ease up, or I'll be finished before we've gotten started," he said breathlessly.

He knelt on the floor in front of Casey and helped him off with the rest of his clothes. When Casey was nude, Trent stood and put his hands on Casey's shoulders and rubbed them affectionately. Trent leaned forward and kissed him, his mouth devouring Casey's, his hands caressing Casey's body.

Trent moved down to Casey's dick, taking Casey's hard-on in his hands. He stroked it gently and then moved in for the kill, sucking Casey's cock ferociously, his warm, wet tongue slavering over every inch of Casey's engorged rod. Casey lay back on the bed, his body alive with pleasure.

He felt Trent's mouth on his balls, then his lips moved higher, kissing his stomach, his bellybutton, his nipples, and finally his mouth.

Trent's jeans and underwear were still bunched at his knees. He shucked them off hurriedly, tossing them across the room. Casey was pleased to see he also took off his socks. He then climbed on top of Casey, straddling his face, his hard cock quivering above the young man's lips.

Casey took Trent's dick into his mouth. His hands glided over Trent's ass cheeks, and then his fingers began to probe his dark, hairy hole.

They got into a sixty-nine position. Trent dived between Casey's legs, swallowing his dick whole then making a slow retreat up the shaft. He cradled Casey's balls in his hand, rubbing them and occasionally giving them a taste.

Casey's mouth moved from Trent's cock to his ass. He lapped Trent's tangy ass ring, prodding it gingerly with his tongue.

Trent let out a groan and sat up. Casey continued to eat his ass, with Trent riding his face. Trent grabbed Casey's legs and pulled them toward him. Casey's butt was now up in the air, his legs resting on Trent's shoulders. Trent leaned forward and buried his face between Casey's legs. His tongue went straight for Casey's pink, puckered hole. His tongue danced around Casey's asshole, periodically making stabs at the opening.

He soon replaced his tongue with a finger. With Casey's ass lubed with his spit, he was able to work a finger in easily. Soon he was finger-fucking him with two fingers, and then three. Casey's body began to tremble; the ecstasy was so intense.

Trent stepped off the bed. Casey sat up and saw him go for his duffel bag. He rummaged through it before returning to the bed with a rubber and a small tube of lubricant.

"You do the honors," he said, handing the condom and lube to Casey.

Casey tore open the condom packet and rolled the rubber over Trent's throbbing cock. He squirted some lubricant into his palm and greased Trent's sheathed dick. Taking a deep breath, he straddled Trent's enormous member and lowered himself onto it.

Trent grabbed Casey's hips as his cock eased into his tender hole. Casey's face became tense as he struggled to accommodate Trent's massive rod. When Trent was all the way inside him, Casey relaxed and began to ride him, his hips making slow, rhythmic movements.

"Yeah, ride my cock, boy," Trent gasped, thrusting deep into Casey's ass. He grabbed Casey's dick and began to jack him off in time to his thrusts.

As the thrusts gained momentum, a sexual delirium took over. Casey's body started to shudder, and he knew he couldn't hold back. He arched his back and gnashed his teeth. His body convulsed and thick torrents of cum shot out his cock, splashing onto Trent's chest and torso.

Trent's hands moved to Casey's waist. He dug his fingers into Casey's flesh. He fucked Casey harder and faster. In an instant, he was grunting like a crazed animal.

"Oh, god, I'm gonna shoot!"

With one prolonged groan, Trent came. Every muscle in his body seemed to become rigid for a second, and then he relaxed.

They lay on the bed, remaining still for several minutes. Casey kissed Trent and climbed out of bed. "Mind if I take a shower?"

"Go right ahead," Trent said groggily.

In the shower, Casey's mind returned to the money. *By this time tomorrow*, he thought, *I'll be on a plane headed for Miami, or maybe the Caribbean.* His whole future seemed like one big vacation.

When Casey stepped out of the bathroom, he saw his future evaporate. Trent was sitting on the bed, fully dressed. He had a gun in one hand, and he was holding a badge in the other. The briefcase was on the bed, opened.

"Don't bother trying to explain, 'cause I won't believe anything you tell me," Trent said.

"You never told me you were a cop!" Casey shouted.

"And, you never told me you were a crook," Trent retorted. "Don't worry. I'm not planning to arrest you. In fact, I should thank you. See, I've been wanting to retire for a while, and you've given me a chance to do that."

Trent stood up and put his badge in his pocket. "Here's a little something to show my appreciation," he said, tossing a couple hundreds on the bed before closing the briefcase. "You can use it to get a bus ticket."

He held up Casey's car keys. *If only I'd left the money in the car*, Casey thought. He was beginning to feel ill.

Trent shoved his gun in his pants and grabbed the briefcase and his bag. Before he stepped out the door, he said, "By the way, you're one hot fuck."

Nocturnal Admissions

I rolled over for the umpteenth time since going to bed an hour before. The glowing numbers on the VCR clock confirmed how much time had passed. It was now 1:08 a.m.

There were many possible causes for my insomnia. I was thrown out of my house last weekend – a house that, after the inevitable divorce proceedings, would be owned by the shrieking harpy I'd once shared it with. She also stood to walk away with the house's contents, one of the cars (probably the SUV) and a sizable chunk of my yearly income. Yet, she was the one who went on and on about how much she was being hurt.

Hal's sofa wasn't exactly the sleeping arrangement I'd been hoping for, either. I knew Hal from work, but I didn't know him all that well. The reason I'd hit him up for a place to stay was he did not know my wife and therefore couldn't take her side, and I knew he had a two-bedroom condo all to himself. Except that he didn't have it to himself.

"Uh, sure," he said when I asked if I could stay for a few days. "But, um, well … my son is home for semester break, so he has the other bedroom. You'd have to sleep on the couch."

Losers can't be choosers.

The real cause of my insomnia, though, was a hard-on so persistent my dick could've been a door-to-door salesman. I could just jack off, except I was in the center of someone else's living room, and even though Hal and his son were both asleep, there was always the chance that Hal might leave his bedroom upstairs to get a glass of water, or his son, Jess, whose bedroom was off the living room, might hear me let out an involuntary grunt and step out to see what was going on. There was just no assurance of privacy. I could've gone into the bathroom, of course, but jacking off while sitting on a toilet made me think of my marriage.

I decided, much to my cock's relief, that a little pud-pounding in the middle of my host's living room was worth possible embarrassment. After all, what's getting discovered masturbating when your wife's already caught you getting sucked off by a cater-waiter at her boss's barbecue?

So I got my little bottle of lube – the one I'd bought for business trips – out of my suitcase, sat up on the sofa, pulled my cock through the fly of my boxers and started greasing it up. I closed my eyes, my mind becoming lost in fantasy as I stroked my throbbing boner. I got so lost, in fact, that I didn't realize that one of my fantasy objects had entered the room. When I opened my eyes I saw Jess standing at the far end of the living room, staring at me. What were the odds?

I moved so quickly to cover up it's amazing I didn't disrupt the space-time continuum.

"Sorry," Jess said. This should've been the moment when he, presumably as embarrassed as I, ducked back into his bedroom. Instead, he started walking towards me. Worse, he turned on a lamp. What the hell was he thinking? I mean, if he'd walked in on me using the bathroom would he stay and chat?

As annoyed as I was with having my now-crimson face illuminated, I did appreciate being able to see Jess more clearly. Now, I'll admit being a bit put out when Hal told me I'd have to sleep on the couch while his college-age son got the condo's only other bed, but after seeing Jess, I didn't mind this sacrifice so much. Jess was, simply put, *fucking hot*! When I first met him, he told me he was majoring in "communications," though he looked like he spent more time at the gym than in class. Every muscle was perfectly toned, the striations almost visible beneath his tan skin. His navel was pierced, and he had a tribal band tattoo circling one of his meaty biceps (interestingly, his father had a similar tattoo). Jess was quite handsome, like his father, though he looked nothing like Hal. I assumed he favored his mother's side.

Jess moved closer. He was wearing his standard leisurewear – that is, a pair of boxer briefs. That's one thing I've got to say about Hal and his son: neither liked to wear a lot of clothes around the house. This fact sent me into heaven and plunged me into hell simultaneously. The heaven part is obvious. The hellish part was, with my being closeted and they being straight, trying to keep my eyes focused on their faces lest Hal caught me ogling his crotch or Jess saw me looking at his ass.

Now, of course, under the guise of looking at the floor in shame, I got a good eyeful of the bulge between Jess's legs. Not much left to the imagination. The swell of his cock and balls were easy to see beneath the cotton fabric, especially since he was semi-hard.

Wait a minute: Jess was getting hard? From watching me? I wondered.

When caught in a compromising position, there's really no right thing to say. You won't find anything in those etiquette books about what to do if caught masturbating in a friend's living room. *This isn't what it looks like* seems to be a popular line, even though no one ever buys it. I certainly know this now. I tried to be casual. "This is so embarrassing," I chuckled nervously, arranging the blanket I'd pulled over my lap.

"S'okay," Jess said. "It's no big deal." He was dealing with the situation much better than my soon-to-be-ex-wife would have.

I chanced looking up at him. He had an odd smile on his face, almost ... seductive.

"So, what were you thinking about?" Jess asked.

The color drained from my face. "W-w-what?" Didn't his parents teach him not to ask such impertinent questions? And was that bulge in Jess's underwear getting bigger?

He moved closer, so close that our knees touched. His crotch was directly in front of my nose, and yes, he had a full hard-on. "You thinking about this?" Jess asked, grabbing his boner and squeezing it.

For a twenty-one-year-old – granted, a rather worldly looking twenty-one-year-old for if I had to guess Jess's age I'd say he wasn't a day younger than twenty-seven – he sure was direct. I started stammering, making indistinct sounds while my mind searched for an appropriate answer.

"You want to suck it?" he asked.

The question required a simple yes or no, yet it wasn't that black and white for me. Yes, I wanted to suck it, but ... well, maybe blowing your friend's son isn't a good idea, though at that moment I couldn't give a specific reason as to why.

Instead I said, "H-how'd you know?"

"Straight guys wouldn't stare at my ass as much as you do."

So I wasn't as sneaky as I thought.

"But your dad might ..."

Jess snorted. "My dad?" Then, more seriously: "Oh, yeah. We'll just be quiet, that's all."

I thought about suggesting we move things to his bedroom. Then again, best to strike while the iron's hot. Not wasting any more time, I reached for the waistband of Jess's boxer-briefs, yanking them down with one quick pull. Jess's dick sprung forward. His cock was so amazing I had to take a moment to admire it. It was as close-to-perfect a penis as I'd ever seen: about eight inches long, thick and uncut, though the foreskin had rolled back, revealing the plump, rosy crown. His cock was so fascinating I wanted suck him off and then, once done, just stare at his dick until it was ready for my mouth again.

It was with that thought in mind that I went to work on Jess's rod. I'm admittedly a little shy about giving head because, being confined to heterosexual circumstances as I was for so many years, I didn't get nearly as much practice as I would've liked. Also, Jess clearly had more experience than I – he was certainly more confident – so I feared disappointing him. I took hold of his cock (it felt so substantial in my hand) and brought my mouth to it, letting my tongue flutter around the head and tasting his salty pre-cum. One of his hands cupped the back of my head. "Go on – suck it," he commanded.

I opened wide and took Jess's cock into my mouth very slowly. I cradled his cockhead in my tongue, circling its smooth contours. Then I eased his dick deeper, managing to take just over four of those eight inches before breathing became an issue. So, I just concentrated on the top half of his dick. While I slurped on the crown my hand stroked shaft

If Jess noticed my lack of experience, he didn't let on. In fact, judging his reaction, I was a better cocksucker than I thought.

"Oh, yeah, man," he hissed, pushing his hips forward. "Suck on it!"

No longer concerned with covering myself, I pulled the blanket off my lap to expose my hard cock. I pulled at my dick as I sucked and stroked Jess's, mindful not to get too carried away; I was so horny that any increase in speed and pressure, and I'd be gushing all over the floor.

I moved down to Jess's balls, swabbing them with my tongue while continuing to stroke his cock. He moaned – a bit too loudly for my comfort. I wanted to scold him, but that would mean taking my mouth away from his delectable low-hangers.

Jess suddenly climbed onto the sofa, straddling my body. His underwear, still around his thighs, made an ominous ripping sound as his spread legs strained the seams. Jess didn't seem the least concerned about destroying a pair of $30 drawers. He rubbed his drooling cock against my face. His fingers combed through my short, black hair. My hands went to his ass, fondling those two firm globes so delicately that my fingers barely touched his skin as they glided over the silky down covering his butt.

Hal's son, though, had no patience for such a sensual approach. Jess slid down to my lap, his underwear finally giving up the fight and tearing open on the left leg. My cock was sandwiched between his buttcheeks, tickled by the curly hairs sprouting from his ass-crack. He took my face in his hands and kissed me, his tongue plunging into my mouth. This surprised me; a kiss seemed a bit romantic for him, but who am I to complain? I responded in kind, sliding my tongue between his lips.

His mouth moved to my left ear. He teased my earlobe with his tongue then traced the grooves of my outer ear.

"I want you to eat my ass," he panted. "Then I want you to fuck me. Then …" He paused, breathing heavily. "… just before you come, I want you to pull out and shoot it all over my face!"

Just hearing this made my cock jump. I was afraid Jess might have to settle for the last item on his sexual list. There was no way I could eat his ass and fuck him without blowing my load in the process.

But, then something happened that immediately cleared my lusty delirium.

An upstairs light came on. "What's going on down there?" Hal called out.

My blood turned to ice water; my cock turned to overcooked spaghetti. Apparently, I just couldn't fuck without someone walking in on me.

I practically threw Jess off my lap. He nearly landed on his ass, but recovered quickly, if not too gracefully. Once again, I frantically covered myself with the blanket. You'd expect Jess to scurry to his room. Instead, he just stood there. Didn't even bother to cover up – in fact, he stepped out of his ripped underwear and stood there with his dick hanging out, like we had nothing in the world to worry about.

"Jess!" I hissed through clenched teeth. "Get the fuck outta here!"

Just as I said that, though, Hal was descending the staircase, tying a red silk robe around his waist.

"What are you guys up to?" he asked before stopping in his tracks. He looked over at Jess, standing naked in the living room, then at me, clutching a blanket to my crotch, and my face advertising my guilt with a neon red glow. Didn't take much brainpower to figure out what was going on.

Hal moved toward his son. Jess said to him: "You owe me twenty bucks."

Hal chuckled. "That right?"

What Hal did next caused my jaw to hit the floor. He wrapped his arms around his son, and kissed him – and it wasn't a fatherly kind of peck on the cheek, either. Tongues were involved. Worse, Hal's hand moved down to Jess's thick cock. He was playing with his son's dick!

Okay, I'm a liberal sort of guy, but this was too much for me. I was so stunned I couldn't speak. I just stared, wide-eyed. Making matters worse was – much as I didn't want it to – that the scene sort of excited me.

Hal and his son stopped making out long enough to look over at me. "What's wrong with you?" Hal asked, like I was the one with the problem.

"What's ... wrong? He's ... your ... son!" I was speaking like I had emphysema.

Father and son had a hearty laugh over that one.

"Apparently Jess was so busy waving his boner at you, he didn't tell you," Hal said.

"Tell me what?"

"I don't have a son. Jess is my boyfriend. I wanted to help you out because I've been in the same situation, but I'm not out at work. So I said Jess was my son."

"Wasn't that clever?" Jess said, rolling his eyes. "I was against the idea. Then once you got here I thought, 'Well, at least he's cute.' I also figured out you were family, but Hal didn't believe me."

"But, you think everyone is gay," Hal chortled.

These revelations certainly cleared up a lot of things. Still, I didn't quite understand Hal's reaction to the scene he discovered in his living room. His boyfriend was getting nasty with another man, so shouldn't he at least be upset?

"Now that everything's out in the open, why don't we have some fun?" Hal said, untying his robe.

His robe opened up, revealing a furry torso and rising cock.

"Oooh, yeah," Jess purred, his hand fondling Hal's hardening prick.

Hal let his robe drop to the floor. "Guests first," he scolded playfully, dismissing Jess with a kiss on the forehead before moving toward me.

Hal was almost old enough to be Jess's father – early forties, I'd guess – yet he'd withstood the passing years better than men ten years younger. His body was armored with solid slabs of muscle and carpeted with dark hair (though his nipples stood out on his fuzzy chest like pink, quarter-sized islands). His circumcised cock, though not as big as his boyfriend's, was a good size.

It tasted pretty good, too. I gulped his dick down my throat hungrily. I still couldn't take the whole length, but I swallowed more of Hal's cock than I did Jess's. My tongue swabbed his pulsing cockhead, and his pre-cum trickled down my throat.

I felt the blanket sliding off my lap. Jess was on all fours between Hal's legs, putting his face between mine. My cock was hard once again, jutting out of the fly of my boxers. Jess seized it, his tongue tracing the seam running up the shaft. He worked a couple fingers into my shorts, hooked my balls and pulled them out, so he could lick those as well. The tickling-tingling feeling of Jess's mouth on my nuts made me squirm with pleasure.

Hal undulated his hips, rhythmically pumping his cock into my mouth, pushing it in as far as I could take it without gagging. He let out a little grunt every time he sank his dripping pole into my mouth.

I ran my hands up his sturdy thighs, feeling the firmness of his muscles. Then Jess closed his mouth over my dick, and I involuntarily pinched Hal's thighs so hard he cried out. I didn't mean to cause Hal any pain, but oh, it felt so fucking good having my cock in Jess's mouth. And, he knew just what to do with it, too. Now, I've never claimed to be huge, but my cock is above average size and pretty thick. Jess swallowed it in one gulp without any hesitation, holding it deep in his gullet.

I was pretty sure if my dick stayed in Jess's mouth just a few minutes longer, he'd be choking on the load welling up in my nuts. Hal, though, pulled me to my feet before that could happen.

"Enjoying yourself?" he growled, encircling my body with his thick arms. His hands cupped my ass.

I chuckled and nodded, not really needing to voice my answer. My hard cock pressing up against Hal's thigh was the only answer he needed.

Hal's tongue slid into my mouth. His mouth was minty, like he'd gargled with mouthwash before catching me with his boyfriend. He pulled at my boxers and Jess assisted in removing them.

"Oh, yeah," Hal purred when my underwear fell to the floor. He kneaded my ass, obviously pleased with it. Not to sound conceited, but I do have a pretty nice ass. ("You can't be straight with a butt that good," commented one of my clandestine tricks from several years ago.) The rest of me is better than average, if I say so myself. I'm not as stocky and rugged as Hal, or as smooth and buff as Jess, but I've logged some time at the gym, building up a respectable physique. A lot of people say I look like that actor who plays the homicidal homosexual in that show about a prison. Given his role, I'm not sure if I'm comfortable with the comparison, though I'd have to say I'd do him if I got the chance, even if it meant getting my neck broken afterwards.

Hal apparently had no problems with my body. He started tweaking my nipples and playfully biting at my ear, all the while grinding his cock against mine. Jess was behind me, his dick sandwiched in the crack of my ass. Next thing I knew, I was being pulled back toward the sofa until I was on my back, laid out for my hosts.

Jess immediately hopped onto the sofa and squatted over my face. "Eat my hole," he hissed. Hal was similarly inclined, only it was my hole he wanted to eat. Pulling my thighs apart, Hal dove between my legs and started licking my asshole. He was real gentle at first, his tongue lightly circling my tight sphincter. It felt nice.

Then Hal forced his way up into my hole, his warm, wet tongue stabbing into my chute. His face was pressed against my ass, his beard rubbing against the walls of my buttcheeks, his hands digging into my thighs – holding me there as if I might try escaping. This was more than a mere rim job; Hal was eating my ass with the gusto of a starving man. It felt fucking incredible!

I was so busy moaning and squirming I was neglecting Jess's succulent hole hovering over my own mouth. He got impatient and sat on my face. I almost suffocated, but I recovered quickly. I lapped his hole tentatively. I wasn't very experienced at rimming, either. Truth is, I always thought it's hot to watch a guy eat another guy's ass, and I certainly enjoyed it when it was done to me, but I've always been reluctant to dip my tongue between another man's cheeks. However, I was so horny now I'd forgotten most of my inhibitions.

I licked Jess's asshole as if I knew what I was doing, gratified to hear his ecstatic moans. Funny thing, hearing him moan and groan the way he was added to my arousal, making me eat his hole with greater enthusiasm. I even managed to work my tongue past his tight ass lips. Jess really got spastic then, his body bucking and trembling atop my head.

"Oh, man, eat it!" Jess was practically shouting. "Shove your tongue up my ass."

There was a sharp tension at my asshole as Hal replaced the urgent probing of his tongue with his spit-lubed fingers. Slowly, he slid his fingers – I don't know how many; at least two – into me, stretching my hole wide.

"That feel good?" he asked, tickling my prostate. It was difficult to answer verbally, what with my mouth full of his boyfriend's butt and all. My cock, however, gave an affirmative answer, pumping out more pre-cum

Hal added another finger, stretching my hole a bit more, though, with my lack of experience, it felt as if he was taking a Jaws of Life to my ass. "Want me to fuck you?" he rasped, his big fingers tunneling up my chute.

I'm pretty agreeable when I'm horny. Though I'd only been fucked once in my lifetime, many years ago, at this moment I would've let Hal ram a fire extinguisher up my butt if he asked. I pulled my lips away from Jess's sloppy hole just long enough to pant out the words, "Oh, yeah. Fuck me!"

Jess said: "And I want you to fuck me!"

We all set to making these desires a reality, gathering lubricant and condoms and rearranging our bodies in the appropriate positions. Jess lay back on the couch, I knelt on the floor between his legs (his ankles were resting on my shoulders) and Hal was behind me, his cock sheathed, lubed and ready. I poured lube onto Jess's asshole (and onto the carpet, but my hosts didn't complain) and inserted an index finger.

Jess's hole was tight, but his butt muscles willingly accepted my finger. I suspected my cock would be accepted just as willingly.

Hal lubricated my butthole. My ass had become much more pliable; I felt a tightness as his fingers slid into me, but no discomfort. Hal picked up on the pliancy of my ass immediately. "Ready for something more?"

"Oh, yeah," I sighed, my body quivering at the thought.

"Shove your cock into me the same time he's starting to fuck you," Jess directed excitedly.

I'd barely torn open the condom packet when Hal pushed my body forward, over Jess, and started inching his cock into my hole.

Let's just say my ass wasn't quite ready for "something more." If his fingers felt like he was stretching me open with the Jaws of Life, his dick felt like a jackhammer. Determined to have this experience, I tried to remain stoic, sucking in my breath between clenched teeth.

Hal moved slowly, his cock creeping up my ass a millimeter at a time. This made it bearable. When he was all the way inside me, he remained still, his chest pressed against my back. "Just take it easy," Hal whispered into my ear. "Relax, and it'll start to feel real good."

I hoped so. My dick had softened from the shock, making it pretty useless for fucking Jess, who lay beneath me pinching my nipples as he waited for my cock.

Hal began to fuck me in short, gentle thrusts. I was numb to the sensation at first, but soon a pleasurable feeling began to smolder inside me. I raised my ass to meet Hal's forward thrust. My cock swelled again.

"Fuck me," Jess reminded, his hard prick rubbing against my torso.

The condom I'd been pinching between my fingers was hastily unrolled over my stiff dick. I coated my tool with lube and aimed it at Jess's asshole.

A note about sandwiches: They're not as easy as they look in the videos. I had to get in a more upright position to actually see Jess's butthole, which in turn threw off Hal's rhythm. When Hal resumed plunging his dick into me, his movements pushed my body forward and off course. My cock stabbed Jess's thigh and then his nutsac. I thought I'd made it on the third try, but it turned out I'd sunk my dick between two sofa cushions.

On the fourth attempt, I was able to hit my mark. The head of my cock butted (as it were) against Jess's asslips and ... stopped.

"Just push it in," he urged, reaching between his legs for my dick, making sure I stayed on target. I pressed on, coaxing Jess's hole open. His sphincter stretched over my pulsing cockhead. Next thing I knew, Jess's hungry ass was swallowing my entire shaft.

"Oh, man, that feels so good," he breathed, his body writhing beneath me.

We all quickly fell into a rhythm, Hal thrusting his dick into me, pushing me forward and causing me to thrust my cock into his boyfriend's hole, while Jess raised his hips to meet my invading dick. While Hal and Jess were clearly enjoying themselves, I felt especially privileged. The dual sensation of simultaneously fucking while being fucked is indescribable. It was ecstasy squared.

Our bodies connected ass-to-cock formed one, big fleshy wave, rolling back and forth with greater and greater force, the pleasure intensifying with each thrust. Hal's meaty hands dug into my sides as he pounded my ass, grunting like an animal feeding on its prey. Jess shuddered and trembled beneath me, his face red, his skin coated with sweat. A constant stream of filthy talk came from his parted lips – unintelligible between his groans, but turning me on nonetheless. Then there was me in between, riding Hal's cock and Jess's butt and squealing like the horny pig I'd so happily become. And I could tell by tightening of my ball sac and the tingling I felt all over, I'd be squealing even louder in seconds.

It was Jess who came first. He was stroking his drooling rod while I fucked him when his body froze and his features twisted into an agonized expression. Letting out a choked yelp, Jess fired his load, splattering cum all over his rigid abs. The thickness of his jizz surprised me; it had the consistency of mayonnaise. I almost wanted to dip my finger in it and taste it – and I almost did, too, except I got distracted with shooting my own wad. Closing my eyes, I gave in to the explosion of pleasure as my dick pumped its juice and Hal pumped my ass.

I fell on top of Jess, our torsos becoming cemented by his splooge. With my head resting on Jess's shoulders, I waited eagerly for Hal to come.

Hal wasn't content to blow his load with his dick buried in my ass, however. He pulled out of me abruptly and, grabbing me roughly by the arm, pulled me off – and out of – Jess. Jess, who had a better idea of what was expected at this moment, hopped down onto the floor, kneeling at Hal's feet. Catching on, I knelt beside Jess. We both looked up at Hal, who'd pulled off his rubber and was stroking throbbing cock, and waited for the inevitable shower.

It wasn't a long wait. Hal let out this deep roar, thrust his hips forward and let his jism fly. I felt the warm, slick drops of his cream land on my upturned face. Jess's face was next to mine, his tongue outstretched, trying to catch Hal's cum. I wasn't so brazen, though I did get a taste of Hal's load when I licked my lips. Kind of sharp tasting, but not bad – certainly not like bleach, as my future ex-wife claimed whenever she accidentally got a mouthful (the bitch always acted like we had to call Poison Control whenever *that* happened).

Hal looked down at our cum-spattered faces and smiled. He joined us on the floor, taking me in one arm and Jess in the other. He and Jess shared a deep, lingering kiss. When their faces separated, thick white beads of jism hung in Hal's goatee. Then he turned to me and pressed his lips against mine, slipping his tongue into my mouth.

"Let's go to bed," Hal said, standing up. He held out his hand, helping Jess to his feet.

I returned to the sofa, about to pull a blanket over my naked, satiated body when I noticed Hal and Jess were just standing there with these what-the-hell-do-you-think-you're-doing expressions on their faces.

"It's a big bed," Hal said.

I certainly didn't need an engraved invitation. I got up from the sofa and followed them upstairs.

Jack's Bounty

He entered the room, number 234. It was the color of a nicotine stain and didn't smell much better. Jack curled his lip in disgust and closed the door behind him. It wasn't the Ritz, but he'd been on the road for three days now. If the room had a bed, that was enough.

Jack dropped his duffle bag on the floor, tossed his keys on the nightstand and pealed off his sweaty T-shirt. So far no one had caught his trail. He hoped his luck held out until tomorrow morning, when he'd exchange the microchip for the 250 grand Vaughn had promised him for the job. Then maybe he could take a vacation and get away from all this industrial theft shit.

He wasn't sure what you'd call his profession. He started out just a simple thief. He was good at it – the cops never could catch him. But, the rich, powerful and greedy did. Jack was ripping off some computer equipment from a company in New Jersey when this joker decided he *had* to come in and work late. Fortunately, though, while the guy was a hard worker, he wasn't an honest one. He cut a deal with Jack: If he'd steal the plans of some project a competitor was developing, then Jack would be a free man. Sounded better than the alternative, so Jack stole the plans.

That one job soon led to others. For the past five years, he'd been hired by some very wealthy, very respectable men to steal the secrets of others. Now this microchip deal. He didn't even know what the fucking chip was supposed to do, but Vaughn wanted it and was willing to pay top dollar to get his hands on it. That was all Jack needed to know.

Jack lit a cigarette and turned on the TV. The reception was bad and he could only get three channels. He turned the set off. This shit-can motel didn't even have cable.

He stubbed out his cigarette in a chipped glass ashtray then unbuttoned his tight blue jeans. A shower was what he needed. The New Mexico heat had left behind a salty, sticky coating on his skin.

After Jack stripped, he reached for his duffle bag to retrieve his shaving kit and a gun – just in case – before heading for the bathroom.

Although alone, he shut the bathroom door behind him. The bathroom walls were covered in sickly green tile. The fluorescent light made everything look so much worse – including him, Jack thought, examining his face in the mirror. Three days on the road with little or no sleep had taken its toll. He had dark circles under his eyes and his short brown hair was now matted in clumps. His face was covered with stubble. Jack considered shaving but decided to leave it alone. He kind of liked it.

Of course the rest of him looked okay. More than okay, in fact: broad shoulders and chest, tapering down to narrow hips and a muscled ass. Then there was the main attraction, his long, thick cock. Jack stroked it a couple times absentmindedly as he turned on the shower. His dick had been neglected lately. Usually he could count on a little fun on these jobs. In fact, there were several occasions when he'd sucked and fucked his way out of dangerous situations. Not this trip. And since this town consisted of the motel, trailer park and a combination diner-gas station-post office, Jack didn't figure the odds were in favor of him finding some bored, young stud to keep him company.

Jack stepped into shower and bowed his head beneath the tepid spray. He took the small, complimentary bar of soap – the motel's only amenity – and lathered up, starting with his hairy chest and working his way down As he soaped up his massive rod and his heavy balls, he closed his eyes and imagined of having his cock sucked by some cute, athletic blond. He would take Jack's prick all the way down his throat, lick his balls, tongue his ass …

His cock was rigid now. Jack began to stroke it harder, the suds acting as a lubricant. He pictured his dick disappearing into that blond guy's mouth. *If only it was happening for real*, he thought, letting out a groan as he kneaded his hard meat, his hips gently thrusting to his rhythm.

Then he heard something, a door closing. Next door, maybe? No, sounded too close. Much too close.

As much as he hated to stop what he'd started, Jack knew he'd better check it out.

Jack rinsed off quickly and turned off the water. By the time he stepped out of the shower stall, his hard-on had already softened to a semi, the mood spoiled by the possibility someone may be in his room waiting to kill him. Not bothering to dry off or cover himself with a towel, Jack picked up the pistol he'd set on top of the toilet tank and approached the bathroom door cautiously. Slowly, he turned the knob. Then he pulled the door open swiftly, hiding behind it. There was no hale of bullets, but that didn't mean he was safe. They could be waiting for him to show his face.

His gun drawn, Jack quickly whirled around and jumped through the doorway, .45 extended in front of him, ready to shoot first.

"Well, don't we make a dramatic entrance."

Standing in front of Jack was a tall, muscular man with long, dark blond hair, wearing a rumpled raincoat and a pair of skintight jeans. His .357 Sig was aimed at the center of Jack's forehead.

Jack lowered his weapon first. "Jesus, El, you mean I got out of the shower to see *you*?"

El Tildon – "El" was short for Elmore, a name he hated – was the bounty hunter who'd been after Jack for the past year. A previous client wanted him dead for a perceived double cross: Jack sold some blueprints he'd stolen this client to someone else. But the client wanted to pay less than what they'd agreed on, so Jack took his merchandise to a higher bidder. The guy was just pissed that Jack wasn't easily screwed – in business, at least.

El's face slid into a smile, revealing a set of perfectly even, white teeth. "Jack, I'm hurt," he said, lowering his gun. "I thought you looked forward to our little visits."

"Can't believe you're still after me," Jack said. "You know I always get away. Besides, why does that old fart keep paying you to hunt me down? It's been a year."

"He holds a grudge," El shrugged. "But he's no longer paying me. He died three months ago."

"So what's this, a sales call?"

"I have a reputation of always getting my man," El said, stepping closer. "You're the only one who's ever gotten away."

"Twice," Jack reminded.

"Twice," El agreed, his smile tightening.

"So why didn't you try to take me out when I opened the door?"

El was very close now. "The old fart wanted you dead," he said. "I just want you."

Jack felt a stirring between his legs. El set his gun on top of the TV and put his hand beneath Jack's chin, raising his face slightly. "Are you as good with your dick as you are with a gun?"

"Why don't you suck it and see?" Jack replied, his swelling cock now pressing against El's thigh. El placed a kiss on Jack's lips, his tongue brushing Jack's lower lip. His arms circled Jack's waist and pulled him closer.

El suddenly pulled away. "I'm overdressed," he said, slipping out of his coat and letting it fall to the floor.

Jack watched as El removed his black T-shirt, revealing a chest that was tan, muscled and smooth. Jack lowered his face to the bounty hunter's firm pecs, his tongue circling one of El's hard, brown nipples. El's breathing quickened.

"I don't think you'll be needing this now," El said, removing the pistol from Jack's hand and setting it on the TV, next to his own gun. Jack didn't protest.

El slowly sank to his knees and grabbed Jack's stiff dong. El was about the same age as Jack – twenty-seven – but looked much younger. This pleased Jack, who liked them young. When Jack saw his big cock slide between those youthful, full lips, he thought he'd shoot his wad right then.

Jack moaned as El swallowed his dick and massaged it with his tongue. El's mouth enveloped Jack's thick meat lovingly. His tongue flicked at the head and traveled down the underside of the shaft. Jack placed a hand on top of El's head and guided him closer.

El fumbled with the fly of his pants, trying to free his aching prick. Jack noticed and slowly withdrew from the bounty hunter's mouth.

"Let me help you out," Jack said lasciviously, getting down on his knees.

El lay back on the floor, not caring about the cleanliness of the ugly burnt-orange shag carpet. Jack straddled El's face and, leaning over him in a sixty-nine position, began to work on releasing the fat cock hidden beneath the denim of his jeans. Meanwhile, El wrapped his mouth around Jack's rod and continued his skillful blowjob.

El's most formidable weapon, Jack discovered when he unbuttoned his jeans, was not his gun. His cock was huge – at least ten inches, Jack guessed. He wrapped a hand around its thickness and, after a couple of preliminary jerks, guided it into his hungry mouth, his tongue licking away the drops of pre-cum that oozed out the slit.

El's mouth continued to do amazing things to Jack's cock, taking the entire length down his throat and holding it deep in his gullet while his throat muscles gripped the shaft. Then the blond who originally had been sent to kill him lapped at his cum-swollen balls and nibbled his silky nutsac.

Jack rose up slowly, his ass directly above El's face. Knowing what was expected of him, El speared the warm depths of Jack's hole with his tongue. Jack closed his eyes as El rimmed him lustily.

"Get on the bed," Jack commanded, standing up.

El did as he was told, kicking off his boots and stepping out of his jeans. He climbed onto the bed and waited.

Hastily retrieving his shaving kit from the bathroom, Jack returned to El's inviting body. El was on his back, his legs spread. Jack put the shaving kit on the bed and leaned over El's naked crotch. He let his tongue dance over El's rigid cock a few more times before moving lower, over his balls then into his ass. El moaned as Jack probed deep into him.

Jack raised his face and smiled. "Think you're ready to get your man now?"

"I've been ready," El gasped.

Jack grabbed the shaving kit and removed a rubber. After rolling the condom over his pulsing shaft, he then took out a small tube of lube and squeezed a generous amount into his hand. He rubbed the lubricant over El's puckered asshole, working his fingers inside to loosen him up. Jack then rubbed the remaining lube over his throbbing tool.

Hoisting El's legs onto his shoulders, Jack entered him slowly, prying his ass cheeks apart with his long, stiff cock. El groaned and gasped as Jack skewered him.

Once inside El's tight hole, Jack began to thrust into him – slowly at first, then picking up the pace. El's face contorted into an expression of agonized pleasure. Jack's breathing quickened. He threw his head back, and a long, low moan escaped through his clenched jaws. He didn't know if he could hold back much longer.

He felt the cold steel of a .38 press against his neck.

"You've got a nice ass," said a gruff male voice, "for a dead guy."

Jack and El froze. From the corner of his eye, Jack could see a tall, athletic man dressed in black standing by the door and holding a gun. The man with the gun at Jack's neck was out of view, but Jack didn't need to see him to know he meant business.

A beefy hand landed on Jack's shoulder and pulled him away from El, sending him onto the floor with a hard thud.

"Ain't so quick when ya' got a piece of ass wrapped around your dick," said the gruff-voiced man. Jack could see him now. He was dressed in black like his buddy by the door, but not as tall and with twice the muscle. He wore his black hair in a spiky crew cut. Altogether, not a bad looking guy, Jack thought. Hell, he actually thought the brute was sexy, even if he did want to splatter Jack's brains against the wall.

"'Spose you know why we're here," the man spat.

"'Cause you're lonely," Jack snapped back.

The man slammed one of his steel-toed boots into Jack's side. "For the microchip, shithead," the man barked as Jack doubled up in pain.

The other man – the tall one – was now at the bed. He had El's neck in a chokehold and the nose of his pistol buried in El's cheek. He was younger than the thug browbeating Jack, but no less good looking and no less dangerous.

Jack slowly rose to his knees. "In there," he said, pointing to the shaving kit on the bed. "It's in a pocket inside."

Not taking his eyes or gun off Jack, the man eased over to the bed and grabbed the shaving kit. Emptying its contents on the floor, Jack's assassin fumbled around inside before he found the interior pocket. He removed the microchip and tossed the shaving kit aside. The chip was about one-inch square and as thin as a credit card.

"Got any idea what this is?" the man taunted Jack.

"Other than one guy paid me a bunch of money to steal it, and you guys are gonna kill me for it, no, I don't," Jack groaned, still in pain.

"This here," the man said, holding up the microchip, "can get into every bank account in the free world. Put this in a computer, and you have access to everybody's money."

"Sounds like a handy thing to have," Jack said, waiting for another vicious kick from the steel-toed boots.

"Shut up, smart-ass," the man snarled. "Now we got what I came for. We're supposed to kill you, and we will. But I want to have some fun first. Whadda you say, Sal. Watchin' these guys in action kind of got me hot, made my dick hard. Whadda about you?"

"This one's got a whopper on 'im," Sal said, still holding El tightly around the neck. "Shame to waste them without getting a taste, Boss."

"My thinking exactly," Boss replied. Slipping the chip in his pocket, he stepped toward Jack, still sitting on the floor. Inches away from him, Boss pointed his gun at Jack's head. "I got a going away present for you in my pants. Why don'tcha unwrap it?"

Slowly, Jack reached up and unzipped the man's fly, undid his belt and slid his pants down to his knees. Boss even wore black underwear. He wasn't lying when he said his dick was hard, Jack noted, admiring the impressive bulge in those Calvin Kleins. He pulled the briefs down, and Boss's massive prick sprang free. It was long, thick and uncut. Jack forgot about the gun pointed to his head and took hold of Boss's rock hard cock, rolling the foreskin back from the plump head. Then he leaned forward and guided it into his mouth.

"This is the last blowjob you're gonna give, tough guy. Better make it last," Boss groaned.

Sal, meanwhile had removed his shirt, revealing a taut, muscular chest and torso. Sitting on the bed, he pointed a pistol at El with one hand while stroking El's dick with the other. El's cock had gone soft, but Sal was quickly reviving it. When El was semi-hard, Sal forgot all about keeping his gun pointed at his head and dove for his prick, inhaling it into his hot mouth. Soft moans issued from El's lips as Sal issued his own delicious torture with his tongue. Apparently, Sal was a more enthusiastic cocksucker than killer.

Jack continued to work on Boss's dick and, judging by Boss's ecstatic moans, was doing a pretty damned good job. Jack had reached his arms around Boss's firm ass and let his fingers toy with his fuckhole.

"Stick your tongue up my ass," Boss commanded. "Make it wet."

Boss removed the rest of his clothes – doing so without once setting down his gun – and bent over, resting one arm on the foot of the bed. Jack spread those perfectly formed ass cheeks and buried his face in the dark, hairy crack. He pushed at the outer edge of his hole and then poked his tongue inside.

Sal had removed all his clothes at this point, too. He and El were locked in a sixty-nine, their tongues and mouths tasting, licking, sucking each other's cocks, balls and asses.

Then Boss, his sexual imagination taking flight, stood upright suddenly and began to arrange everyone on the bed.

"Okay, tough guy, I want you on all fours. I'm gonna plow into that ass so hard you'll wish I killed you. And you, blond boy, get underneath your friend here so you can suck his cock and lick my balls as I'm ramming him. Sal, feed your dick to tough guy here. He likes cock, and he'll love yours."

Thus arranged, the four of them began their frenzy of sucking and fucking. Boss smeared lube on his cock and on Jack's ass, but it still wasn't enough to ease the shock of that massive rod ramming into Jack's hole. Jack sucked in his breath as Boss's cock stretched his asshole wider than it ever had been stretched before. But the pain soon gave way to a near unbearable pleasure, the sensation heightened when El coiled his tongue around Jack's prick.

With Sal's pole poking him in the face, Jack's lips covered the dewy cockhead, prodding it with his tongue. Sal's cock quivered with each touch. With Boss slamming into him from behind and El slurping on his cock it was difficult to concentrate on giving head, but Jack soon took Sal's prick in his mouth, eagerly sucking on the engorged flesh. Sal thrust his hips forward, fucking Jack's mouth in wild abandon. Not wanting to ignore El, Jack reached down to fondle his prick.

Sal was the first to come. His thrusts into Jack's mouth became faster, as did his breathing. He was soon whimpering as he fought back his orgasm. Then, letting out a sharp cry, he shot his load. The heavy cream hit the back of Jack's throat, and he swallowed every last drop.

El was next. His body shuddered and his thick juice spurted from his cock in a wide arc. He came with such force that drops of his load hit Sal's thigh. Another heavy spurt of cum cascaded over Jack's hand and landed in El's pubic hair, hanging there like drops of pearly dew.

Before El could catch his breath, Jack let his jism fly into his welcoming mouth. Although it had been merely a number of days since Jack last came, it might as well have been years. By the time the last drop of his cream dribbled from his cock and onto El's wet, pink tongue, Jack felt weak, as if his energy had been drained along with his balls.

Boss pounded Jack's ass with greater ferocity as he reached his peak. His animal-like grunts became louder and louder until he suddenly withdrew. Sal immediately rushed around and kneeled beside him.

"Shoot on me, Boss," he pleaded. "Come on my face."

Vigorously stroking his cock, Boss aimed it at Sal's face. The first spurt of jism hit Sal right between the eyes, dripping down his cheeks and over his sensual lips. Sal's tongue darted out to lap up the bitter man-juice.

Boss's eyes were closed and his face relaxed into an expression of contentment as he sank down on the floor next to his partner. The two of them embraced and Boss gave Sal a long, loving kiss.

So, the killer is a romantic at heart, Jack thought.

While the Boss and Sal were canoodling, Jack grabbed his car keys off the nightstand and his duffle bag off the floor. El snatched up Boss's pants, which had the microchip in the pocket. Naked, Jack and El ran out of the motel room.

By the time Boss and Sal had grabbed their guns and chased after them, Jack and El were speeding down the highway.

The Vertel Project

Tory circled his tongue slowly around the bulbous crown of Dr. Vertel's cock, savoring the feel and taste of the engorged organ. His tongue treatment elicited muffled groans from the doctor. Encouraged, Tory opened wide then took Dr. Vertel's prick into his mouth, taking it down his throat until his nose almost touched the doctor's cum-heavy balls. More groans of pleasure.

The doctor was delivering a fair amount of pleasure himself. Tory was positioned above him on the doctor's bed. Dr. Vertel had been slurping his young assistant's dick, but now his mouth was wandering. The doctor's wet tongue caressed his balls then tongue probed Tory's ass. Dr. Vertel's mustache felt scratchy against Tory's ass crack, but his tongue was smooth as silk.

Tory sucked the doctor's cock more fervently. Dr. Vertel slid a finger into Tory's spit-lubed asshole while stroking the young man's dick with his other hand. Tory was practically grinding his ass into the doctor's face. Meanwhile, he continued to worship Dr. Vertel's cock, licking it, sucking it and swallowing it.

Before long, the doctor was thrusting his pelvis upward, fucking his assistant's mouth. The more pleasure Tory gave, the more forceful Dr. Vertel became, gnawing at Tory's puckered ass ring and pulling at Tory's dick until ...

They came almost simultaneously. Tory pulled his mouth away just in time before the doctor released a thick, syrupy load from his cock, his cum hitting Tory on the chin. At that instant, Tory let loose with his own gooey eruption.

Minutes later, Tory was lying next to Dr. Vertel, his head on the doctor's shoulder and his hand running through the forest of coarse black hairs that spread across the doctor's broad chest. Tory's spent load had formed sticky puddles on Dr. Vertel's nicely rounded pecs.

Dr. Vertel grabbed the remote from the nightstand and kissed the top of Tory's blond head. "Time for the news," he said, clicking on the TV.

They stared at the screen as a perpetually smiling newscaster told of the tragic goings-on in the world.

"I treated him a year ago," Dr. Vertel said of the anchorman.

"Yeah, you told me," Tory said dully. Dr. Vertel mentioned it whenever the news came on.

"He's got the hots for the sportscaster," Dr. Vertel continued. "Never said that was who, but he described him to a T. Apparently played golf with the guy one day, saw him naked in the locker room, and came running to me with all these fantasies of how he wants to suck the guy's dick. Kinda' sad. Anyway, it gets me thinking."

"About what?"

"My theory – or rather, my experiment to prove the theory."

"The one about how all men – even those most staunchly heterosexual – really prefer sex with other men?" This, too, Tory had heard many times.

The doctor chuckled. "Yes, that one. Anyway, I think it's time to go through with it. All I lack is a subject, which will be tough because the type of man I need won't volunteer."

It was to be one of the doctor's more questionable escapades. The Vertel Clinic had long been a thorn in the side of the AMA. Though most of the doctor's practice was legit – he specialized in treating sexual dysfunction among men, particularly gay men – some of his other treatments wouldn't have been viewed kindly by the medical community. Among these treatments were Group Fantasy Therapy, which was nothing more than glorified circle jerks, or the One-on-One Encounters, which, by most professional standards, were considered nothing short of prostitution.

Suddenly, an item on the news caught Dr. Vertel's attention. The story concerned a man who was beaten up by three college students as he left a gay bar. Two of the students had escaped but one was arrested. The young man was shown snarling at TV cameras as he was led handcuffed to a police car. The man's name was Stephen Bixley. He was in jail waiting to make bail.

Dr. Vertel turned to Tory and smiled. "I think we just found our subject," he said.

It was nearly dawn before one of Stephen Bixley's fraternity brothers arrived at the jail to bail him out. "Can't believe they arrested me for beating up a faggot," he muttered as he collected his personal items from the desk sergeant.

The sun was just beginning to rise as the two young men left the police station. Even though he had been in jail for a mere seven hours, Stephen felt dazed by the fresh air and sunlight. As they headed for the parking lot next to the station, two men approached them from the opposite direction. Both the men looked like bodybuilders. The two fraternity brothers tried not to appear intimidated.

"'Scuse me," one of the men said, stopping Stephen's college friend. "Do you have the time?"

While his friend checked his watch, Stephen looked out at the street, trying to ignore the steroid freaks.

A fist slammed into the base of his neck. Stephen was unconscious before he felt the pain.

Stephen came to in a sterile white room. He was naked and sitting on a small bed. His hands were tied behind his back, his feet were bound and his mouth was fitted with a ball gag. He felt like someone had driven a railroad spike through his skull.

His eyes focused on two men in front of him, one sitting and one standing. The one sitting was older, had dark brown hair, a moustache and wore a white lab coat. He stared at Stephen through a pair of wire-rimmed glasses. The other guy was younger, maybe in his early twenties. He had shaggy blond hair and wore a white uniform, as if he was a nurse or something, except most nurses Stephen had seen didn't wear pants so tight you could see the shape of their cocks.

"Hi, Stephen," the older man said, his voice deep and commanding. "I'm Dr. Vertel. Behind me is my assistant, Tory. You're at the Vertel Clinic. I won't tell you why we brought you here – yet – but I can assure you that you won't be harmed. I apologize for the manner in which we got you here, but suffice it to say you would not have come willingly had we given you that option.

"We will provide you with all the necessities, such as food and shelter. Clothing isn't a necessity here. You will be unbound after we leave, but you will not be able to leave this room. I've had you gagged because I have no interest in what you have to say.

"Tory and I will leave you now. One of my interns will be arriving shortly to untie you and give you your lunch. I trust you won't give him any trouble."

After the two men left the room, Stephen was more confused than when he had first regained consciousness.

#

"Think we'll experience our big breakthrough today," Dr. Vertel announced as Tory entered the viewing room. The doctor was sitting in front of a bank of six television monitors covering one wall, monitors that could serve as a window into six different rooms or into one room.

All six TV screens were tuned to room 12, Stephen's room.

Stephen had been at the Vertel Clinic for three weeks now. Much to Dr. Vertel's amusement, the police weren't buying the story that Stephen was kidnapped, particularly since there were no ransom demands. They wrote his disappearance off as some scumbag who jumped bail.

Since being brought to the clinic, Stephen had followed a predictable course of behavior. For the first couple of days, he'd spent his time cursing his situation (he was gagged frequently) and trying – without success – to escape.

He'd been more subdued the past couple weeks. It was during this time Dr. Vertel actually implemented his experiment. First stage: Sexual depravation. Stephen was to be exposed to no sexual stimuli at all and his hands were bound, so he couldn't jack off. Second stage:

Redirected orientation. Stephen would receive subtle stimuli to induce sexual thoughts, but all suggestions were about men. This was tricky, for Dr. Vertel had trouble finding material that was subtle but did not include images or references to women. The best he could do was a men's clothing catalogue and some lame sports videos. Still, these did have the desired effect. Although Stephen's initial reaction upon receiving a copy of the clothing catalogue was to hurl it across the room, he did eventually pick it up and leaf through it. Dr. Vertel was careful to note his homophobe captive got semi-hard while studying the catalogue's underwear section.

Now the third stage, fantasy confrontation, was in progress. The closed circuit TV in Stephen's room was now showing all-male porn videos. He had been strapped to his bed. The straps went across Stephen's chest and legs, but not his wrists. He couldn't raise his hands over his head, but he had easy access to his crotch.

Tory stood beside the doctor's chair. "Check this out," Dr. Vertel said excitedly, pointing at the six TV screens.

Not that Tory hadn't already noticed: Stephen was stroking a raging boner as he watched a young performer get stuffed from both ends on the TV in his room. Tory felt stirring in his groin. He didn't know if Dr. Vertel's "project" would turn a homophobe gay, but it sure was making him horny.

"How long has he been watching the movies?" Tory asked.

"Almost 10 hours now," the doctor said, glancing down at the notes in his lap. "He first started shouting that the films were 'gross' and 'sick' and shutting his eyes, which is to be expected, given his mentality. But, he soon began to stare at the screen. As you can see, he doesn't find the films so gross anymore."

Tory watched as Stephen massaged his cock, his strokes more intent now. Tory dug at his own crotch, adjusting his stiffening dick. Stephen may have been a homophobic asshole, Tory thought, but god, he was a feast to the eyes. His handsome face contorted in a look of rapture; his sculpted body writhed beneath the straps holding him to his bed; and the way he pulled at his pulsing prick – it had Tory wishing he could rush to room 12 and give Stephen what he obviously desired.

"You appear interested in Mr. Bixley's progress," Dr. Vertel said, reaching out and taking Tory's hand.

"Um, just watching," Tory said as the doctor pulled him close.

"So I see," Dr. Vertel said, dropping his clipboard to the floor and unzipping Tory's pants.

Tory's cock sprang forward.

The doctor flicked the tip of Tory's dick with his tongue then slowly swallowed the organ all the way down to the hilt. Tory was torn between watching the TV monitors and devoting his attention to the doctor. But, it was no contest, really: Stephen may have been a pleasure to watch, but what Dr. Vertel was doing to his cock was ten times more compelling.

Tory leaned down and fumbled with the doctor's belt and zipper, freeing Dr. Vertel's own granite-like cock. As he stroked Dr. Vertel's hard-on, the doctor gulped and licked Tory's dick with greater enthusiasm.

Tory shut his eyes. "Oh, yeah, I think ... I'm gonna ... come!"

His whole body jerked. Dr. Vertel withdrew his mouth just in time to receive Tory's load right in his mustached face. The force of his orgasm was so incredible, Tory almost lost his balance. In fact, Tory was so lost in the feeling that he almost didn't notice Dr. Vertel spilling his own man juice all over the leg of his gray trousers.

When the pleasure had subsided, they shared a leisurely kiss. Tory playfully lapped up the droplets of his load that stippled the doctor's face. Then he noticed something out of the corner of his eye.

"Dr. Vertel, look!" he said, pointing at the TV monitors.

Stephen was releasing a geyser of white, gooey man cream. But that wasn't the interesting part. The two men couldn't help but notice that their subject had worked two of his fingers into his ass while he brought himself off with his other hand.

"I believe we may be witnessing another success story for the Vertel Clinic," the doctor said, his mouth widening into a proud smile.

# # # # #

From the other side of a two-way mirror, Dr. Vertel and Tory watched as Stephen was ushered into the next room. It was time for the final test.

There wasn't much to observe at first: Stephen wandering about, naked, giving a curious glance at a pack of condoms and a bottle of lubricant set on a table in a corner of the room. The room's only other furnishing was a leather-upholstered chaise lounge. Dr. Vertel pressed a button on the intercom sitting on the table next to him. "Send in the other two subjects," he commanded.

Things quickly got more interesting. In walked a muscular blond man sporting a generously proportioned cock and a brunette woman with a centerfold's body.

Tory shot a glance at Dr. Vertel, who quickly explained. "To prove my theory, I'm afraid I will have to offer the temptations of the opposite sex. The woman is a very successful call girl, charges upwards of $500 a night. For this job, she will get $1,000 if Stephen does to her what I expect, which is nothing, and $5,000 if this experiment blows up in my face, and he fucks her."

"And the guy?" Tory asked. "He looks familiar."

"I cheated a bit. That's Billy Buldick, star of many of Stephen's now-favorite videos. Let me tell you, the hooker is a bargain compared to his asking price."

The doctor and his assistant watched as Stephen, who had only been instructed to "do what comes naturally," studied his two companions.

Stephen eyed Billy, but gave no visible indication that he was interested in, or that he even recognized, the porn star. He then turned his attention to the girl, who flashed her best $5,000 smile. Stephen walked toward her.

"Oh, shit!" Dr. Vertel shouted, pounding his fist onto the table beside him. "Please don't let this happen."

Stephen was now in front of the girl. Cautiously, Stephen raised his hands, reaching for her tits.

"No! No! No! You stupid son of a bitch!" Dr. Vertel shouted again, as if he'd just witnessed a bad play at a football game.

But before Stephen's hands made contact with the hooker's flesh, he looked over at Billy. The porn star smiled and slowly rubbed his hand over his fat cock. Stephen quickly redirected his interests, turning away from the girl and walking toward Billy. It appeared the call girl was only going to get $1,000 for this job.

Tory and the doctor watched anxiously as Stephen stood before Billy, obviously unsure of how to proceed. Billy reached up and playfully pinched one of Stephen's nipples. Stephen didn't resist. He instead rubbed a hand across the chest of one of gay porn's favorite leading men.

Dr. Vertel was positively giddy. "Yes! Oh, thank Christ, my plan is going to work!"

Proving one's hypothesis was fine, Tory thought, but he was more interested in watching these two hunks fuck.

Billy wrapped his arms around Stephen and grabbed his ass, pulling the young man closer. When he kissed Stephen, Dr. Vertel became visibly tense.

Stephen opened his mouth and slid his tongue between the lips of Billy Buldick. The woman shrugged and quietly left the room; Stephen's choice had been made.

Stephen had his arms around Billy now, pressing his body hard against him. He gyrated his hips, grinding his cock against Billy's. Soon, Stephen was sinking to his knees, his tongue gliding down Billy's spectacular torso as he went.

Billy's famous nine-inch cock was rigid now. Tory rubbed his crotch as he watched Stephen make the first tentative jab at Billy's cock with his tongue. He then slowly wrapped his mouth around Billy's dick. He sucked the porn star's cock clumsily, but it was obvious by the expression on Billy's face that Stephen's lack of skill wasn't hindering the pleasure. Billy began to gently fuck Stephen's mouth.

Tory unzipped his fly and took out his stiff dong, fondling it as he watched the action in the next room. He glanced over at Dr. Vertel;

the doctor, staring intently at the progress of his "study," also had his cock out and was stroking it.

Tory stood up from his chair and stripped off his white uniform. "I have a treatment of my own for that," he said, pointing at the doctor's hard-on.

Dr. Vertel only smiled in response as his assistant, now nude, knealed between his legs and took his swollen prick in his mouth. The doctor sighed. Tory's hot mouth was definitely the ideal prescription.

In the next room, Billy and Stephen had moved to the lounge chair. Stephen was reclining on his back, his eyes shut and his chest heaving as Billy gnawed at one of his nipples and stroked his cock. He then moved his mouth down to Stephen's dick, swallowing it whole.

This sent Stephen into a pre-orgasmic frenzy. Through clenched teeth, he let out whimpers, gasps and moans as Billy sucked and licked his man-meat. In the next room, Dr. Vertel was having a similar reaction as Tory swirled his tongue over his balls.

Billy stood up suddenly and reached over to the table, grabbing the bottle of lube and the condoms that had been provided for them. Kneeling at the foot of the chair, Billy buried his face between Stephen's thighs, burrowing his tongue into Stephen's hole. His body writhing, Stephen placed both hands on Billy's head and pulled his face deeper into his splayed ass.

The porn star pulled away, grinning. He removed a condom from the box and slipped it over his dick. He then squeezed a generous amount of lube into his hand. Billy first greased his sheathed cock, then reached between Stephen's wide-open legs, sliding his fingers inside the ex-homophobe's tight, virgin hole. It was clear by the look on Stephen's face that he was eager to be deflowered.

Much as he hated to, Dr. Vertel's duties as a scientist demanded that he interrupt Tory's energetic cocksucking to point out the action on the other side of the glass. They both watched as Billy carefully entered Stephen. Stephen, unprepared for the pain of the initial thrust, let out a howl that penetrated the soundproof walls. But, Billy was gentle; once inside, he began to pump Stephen's ass slowly and soothe him with a tender kiss.

Inspired by the scene in the next room, Dr. Vertel removed a lubricated condom from his lab coat and handed it to Tory before standing up and peeling off his clothes.

"I think our subjects have the right idea," the doctor said.

Once naked, the doctor returned to his seat. Tory quickly tore open the condom packet and unrolled it over Dr. Vertel's large prick. He stood and, turning so he faced the glass and could continue watching Billy ram Stephen, eased himself onto the doctor's cock. He leaned back against Dr. Vertel's muscular chest and moaned as the doctor thrust deep into his chute.

In the other room, Billy was delivering some deep thrusts of his own. Stephen had his hands locked around the porn star's ass cheeks, as if he feared Billy would flee at any minute. Billy was furiously fucking Dr. Vertel's subject. It was hard to believe that only a couple months ago Billy was perpetrating hate crimes against "fags"; now he was gleefully getting his ass pounded by one.

The imminence of Billy's orgasm was soon evident on his face. Even though he was a seasoned pro, Billy couldn't hold back indefinitely. With one final stab into the depths of Stephen's ass, he came, his body jerking each time his cock pumped out another spurt.

Tory could feel the doctor nearing his peak as well. Dr. Vertel's breath hit the back of his neck in hot gusts, and his fucking became more intense. The doctor reached around Tory's waist and stroked his young assistant's drooling rod. Any minute now, Tory thought ...

Next door, Billy had slid out of Stephen's ass and was now jacking him off while tonguing Stephen's tight nutsac. Stephen's head was thrown back, his eyes shut and his mouth contorted into a grimace. In an instant, he was showering Billy with thick streams of jism.

Watching Stephen come triggered Tory's orgasm. Jets of hot jizz spilled onto the floor and dribbled over Dr. Vertel's hand. Dr. Vertel came, too, crying out as he fired his load.

After catching their breath, the two men enjoyed a long, passionate kiss. The doctor continued fondling Tory's dick, petting it as if it were a purring kitten.

On the other side of the glass, they could see Billy and Stephen lying next to one another, kissing and running their hands up and down each other's bodies.

"Isn't science fascinating," Dr. Vertel commented.

"Yeah," Tory smiled. He then asked, "What about when Stephen leaves here? Aren't you afraid he'll tell the police?"

Dr. Vertel grinned. He had a parting gift for Stephen: a copy of a videocassette on which his session with Billy Buldick had been recorded.

"He won't tell," the doctor said confidently.

The Center Ring

Ari knew his fate before his father told him. He knew the moment the blond man in the black car arrived.

He had heard of him, the Talent Scout. He searched the outlying villages for young men to take to the Center Ring. It was supposed to be an honor to be chosen. In return, the family got a substantial sum of money.

So, when his father returned to the garden where Ari was half-heartedly hoeing the dry soil, he wasn't surprised by what he was told.

"You're leaving with the Scout," his father said, clasping Ari's shoulder and squeezing it affectionately. "You've been chosen." Tears welled in his eyes.

"Now?" Ari was incredulous.

"Now," answered the Scout, walking up behind Ari's father. Ari suddenly felt anxious upon seeing the man he'd heard so much about but had never seen. The Scout's thickly muscled body was clothed entirely in black: black T-shirt, black leather pants, black motorcycle boots. He wore a long, black leather trench coat that flapped behind him in the breeze. A pair of black sunglasses shielded the Talent Scout's eyes.

The Scout was puffing on a long brown cigarillo. "He can come as he is. Everything will be provided for him where he's going," the Scout told Ari's father, exhaling a large cloud of smoke that immediately disappeared in the wind.

Ari looked first to the Scout then to his father. Ari wore only a pair of tattered cotton shorts. He wasn't even wearing shoes.

As if sensing Ari's concern, the Scout smiled. "Don't worry, clothes aren't going to matter much."

Ari's father took the hoe from his son. "Go, now," his father urged, pushing him toward the Scout.

He slowly walked toward the Talent Scout. The Scout's hair was short, spiky and bleached blond, almost white. He had a closely cropped beard, a few shades darker than his hair. Ari could see the outline of the man's cock beneath the leather pants; it was semi-hard. The tension Ari felt was now out of desire, not intimidation.

The Scout threw an arm around Ari's shoulder and walked him to the long black car. It would be the first time Ari had ever ridden in a motor vehicle; gas was so expensive only the very wealthy could afford to have cars. Hard to believe that before the Great Winter almost everyone had a car. His father had told him that before nature was thrown off balance by the abuses of man, most people had electricity and water piped into their homes, things now only attainable by an elite few.

The Scout opened the door and ushered Ari into the back seat. The Talent Scout tossed his cigarillo away and climbed in after him. The moment the car door shut, the driver, concealed by a wall of black glass, put the car into the gear and sped away. Ari looked out the back window and watched the small house, the meager plot of land, and his father disappear in the dust.

"You afraid?" the Scout asked.

Ari shook his head.

"Good. Nothing bad is going to happen to you. In fact, you'll probably enjoy it very much."

The Scout took Ari's hand and placed it on the mound in his crotch. Carefully, Ari squeezed the Scout's cock through the leather.

"Like that? Want to take it out? Go ahead," the Scout encouraged.

Ari carefully unbuckled the man's belt and unzipped his fly. The Scout's dick popped out, red and swollen with lust. Ari felt his own cock start to rise and a pleasurable warmth spread through his body.

"Touch it," the Scout commanded.

Ari obeyed. His hands gently glided over the Scout's long member, caressing the raised veins on the shaft and gliding over the bulbous crown.

The Talent Scout leaned over and whispered in Ari's ear: "Suck it. I want you to suck my cock and lick my balls."

Ari's eyes widened. He'd never done this before, though he'd thought about it. He'd fantasized doing it as he jacked off, but he had never had the chance to act on that fantasy – until now. His heart quickened, out of fear and excitement, as he tentatively lowered his head toward the man's crotch.

"Ooohhh, that's right," the Scout gasped as Ari's mouth enveloped his stiff prick. Sampling the new ones wasn't expressly forbidden, but the Talent Scout knew it was not approved of either. Still, he considered it one of the perks of his job, an audition of sorts. As Ari took his cock down his throat, the Scout couldn't help but pat himself on the back for getting this one. An innocent looking, handsome face coupled with a well-formed, manly body. And, he was young, too. Just turned nineteen, the boy's father said. They liked them young in the Center Ring.

Ari began to suck the Scout's dick more aggressively, trying to swallow its entire length. The Scout was squirming now, running his gloved fingers through Ari's long, dark blond hair. Ari himself was now rock hard. He massaged his rod through his shorts. He hoped the Scout would suck him off, too.

The Scout began breathing faster. He thrust his hips upwards, trying to feed the young man more of his cock. Suddenly, he let out a loud, satisfied groan. His hot, gooey load washed over Ari's tongue and down his throat.

The Talent Scout relaxed, leaned back against the seat and let out a heavy sigh. Ari raised his head. The Scout smiled at him and put his hand beneath Ari's chin, wiping away a drop of his own cum. Yes, he had made a good choice.

They arrived in Voltare in an hour's time, as the sun was starting to set. It was an ugly city. To Ari, it resembled a giant, abandoned factory. Tall, dirty concrete and brick buildings jutted into the horizon. Smokestacks spilled out clouds of black smoke. "That's where the fuel is burned for power," the Scout explained. Ari nodded, though he did not fully understand what the power was. Where he grew up there was no electricity.

Though the city looked lifeless from a distance, it was, in fact, a hub of activity. The streets were filled with people and the long black car had to slow to a crawl as it maneuvered through the bustling crowds to its ultimate destination. Their arrival at the Center Ring was something of a letdown for Ari. For all the stories he had heard about the place, it didn't appear to be much from the outside, just a large brick warehouse with a heavy black door.

The car stopped. The Talent Scout lit another cigarillo and grabbed Ari's arm. "Come with me," he said, leading Ari out of the car and into the building.

It was dark inside. Ari's eyes barely had a chance to adjust before the Scout was ushering him upstairs. On the third floor, they entered an empty room. "Wait here," the Scout said, before disappearing through another door. He came back moments later with another man. This man was tall and thin. He was older than the Scout, his hair a bushy mass of steel grey and his face, though attractive, had the distinct lines of time. He wore a long purple robe. To Ari, he looked like a priest.

"And who do we have here?" the man said.

"Ari, this is Farrell. He runs the place," the Scout said.

"Ari," Farrell repeated, taking the young man's hands into his own. "Like the name. Where did you find him?" he asked the Scout.

"In Tormaine, about 75 miles from here. Slaving away on a small farm with his father," the Scout said.

"Hard labor," Farrell smiled brightly. "That explains the muscles. You've done well. Get him ready right away. He can debut tonight." To Ari, Farrell said, "I think you'll be very popular here."

Farrell let go of Ari's hands and left the room.

The Scout took Ari down another corridor and into a large, white tiled bathroom. The Scout told Ari to remove his shorts. Ari noticed a wry smile crossing the Scout's lips as he stepped out of his only article of clothing. Ari thought they might do more of what they did in the car and felt a stirring in his groin. But, the Scout just told him to step into the showers.

"There's soap and shampoo for you in there," the Scout said as Ari stepped into the shower area. "Take as long as you like."

Ari turned a knob on the wall and hot water shot out of the shower, the spray pelting his flesh. Soon he forgot about the Scout being there and relaxed, lathering up his body with the perfumed soap provided for him. So much nicer than the harsh soap his father made. After twenty minutes, he turned the water off. He turned and was startled by the sight of another man standing in the room, holding a towel out to him.

"I'm Joshua," he said as Ari took the towel from his hands. Joshua was about Ari's age and very beautiful. The shapeless white tunic Joshua wore stretched tight across his broad shoulders and firm pecs before falling like a curtain over the rest of his body.

Once dry, Ari wrapped the towel around his waist and followed Joshua into another room. "Hop up here," Joshua said, patting a massage table.

Ari got up on the table and lay down on his back. Joshua got a bottle of oil and poured it on Ari's body. The oil was warm and had an earthy scent. Ari closed his eyes as Joshua rubbed the oil on his chest. It felt good having Joshua's hands on him. Real good. His cock began to stiffen.

"Take the towel off," Joshua said, his hands gliding over Ari's abdomen. Ari took off the towel, embarrassed that his dick was now rigid. But, Joshua didn't say a word. He kept rubbing the oil on Ari, his hands lightly brushing Ari's balls as he rubbed down the inside of his thighs.

"Turn over," Joshua said. Ari did, and Joshua continued. His hands traveled over Ari's shoulders, down his back. He squirted some oil onto Ari's ass. His hands caressed him much slower now. Ari felt his fingers work their way inside him, spreading the oil into his tight hole. He let out an involuntary gasp. It felt so good. Ari's cock was now like stone.

Abruptly, Joshua said, "Okay, you're ready. I'll take you to the Ring now."

When Ari sat up and hopped off the table he noticed Joshua's cock was poking at the front of his tunic. He wanted to touch it, take it in his mouth like he had done with the Scout's dick. He wanted Joshua to do the same to him. But, Joshua just silently led Ari out of the room, through a dark corridor and down a short flight of stairs.

"What's going to happen to me?" Ari asked, trying to keep the fear out of his voice.

Joshua smiled. "Nothing bad. Just enjoy it."

There was a door at the foot of the stairs. Joshua removed a key from a pocket in his tunic and unlocked the door. "Whatever happens, don't resist," he said. Then, with a sly grin, he added, "Though you appear more than eager."

Joshua opened the door and pushed Ari through, immediately shutting it behind him.

More darkness. Ari could hear the din of conversations from an unseen crowd. His cock began to shrink. He wasn't afraid; he was terrified.

A shaft of bright light rained down on him suddenly, followed by the roar of approval from the crowd.

Ari was on a stage, enclosed by a chain link fence. The bright light prevented him from actually seeing the audience on the other side of the fence, but judging by the noise they made, it was a large one.

"Gentlemen," said a voice through loudspeaker, "thank you for joining us. Tonight, we present Ari, brought to us just today. I'm sure you'll find him a welcome addition to the Center Ring."

Ari recognized the voice. It was Farrell. The crowd cheered again. When the noise died down, Farrell told the audience, "And now the Ring Master, and his two apprentices, Ty and Joshua."

The crowd roared and stomped its feet as three men joined Ari on stage.

Joshua was no longer wearing his tunic; on stage his costume consisted of a heavy chain around his waist and chains around his wrists. His dick was long and semi-erect. The other apprentice, Ty, was adorned in a similar fashion. Ty was shorter than Joshua, but just as attractive. His hair was black and curly, and beneath his thick eyebrows were seductive brown eyes. His compact body was muscular and hairy. His cock was fat, uncut and bounced slightly as he walked.

Ari's fear dissipated, replaced with desire.

The Ring Master walked slightly behind the other two. Ari was immediately transfixed. The Ring Master's physique was incredible, each muscle thick and exquisitely defined, from his broad shoulders to his narrow hips to his solid legs. He had the regal features of an ancient Roman statue, and his head was capped with dark, closely cropped hair. Unlike the apprentices, the Ring Master wore leather: leather bands around his upper arms and a pair of leather briefs that had a zipper going down the front. The thought of what lay beneath that zipper had Ari's cock rising quickly.

Ty and Joshua came to a stop at either side of him. The Ring Master stood in front of Ari, his green eyes boring into him. A trace of a smile crossed his lips, and he leaned forward and kissed Ari. It was a slow, sensual, probing kiss that almost brought Ari to his knees.

The Ring Master pulled away. "Do you think you can please me?"

Ari nodded feebly.

"First, I want to watch you. Suck off my apprentices. I want to see both their cocks in your mouth. I want you to suck them until they come. I want to see their juice spill over your pretty face."

The Ring Master's deep, serious voice gave his request a sinister edge that made Ari's stomach quiver with fear. Still, he was determined to please the Ring Master and slowly kneeled between the apprentices.

The two men closed in on him. Ari took their dicks, now hard and quivering, in his hands. He first started on Joshua, licking the head of his cock before taking its full length in his mouth. He turned and did the same to Ty, pushing back his foreskin with his tongue.

"I said at the same time," the Ring Master's voice boomed.

Ari opened his mouth wide, letting Joshua and Ty crowd their throbbing cocks inside. At first he feared he would gag, but he soon adjusted, enjoying the feel of two dicks in his mouth, stretching his lips wide. The apprentices tried to force themselves deeper, groaning as their cocks rubbed together within Ari's hot mouth.

Ari reached down to pull at his own prick, only to be scolded by the Ring Master. "Don't touch yourself!" he said. "You can only touch us." Ari immediately moved his hands away. He decided to keep them occupied by letting his fingers explore the apprentices' asses and working his fingers into their holes.

Joshua and Ty's lips and bodies were pressed against each other. They kissed urgently as their pleasure intensified. Ari could sense they were nearing their peak and pulled his mouth away. He grabbed their cocks and jacked them off simultaneously. Both let out loud cries as their thick cream hit his face in rapid spurts. Rivulets of cum cascaded over his cheeks, lips and chin.

When the two men had finished coming, Ari looked up at the Ring Master. He was grinning. The audience's cheers were deafening.

The Ring Master knelt down in front of him. "You did very well," he said. He reached to stroke Ari's dick. "Bet you're so hot you can't stand it," he teased, pulling at Ari's cock a little faster. "Bet you're about to shoot any second."

Ari was breathing heavy. His balls were tight, on the verge of releasing his load.

The Ring Master withdrew his hand abruptly.

"Later," he said, standing up. He rubbed his bulging crotch. "Bet you want this even more, don't you? You want to suck my dick. Bet you've wanted to open this zipper, so you can get at my cock and swallow it all. Am I right?"

Ari nodded timidly.

"Then go ahead. Unzip it."

Ari reached up and, hands trembling, unzipped the leather briefs. They fell to the floor, and the Ring Master's rod sprang free. It was much larger than either Joshua's or Ty's, jutting over Ari's face like a flagpole. Ari began to salivate, wanting to trace the rigid veins of the Ring Master's cock with his tongue. He reached up for it, only to have the Ring Master turn around, suddenly and cruelly.

"I want your tongue in my ass first," he said, presenting his firm, round butt to Ari's face. "Nothing would get me hotter than your little pink boy tongue up my hole."

The crowd applauded. One member of the audience shouted, "Hell YEAH!"

Ari leaned forward, grabbed the Ring Master's butt cheeks, and, taking a deep breath, buried his face in the crack of his ass. His nose filled with his manly scent. Cautiously he touched his tongue to the Ring Master's rose-hued ass lips.

"Shove it inside," the Ring Mastered said. "Fuck my ass with your tongue."

Not wanting to disappoint, Ari forced his tongue into the Ring Master's chute. He probed and prodded it, thrilled when he heard the Ring Master moaning softly.

One of the apprentices – Ari couldn't see which one – began exploring Ari's ass, first with his tongue, then with his fingers. Ari savored the feeling. As his pleasure increased, so did his efforts to please the Ring Master. He rimmed him eagerly, making his hole wet with his spit.

The Ring Master turned around again. "You know what to do now," he said, grabbing the base of his dick and waving it tauntingly at his young performer.

Ari immediately wrapped his mouth around the Ring Master's engorged cock, inhaling it down his throat. The Ring Master threw his head back, grunting and groaning. Ari's tongue circled the corona of the Ring Master's prick and glided down the length of his shaft. He sucked on his balls and then returned to the tip of the Ring Master's cock, circling the crown with his tongue before opening wide and swallowing as much of the meaty pole as he was able.

The Ring Master was practically breathless when pulled away. "Get on all fours," he said. Ari did as he was told. The Ring Master moved behind him and the crowd began to chant.

"Fuck him! Fuck him! Fuck him!"

The Ring Master got down on his knees. He lowered his face to Ari's ass, until Ari could feel his breath against his butthole. Then he stabbed his tongue deep into Ari's chute. The young man yelped from the shock, but quickly became lost in the sensation, closing his eyes and smiling as the Ring Master ate his ass.

A much more brutal shock followed when the Ring Master replaced his tongue with his cock. The sharp, sudden pain of his ass-ring forced open by the larger man's huge dick nearly brought Ari to tears. He felt as if he were being split apart. He cried out, begging the Ring Master to stop, but the other man continued to drive his cock deeper into his hole.

The pain soon subsided, giving way to a delight Ari had never experienced. Ari writhed ecstatically as the Ring Master thrust into his ass.

While the Ring Master plowed into him from behind, Joshua sat down in front of Ari, spreading his legs invitingly. Ari didn't need to be told what to do this time. He slowly licked Joshua's hard prick. Ty stood over his fellow apprentice, moaning as Joshua sucked on his hairy balls.

The audience had lost all control. Men leapt onto the chain link fence and offered their rigid cocks to the men inside the Ring. Some were content with each other, climbing up on tables and letting other members of the crowd suck their hard dicks or fuck their eager asses.

Ari continued to swallow Joshua's cock, while Joshua, in turn, worked Ty into a joyful frenzy with his mouth. The Ring Master's thrusts were quickening, his groans becoming louder. Suddenly, he clenched Ari's ass and with one final thrust, sent a stream of hot cum into the young man's gut.

As if responding to the Ring Master's release, Joshua shot his load down Ari's throat. Ari quickly swallowed the tart cum, not letting go of Joshua's cock until he'd gotten every drop. When he finally looked up from Joshua's crotch, Ari saw that Ty had also spilled his load, his pearly-white jizz dribbling off Joshua's chin.

The Ring Master pulled out of Ari's ass and told him to stand up. Once he was on his feet, the Ring Master embraced Ari and gave him a long, sensual kiss. Then his mouth traveled down the length of his young, firm body, starting from Ari's neck, over his chest, down his abdomen. His mouth stopped at Ari's dick, now aching for release. The Ring Master gave him a wink and a smile before taking Ari's cock between his full lips.

Ari came almost instantly. His body convulsed as he sent a torrent of cum into the Ring Master's mouth. The Ring Master gulped down every last drop that oozed from the head of Ari's dick.

Ari crumpled to the floor. The Ring Master lay beside him, his hands lightly caressing Ari's smooth, sweaty chest. Joshua and Ty kneeled beside him, Joshua stroking Ari's hair; Ty played with his balls.

The crowd rattled the fence, waving their cocks and shouting for their turn with Ari. Many of them had jacked off through the fence, dotting the Ring's perimeter with sticky puddles of jism.

The Ring Master kissed Ari on the forehead. "And now," he said, "it's time to meet your public."

He sat up and made a signal with his hand. Two sections of the chain link fence were pulled apart. Ari tried to protest as the crowd surged forward, but a large, bearded man shoved his dripping cock between Ari's lips before his pleas could be heard ...

11:30

Nick, a towel tied around his waist, stepped out of the bathroom, a trail of steam following close behind. The rest of his studio apartment wasn't much bigger than the bathroom he just exited. An unmade bed dominated half of the front room; a set of weights and a weight bench took up the other half. *Good thing I don't entertain*, Nick thought.

He went to the kitchenette in the corner and poured a cup of coffee, the last of a pot he made two hours earlier. It was bitter, but Nick drank it anyway.

Nick sat down on the bed. A digital clock on the dresser said it was 10:54 a.m. Staring out the window at the abandoned warehouse across the street, he wondered why he had awakened so early. *Not like I have anything to do*, he mused.

He turned his attention to the phone, hoping it would ring but doubting it would. Damn thing seldom did. Bought an answering machine, in case The Man called with one of his legally questionable jobs while he was out (The Man didn't trust cell phones), but it was rare for Nick to come home and find the message light blinking.

Nick reclined on the bed and gulped the rest of his foul coffee, wondering why he was seeking a caffeine rush when being awake nowadays only depressed him. He set the cup down and stared down at his body. This cheered him somewhat. *Looking good, looking good*, he told himself. Every muscle bulged, rippling beneath his golden skin. His pecs were two plush mounds of muscle, his stomach flat and firm; definitely a body to be proud of. *Maybe*, he pondered, *if I don't get a call from The Man, I can see about a job at that bar, the one that's always looking for "men, 18-25, with model-type physiques."* Maybe his looks would help them forgive the fact that he was on the wrong side of twenty-five.

He imagined working at that bar, all eyes on him as he took off his clothes, guys waving money at him to entice him to peel off his shirt, his pants, his jock. They'd offer him more if he'd let them touch it. His cock twitched beneath the towel. Nick removed the towel and watched his dick thicken and stretch. He often got hard in the time between taking his shower and getting dressed; his own nakedness excited him.

Nick took his stiffening cock in his hand, wrapping his fingers around the smooth, sensitive flesh. He fingered the head, closing his eyes as a sexual current shot through him. His fist pumped up and down the shaft in slow, even strokes. He could feel his cock get harder with each stroke, until it was a huge, meaty tower rising from his crotch.

The sexual voltage surging through his body increased. He reached down and grasped his balls, giving them a gentle squeeze. *Oh, yeah, any minute now ...*

The phone rang.

"Shit," Nick cursed. "Now it rings." For a moment, he was tempted just to let the machine get it, but his need for work was more important than his need to get off. Reluctantly, he picked up the phone.

"This is Nick," he said tersely.

"Got something for ya'," wheezed an old man on the other end of the line. It was The Man.

"Great," Nick said, trying not to sound overeager. "What is it?"

"How many times I gotta tell you ..."

"Oh, yeah. Not over the phone, right. Okay, where can I meet you?"

"Ya' know where Chinook Park is? Bathrooms, north side, 11:30 tonight."

"Okay, okay," Nick said excitedly, "that's Chinook Park, 11:30, bathrooms ..."

But The Man had already hung up.

#####

Neal Cannon jogged through the neighborhood, dodging children on bikes and stepping out of the way of harried mothers in Volvos and SUVs.

He usually jogged in the morning before work, but today he had overslept, and his whole routine had been shot. He was supposed to go to the gym after work, but he went at lunch, so he could do his jogging now.

As he headed for Chinook Park, Neal stripped off his soggy tank top and tucked it in the waistband of his shorts. A car of teenage girls whistled. He waved, never slowing his pace.

Some of his friends thought Neal was too obsessive about his fitness routine, but it had taken two years for him to get his body in the shape it was now. He'd be damned if he'd let that muscle turn to fat.

Then again, he wondered as he entered the park, having a great body hadn't paid off like he'd hoped. When he was flabby and out of shape few guys approached him. Now plenty were attracted but assumed someone with his looks and physique was already taken. He had toned and sculpted his body, so it was built for sex, and he hadn't been laid in nearly four months.

He slowed his pace as he rounded the playground, young mothers and a couple of young fathers sneaking a peek as he jogged by. Up ahead, near the restrooms, he saw a bicyclist rest his ten-speed against the wall of the building. Neal watched the young man remove his helmet and shake his head vigorously, sending a spray of sweat from his damp, curly blond locks. His body was lean and taut, and Neal could make out a provocative bulge in the crotch of his blue Spandex biking shorts.

The bicyclist stepped into the men's room. Neal decided to follow, though he had no idea how he'd start a conversation.

The restroom was dark, the room's only light coming from a small window near the ceiling. The bicyclist was at one of the urinals. Neal walked up to the one beside him and, even though he didn't have to go, feigned taking a leak.

"Damn it's hot," Neal muttered under his breath.

"Sure is," the bicyclist agreed.

Neal tried to get a look at the cyclist's dick, but when his eyes darted sideways, the bicyclist already had his shorts up. Then he flushed and walked out, not even bothering to wash his hands.

That was futile, Neal thought disgustedly, pulling up his shorts. He was about to leave when he noticed the graffiti. The walls were covered with it, almost all of it promising – or asking for – some sexual favor. "Blond, 6'4", wants to suck your dick. WM only," read one. "Looking for young, slim black/Latin to suck cock. Leave date and time," read another. The whole wall was like the personal ads in the back of a porno magazine.

Neal immediately felt a twinge of excitement that went right to his cock. He'd seen such graffiti in restrooms before, but always dismissed it as trashy, maybe even dangerous. But Neal was getting awfully horny. He scanned the wall for an "ad" that looked appealing.

"Will suck the cum out of your cock. Here, 11:30 p.m., M-F."

Maybe, Neal thought, *I'll see about taking a late night walk in the park.*

# # # # #

Nick parked his aging Chevy at the curb and got out of the car, the door making a loud creaking noise that ricocheted off the trees. It was 11:20; the park was abandoned. Still, Nick got the sensation he wasn't alone.

He walked toward the small building near the playground, figuring it housed the restrooms. *What else could it be?*

As he got closer, he looked around for The Man's black Lincoln but couldn't see it. "Bastard's late," he grumbled to himself, forgetting that in fact *he* was early.

Nick stopped outside the restrooms. A faint glow emanated from the light inside. He checked his watch again. 11:25. Where was the old guy?

Well, he did have to take a leak. His nerves and the two beers he had before leaving his apartment put his kidneys in overdrive. Giving up on The Man, he stepped through the door.

# # # # #

Neal almost chickened out. At 10:45 he told himself there was no way he was going to some public restroom for a blowjob from a stranger. Then, at 11:00, as he was getting dressed, he tried to talk himself out of it. *It's sleazy*, he reminded himself. *Only perverts do this sort of thing. What if the cops bust me? What if the guy's a serial killer?*

Then he agonized over what to wear. Certainly nothing you wanted to get dressed up for, but he didn't want to look like a slob either. Neal put on a fresh pair of underwear (the black bikini briefs he usually wore when he hit the bars) and slipped into a pair of faded blue jeans. Then he put on an old, purple T-shirt. Nothing special, but as he checked himself out in the mirror on his closet door, Neal had to admit he looked pretty damn hot.

But, I'm not going through with this, he told himself.

At 11:15, he put on a blue windbreaker – careful to put a condom in the pocket – and headed out the door.

He reached the park at 11:27. It appeared deserted, though he did see a battered Malibu parked at the curb. *Could that be the other guy's car?*

Neal strode toward the bathrooms, his heart pounding in his chest. He alternately hoped the man would be inside waiting, or that he wouldn't show. Neal would have an easy out if the guy wasn't there. But if he was ... well, it could be worthwhile.

He stopped at the men's room door. *Was someone in there?* He thought he heard someone. *Okay*, he bargained with himself, *if he's relatively good looking, or even just average, I'll go through with it. If he's beneath even my lowest standards, I'll say I'm just here to take a piss. That's all.*

Then he took a deep breath and opened the door.

# # # # #

Nick was standing at the urinal when he heard the door open. He looked over his shoulder, expecting to see The Man, with his scowl and that ill-fitting black suit he always wore. What he saw instead was a very attractive man looking somewhat surprised, then expectant.

Nick turned toward the wall again, draining his dick and glancing over the writing on the wall. "Want to suck your cock. White boys only!" he read. "Blk. Male, hung, wants to show you a good time. Call ..."

Who did this kind of shit? Nick wondered, though he was more than a little intrigued.

He reached up to flush the urinal and heard the guy at the door clear his throat. Nick turned and saw he was still staring at him. The guy raised his eyebrows in a funny way, like he wanted Nick to do something.

"What the fuck's your problem?" Nick snarled. Then he turned to the wall again.

"Will suck the cum out of your cock. Here, 11:30 p.m., M-F," he read on the wall.

Zipping up his pants, Nick turned toward the good-looking guy at the door.

"Now I get it," he said, grinning.

# # # # #

Neal couldn't believe it! This guy was better looking than half the hunks he saw at the bars. When he opened the door and saw him standing there, that firm, round butt straining those tight, black jeans, he was mesmerized. And when Neal saw that face – high cheekbones, deep-set eyes and full lips – he practically fell in love.

Then the guy turned away.

Maybe there was some sort of signal I am supposed to give, Neal thought. But when he got the guy's attention again, he nearly got his head bitten off. *I guess this isn't the guy*, Neal thought, ready to retreat from the restroom in a hurry.

Now the guy had turned around again, grinning at him. "Now I get it."

"Um, hi, I'm Neal," he started, trying to sound calm. "I don't usually do this sort of thing ..."

"Last stall," the guy said, zipping up his pants. Neal's eyes dropped to the guy's crotch. Looked like he was hiding a boa constrictor in there.

Neal followed him to the last stall, the guy motioning for him to enter first. When Neal was inside, the guy followed, closing the door behind him. They were standing inches apart.

"Ain't you gonna sit on the toilet?" the guy asked. "Won't it be easier?"

Suddenly, Neal realized there had been a misunderstanding. This guy thought Neal had written that note on the wall.

"This is kinda' embarrassing," Neal began, "but I'm not ... Well, I thought ..."

The guy unzipped his pants. He pulled out his cock, all eight inches of it. Thick, with a network of veins crawling up the shaft and a plump, red crown.

Neal sat down.

Nick hovered over the good-looking guy in the windbreaker. Said his name was Neal. Nick was waiting for Neal to get down to business.

He took Nick's cock into his hand. It was kind of sweaty but smooth, and Nick's rod immediately twitched in response to his touch, getting a little harder. Neal stroked it a few times, examining it with awestruck eyes. Nick was glad this guy was so admiring, but this wasn't what he wanted.

"C'mon, suck it," he hissed.

Neal's tongue glided across the head of his dick. He licked the underside of the shaft, tracing the engorged veins. After that, he slid Nick's cock into his mouth, swallowing it. "That's it," Nick groaned.

Neal gulped his dick all the way to the base, his chin digging into Nick's ballsac. Nick thrust his hips forward, fucking Neal's warm, moist mouth. The guy almost gagged, but recovered quickly, slurping his rod lustfully. Nick ran his hands through Neal's short, brown hair.

He didn't care if The Man ever showed; this was worth being unemployed.

Neal put his mouth on Nick's balls, his tongue rolling over them lightly. Nick was in ecstasy and wanted more. He slid his jeans down, over his ass and down to his knees. Neal immediately reached up and fingered his dark, hairy hole. Felt so good, this guy's mouth on his cock and balls, his smooth fingers at his asshole. But Nick wanted more.

He turned around. Grabbing the top of the stall door, Nick bent at the waist, his hard, round ass at Neal's face.

"How's 'bout tongue-fucking my ass while you're down there?" he said.

Neal palmed his ass open and ran his tongue slowly up the crack, giving Nick's tailbone a little kiss before diving in again. His tongue fluttered at Nick's tight, puckered ring. Neal then dove deeper, forcing his hole open. Nick groaned loudly as the other man's tongue pushed into his ass, forcing his ass-ring open. Nick shuddered as the pleasure rocketed through his body.

He heard the guy unbuttoning his jeans. Nick wondered what kind of weapon Neal was carrying. *Bet it's about to burst*, he thought, *cooped up in his pants while my ass is rubbing against his face. Bet the guy needed a little manly attention of his own.*

Nick turned around. Neal's dick was as attractive as the rest of him. "Does it taste as good as it looks?" Nick asked, sinking to his knees.

# # # # #

Neal spread his legs open, his cock hard and throbbing, the head glistening with pre-cum. The guy was on his knees, pulling Neal's pants down to his ankles. He grabbed Neal's dick in his big, meaty hand. Neal leaned back on the toilet, trying to think of other things (that project at work due next week; need to do laundry; a past-due credit card bill) lest he shoot his load all over the stranger's hands.

The anonymous stud bent down and teased the head of Neal's cock with his tongue. Ecstacy shot through him like a bolt of lightning. He felt the man's lips slide along the shaft, down to his cum-swollen balls. Then he took Neal's dick into his mouth, greedily gulping Neal's meat down his throat. Neal's breath quickened. As the stranger's head bobbed between his legs, Neal ran his fingers through the man's wavy black hair.

The man started pulling at his windbreaker, unzipping it while he sucked Neal's dick. His hands slid underneath Neal's T-shirt, grasping his firm pecs and giving them a squeeze.

Neal's body trembled with pleasure as the stranger licked his cock like a lollipop. Then he pulled Neal's body forward and forced his legs wide apart. His tongue slithered into Neal's ass, probing the rosebud nestled between his butt cheeks.

"Oh, yeah, baby, oh yeah!" Neal panted, riding the guy's face.

The man stood up suddenly, his prick swinging over Neal's face. "Sure like to fuck that tight little ass." His voice was a low growl.

Neal's hand dove into the pocket of his windbreaker and retrieved the rubber. The stranger smiled, taking the condom from Neal's hand.

They traded places. The guy sat on the toilet, quickly rolling the rubber down his long, thick cock, then lubing it up with a palm full of his own spit. Neal pulled his jeans off over his tennis shoes and straddled the man. Slowly, he eased himself onto the stranger's dick.

A fierce pain stung Neal's asshole as his sphincter stretched over the man's cock. Gnashing his teeth, Neal continued his descent until he felt the stranger's rod deep in his bowels.

The man fucked him in quick, hard thrusts. Pain soon became pleasure, Neal savoring the feel of the guy's fat pole sliding in and out of his chute. He grabbed the stranger's muscular shoulders as he bounced on his cock. The man cupped Neal's ass, leaned forward and bit at his neck, snarling like a wild dog.

"Fuck me! Fuck me! Fuck me!" Neal panted, riding the stranger like a mechanical bull.

The man grabbed Neal's cock, jacking him off roughly as Neal bounced up and down on his stiff pole. Neal felt the first tremor of an orgasm ripple through his body almost immediately. *Not yet*, he told himself. *Just a little while longer.*

But his cock was beyond his mind's control. An explosion ignited in the base of his prick and fired throughout his body. Thick streams of cum splattered the stranger's shirt.

The man continued to fuck Neal, barely noticing the jism staining his shirt. In an instant, the guy seized Neal's waist in a backbreaking bear hug and let out a harsh groan. The man's body convulsed as he shot his load. The man let out a contented sigh as Neal milked his condom-sheathed cock with his ass muscles.

"Not that it matters much now," Neal said, resting his cheek against the stranger's forehead, "but what is your name?"

"Nick," the man said, giving Neal's ass a hearty slap.

# # # # #

Nick left the restroom with Neal's phone number. "Maybe next time we could do this at my place," he suggested.

"Probably safer that way," Nick agreed, though he had to admit that fucking in public was pretty damn hot, even if it was in a dank toilet stall.

As he walked across the park toward his car he saw the familiar Lincoln come around the corner. *Shit!* He'd forgotten about The Man.

The car's headlights caught Nick's face and stopped. Nick moved toward the car, shielding his face from the glare of the lights. A window in back rolled down, and the corrugated face of The Man appeared.

"You stupid bastard! Where've you been?"

"At the bathrooms, like you said," Nick said, pointing toward the building behind him.

"You shithead!" The Man screeched. "I said the *north* side bathrooms. That one there's where the perverts hang out!"

"You don't say." Nick tried to suppress a smile.

Mr. Sheppard's Son

"Oh, yeah, fuck me," Channing groaned, riding Phillip's dick. "Fuck me!"

"Easy," Phillip whispered, cupping the young man's smooth, round ass, holding him steady. Phillip gently thrust upward, keeping his movements restrained as Channing worked his ass muscles against his cock. He didn't want to come too soon.

They met before, earlier, on the elevator at RTG Industries. Phillip, holding his personal belongings in a box, was getting on as Channing was getting off. Phillip would just as soon kill someone as look at them, but he wasn't so pissed off he couldn't look at Channing – blond, blue-eyed, young, athletic, showing off some nice arms in his tank top. And Channing was checking him out. He, Phillip – black, handsome, sturdily built and now unemployed. Despite being told twenty minutes earlier he was no longer a part of the RTG team – "I have to downsize, Phil," Mr. Sheppard said – Phillip could spare a smile for this cute stranger getting off the elevator.

"Harder," that cute stranger now begged, bouncing on Phillip's cock, wanting to feel it deeper in his ass. He gyrated atop Phillip wildly, as if he'd been possessed by some outside entity.

They met again, much later, at Chess, one of the few gay bars in town that didn't overwhelm patrons with deafening disco and pulsing strobe lights. Here, the only thing competing with your conversation was Celine going for the high note or the bartender's full and frequent guffaws. Phillip had come here to get drunk, not laid. But then there was the blond guy from the elevator, now dressed in a crisp white dress shirt and a pair of khakis that fit as if they were tailored to hug that ass just so.

"I remember you. From the elevator at RTG, right?" he said, much too cheerfully. Phillip was interested, just not now. But then the blond guy, Channing – who the fuck names their kid *Channing*? – offered to buy him a drink, and Phillip couldn't refuse. He took the seat beside Phillip. By his second drink and Phillip's fourth, Channing was suggesting they go to Phillip's apartment. "I would take you to my place, but I'm staying at my parents' and ..."

"Understood."

Now they were fucking on the living room sofa, Channing astride Phillip's lap, gasping and whimpering, begging for more of Phillip's cock. "I'm so close, *soooo close.*" His hard, muscular body froze, then jerked. His load splattered Phillip's smooth abdomen, Channing's thick jism forming puddles in the crevices of the six-pack that plated Phillip's stomach. Channing looked down at the sticky, white mess he produced, then, smiling, guided Phillip's hand one of the puddles of jizz. "Feed it to me," he whispered.

Simultaneously taken aback and intrigued, Phillip raked up some spooge with two fingers and raised them to Channing's lips. Channing took hold of his wrist once again and guided the dripping fingers to his mouth. He made a big show of licking the cum off Phillip's fingers, scooping it up with his tongue, making sure Phillip saw the dollop of cream that now rested on the tip of his tongue. Then, slowly, that tongue disappeared inside his mouth. When it curled out his lips again, it was clean.

It was while Channing sucked on his fingers that Phillip came. There was no restraint in his movements now as he stabbed his cock upward into Channing's hot ass. Suddenly, the pleasure got unbearably great, then a catch in his breath and a tensing of muscles, and finally release as his cock pumped out a hot load, filling the rubber.

"Oh, yes," purred Channing, clenching the walls of his ass against Phillip's throbbing dick and pinching his hard, chocolate-brown nipples.

They met before, and they'd meet again.

#

That next meeting happened a week later, when Phillip stopped by the office to pick up his final paycheck ("We can mail it to you," bitched the secretary in payroll) then stopped by his department to say hello – and goodbye – to a few former co-workers, none of whom were "downsized." And, there he saw Channing, at his old desk.

"Fancy meeting you here," Phillip said.

Channing, spun away from his computer and stood. He looked at once mortified and pleased. "Hi! How're you!" he said quickly. Then, conspiringly, "I was hoping I'd see you again after that night."

Hoping, even though Phillip gave him his number and there hadn't been one phone call since "that night."

Phillip's gaze went down, ostensibly to check out how nicely Channing filled out his tailored, blue pinstripe trousers. He saw the nameplate: Channing Sheppard. Didn't his former boss, Mr. Sheppard, say a couple months ago he had a son about to graduate from State?

Downsizing, my ass, Phillip thought.

"You're seeing me now," Phillip said, forcing a smile.

Channing blushed. "You know what I mean."

"You still at your folks'?"

Channing nodded.

"Then how 'bout my place, tonight. Around nine?"

"Sounds good."

Though he'd been invited, it was almost a surprise when Channing showed up at Phillip's door. He half-expected to be stood up. "I brought wine," he said goofily, holding up a bottle of Château de Something.

Phillip grabbed Channing by the belt and pulled him inside. "We'll drink it later."

He tore into Channing ferociously, his lust fueled by rage. Phillip jerked down Channing's zipper and pulled out his semi-hard, cut cock. It hardened instantly. He pushed his tongue deep into Channing's mouth, nearly drawing blood as he gnawed at his peach-colored lips. He tore away Channing's shirt, fabric ripping and buttons popping.

"Hey! That shirt's brand n ..."

"Get on your knees," Phillip ordered.

Channing looked perplexed, but his bewilderment was immediately followed by a smile. He did as he told.

Phillip pulled out his cock. It was like steel. Its dark brown shaft pulsed, and pre-cum oozed out its rosy-tan head, collecting in the folds of his foreskin. Grabbing a fistful of Channing's dark blond hair, Phillip pulled his face to his dick. "Suck it!" he commanded and then shoved his cock down Channing's throat.

Channing sputtered and gagged, but he never asked Phillip to stop.

He fucked Channing's mouth. "Take that cock," he hissed. "Take it *all*." He wanted to say: *Take it all, you rich, candy ass fuck! Just because Daddy says so, you can just waltz into an executive spot while someone else is kicked to the curb – just to make room for your privileged ass.*

Wanted to, but didn't.

Phillip pulled his cock out when he felt the first twinges of an orgasm. "Open up," he growled, "cause I'm about to shoot. Right. Down. Your. Throat!"

Ropes of cum spewed from Phillip's cock and onto Channing's expectant face, covering his forehead, his nose, his cheeks. He shot into Channing's mouth then pushed his dick inside, making Channing suck the last few drops from his prick.

"Now we'll have some wine," Phillip said.

Later, after a couple glasses of wine, Phillip fucked Channing. Fucked him *hard*. With Channing on all fours on the bed, Phillip rammed his ass, plunging his thick cock deep into Channing's pliant butt. He dug his fingers into Channing's thighs; he leaned down and bit his neck and shoulders. He called him a filthy slut and promised to fuck him so hard he'd have trouble walking for the next week. Channing moaned, groaned and sighed. Phillip came, letting out a deep roar as he drained his balls a second time that evening. Channing came on the comforter. Phillip rubbed his face in the spooge, as if he were housetraining a puppy. Then he pulled Channing's cum-smeared face up to his and kissed him. Channing melted against his body.

Channing kept coming back, and after each night of brutal fucking, Phillip thought it was over. But the next night, there was Channing.

That's when Phillip got "The Idea."

"This should be fun," Channing giggled when he saw the camcorder set up on a tripod in the living room. His hands went for Phillip's crotch. "Turn it on and let's get started."

Phillip pushed him away. "No. It won't be like that"

"What will it be like then?"

Phillip responded with a mischievous smile.

# # # # #

Channing left around 1:00 a.m., and Phillip took a shower. Then he watched the tape.

Wrapped in a soft cotton robe, Phillip eased back on the living room sofa and hit the "play" button on the remote.

The tape began abruptly. For the first few seconds the image was out of focus, and there was some jerky camera movement. When the image came into focus, Channing, shirtless, was visible from the chest up. Phillip heard himself say: "Ready now?" Channing nodded.

"So, ever done something like this before?" Phillip asked his star.

Channing shook his head.

"Ever watch yourself?"

"Jacked off while looking in a mirror once," he said. "Kinda' felt silly afterwards. And one time I got fucked in front of a mirror, but the other guy was watching more than me."

"Never been videotaped then?"

Channing smiled. "This is my debut."

Phillip changed his line of questioning: "Are you gay?"

"We've been ... *doing it* for how long? And you have to *ask*?" Channing giggled.

"I've fucked guys six ways sideways and have them turn around and say they're straight and just experimenting, or bi, or drunk, or some bullshit. So I ask again: Do you consider yourself a homosexual?"

Channing looked away from the camera. His answer was barely audible. "Yes."

Watching Channing's discomfort on tape affected Phillip in a way he didn't expect. Pangs of compassion and empathy welled within him as he remembered, years ago, how difficult it was for him to realize and accept his own sexuality.

The interview next focused on Channing's favorite qualities in men. What attracted him: A nice face. His favorite body part (besides the dick): Chest. Did he prefer black men? "I just like hot men," he giggled again. How many guys had he been with: About 13. He thought.

Then Phillip asked: "What do you like to do?"

"In bed?"

"No, in church. Yes, in bed."

"Um, well ..." Though the video's picture quality was muted, Channing was clearly blushing. "I like to get fucked."

"I've noticed," Phillip said. "You ever top?"

"A few times, but, well, I guess I'm a better bottom."

"What else you like?"

After much stuttering and stammering, Channing said: "This is embarrassing," Then, looking down, the camera making him uncomfortable, he answered the question. "Sucking dick."

"Do you swallow?"

The question made him wince. "You ... you *know* this."

"Answer the question." Phillip's voice was authoritative. There was no negotiating.

"Uh ..." Channing sighed, looked away and attempted a sideways smile. "Yeah. I swallow."

"You like the taste of cum?"

"It's not the taste," he replied, turning back to the camera. "It's ... the moment, I guess ... the *idea* of it. Like you're so into the other person you *want* to taste their load."

"You make it sound romantic. I just thought it was because you're a freak."

Channing grinned. "That, too."

"Rimming?"

"That's okay, but I like receiving more than giving."

"You'll drink a guy's cum, but not lick his asshole?"

"It's not that. I just ... I dunno, don't get into rimming as much. I love feeling a guy's tongue up my ass, though." Channing blushed again.

"You *do* have a pretty edible ass," Phillip purred.

"You can eat it now, if you want," Channing suggested.

The camera jerked away, showing the opposite wall, the floor, Phillip's foot, and then another wall. Once the camera movement settled, and there was a wide shot of Channing sitting on a wooden chair, wearing only a pair of white boxer briefs (designer brand, naturally). The image blurred as the camera zoomed in on Channing's crotch, getting the outline of his boner on tape. Pulling back for the wide shot, Phillip ordered Channing to "show me that ass."

Channing stood up. His movements were stilted, uncertain; he turned around and looked over his shoulder, as if needing Phillip to confirm he was following the script correctly. With his back to the camera, he started pulling down his underwear.

"Slowly," Phillip directed off camera. Channing pulled his shorts down halfway, revealing part of his crack, the elastic waistband hugging his voluptuous butt. "Now, slide your fingers down into your butt crack, underneath your underwear. Want you to touch your hole."

He did as he was told, tracing the divide of his ass cheeks. Another zoom to capture his fingers disappearing beneath his boxer briefs. Though his fingers were hidden beneath fabric, it was clear Channing was rubbing his asshole.

"Okay," Phillip said, "show it all to me."

The camera pulled back to get the removal of the underwear. Channing seemed less self-conscious now, starting to get into it.

Watching the video now, barely an hour after taping it, Phillip was getting into it, too. His cock was hard, and his hand slipped beneath his robe periodically to manipulate his erection and fondle his balls.

On screen there was a tight shot of Channing's ass. More jerky motion, and then the picture moved to an upward angle, so it looked like the camera is just below Channing's butthole, which, of course, it was. Though crudely executed, Phillip was proud of the shot. *I might have a future in porno*, he thought wryly.

He instructed Channing to stick two fingers in his mouth and then work those fingers into his ass. The camera didn't catch Channing lubing his fingers with spit, but it got him sliding them into his asshole in graphic detail. It had excited Phillip while taping it, and it excited him watching it now. He untied his robe and pulled it open, exposing his hard-on and allowing easier access.

Channing sank two fingers up his hole, deep. There was a minute or so of him finger-fucking himself, then Phillip said: "Put those fingers back in your mouth and suck on them."

Abruptly, the camera shifted, swirling about as Phillip got to his feet, before settling on a medium shot of Channing slowly bringing the two fingers used to massage his prostate up to his mouth. He flashed a sexy grin, playing to the camera. Opening his mouth, Channing touched his tongue to meet his index finger. Tongue and finger went into his mouth, and his lips closed. He sucked on the finger. His other finger went into his mouth – again, nice and slow.

"Suck on those fingers like you suck my cock," Phillip said. The fingers went all the way into Channing's mouth, then were withdrawn a millimeter at a time. Just before the tips popped out of his lips, he shoved the fingers back into his mouth.

The camera moved back for a wider shot. Channing was told to sit back down. His cock was like steel. It was not the biggest dick Phillip ever played with, but was a nice one all the same. The camera caught the light glinting off the pre-cum glazed the head. Channing was instructed to rub his fingers over his cockhead and lick his juice off them. Channing obeyed without protest. The camera followed his fingers to the head of his dick, staying with them as they returned to his mouth, Phillip zooming in to get a close-up of Channing sucking his pre-cum off his fingers.

Phillip's cock was pumping out some serious pre-cum as he watched his sex tape. Without thinking, he imitated the action on his TV screen, tasting his own salty juices.

On the video, Phillip asked Channing what he wanted to do next. There was another close up of his face, slightly out of focus. "I want you to fuck me," he said to the camera, his voice almost disappearing into the hiss of white noise. Phillip asked him to repeat himself, louder.

"I want you to fuck me."

"Louder."

"I. Want. You. To FUCK me."

"Not slower. Louder!"

"FUCK ME!" Channing shouted.

"You're ready for this?" The camera pulled away and the picture plummeted downward. After some hasty adjustments, the camera was pointing down at Phillip's hard cock. "You want this up your ass?"

"Yes. Fuck me."

"Fuck you with *what*?"

"Fuck me with your big cock."

"Fuck you with my big *black* cock," Phillip corrected.

Channing was clearly uncomfortable by this command.

"You don't say it, you don't get it," Phillip taunted.

A deep breath, then: "FUCK ME! With your BIG! *BLACK!* COCK!" Channing practically shrieked the words. There was a desperate edge to his voice, and his expression on camera could be read as rage. As he watched it on tape, Phillip felt his balls tighten up in their sac.

Suddenly the screen went black. A few seconds later, the tape resumed. The camera was on the tripod now, trained on an easy chair on which Phillip sat. His cock was covered with a condom and lubricant. He smiled at the camera. "Ready for your close up?" he chuckled as he stroked his dick. It was the only time his face was on screen.

Channing moved into the frame, his head out of view. He was told to turn toward the camera, then sit on Phillip's cock, reverse cowboy style. He did so, slowly easing down onto Phillip's dong. It wasn't a position they tried before, and really, Phillip didn't see doing it that way again. But for cinematic purposes, it worked.

The camera caught Phillip's cock sliding up Channing's lubed ass. As Channing sat on Phillip's prick, his face came into view, obscuring Phillip's. His expression was one of extreme concentration. When Phillip's cock was all the way up his chute, his expression turned rapturous.

Phillip fucked him roughly, driving his cock up Channing's ass in forceful stabs, calling him a "horny slut" and "fuck toy."

Channing moaned, his muscular body twisting against Phillip's. "Fuck me," he panted over and over, the words becoming a mantra. Channing wore a dreamy expression. He held Phillip's hand in place while licking up his own spooge. Still, it was pretty fucking hot without the zooms and additional angles. Phillip started jacking off as he watched the action on his TV, his hand sliding up in down his cock the same way Channing slid up and down it barely an hour earlier that evening.

On screen, Phillip's hands moved up and down Channing's body, their dark hue contrasting nicely with Channing's pale skin. His fingers pinched Channing's coral-pink nipples. His hands glided down Channing's hard torso, down to his purple-headed cock. Phillip gripped his drooling hard-on, stroking it and mumbling something to Channing. (Phillip remembered something like, "How you like that big cock up your ass?" or something to that effect.)

Channing moaned loudly. His muscles tensed up, his body twisted. He was close to shooting his load. Phillip pulled his hand off Channing's cock and told him to jack off. Cupping his hand beneath Channing's cockhead, Phillip said: "Come in my hand."

Channing pumped his dick – just as Phillip pumped his now while watching. It was obvious he was trying to hold back, make the moment last, but he was powerless. Making a noise that sounded like the beginning of a sneeze, he blew his load. Phillip caught most of it, though a few thick drops hit the floor. Phillip wished he had a cameraman for that part, too, to get the cumshot. It was exciting nonetheless.

Phillip brought the handful of jizz to Channing's face and clamped it over his mouth. "Lick it clean," he hissed.

Channing wore a dreamy expression. He held Phillip's hand in place while licking up his own spooge.

Phillip was close to coming, both on the video and now. In both cases, he quickly stopped what he was doing, be it fucking or jacking off, holding off for the finale.

The screen went black again for a few seconds, starting back up with a new angle. The camcorder was back in Phillip's hands, pointed down at Channing kneeling before his cock. Channing's face was shiny, still glazed with his own load.

"Make me come in your mouth," Phillip said, the words coming out as a gasp.

Channing took Phillip's cock in his hand, holding it as he closed his mouth over it. He took it deep into his throat then eased back.

Phillip's grunts on the tape mixed with the grunts that pushed out his mouth now while he beat off watching it. It was impossible not to jack off watching the action on screen, even if the image of

Channing slurping on his dick was shaky and blurry. He didn't want to come yet and struggled to keep control of his pulsing cock. He wanted to come at the same time he came on the tape.

That moment happened quickly. Through heavy breaths, Phillip announced he was about to come. He ordered Channing to open his mouth, telling him he wanted to see his load shoot out his dick and into Channing's mouth.

Channing pulled on Phillip's cock while looking up at the camera, his mouth open wide. Phillip's heavy breathing filled the soundtrack. In a harsh whisper, he panted: *"I'm-coming-I'm-coming-oh-god!"*

His thick load splattered Channing's face, making him jump as the jizz nearly hit him in the eye. More streams of spooge followed, these landing on Channing's tongue. Mr. Sheppard's son swallowed those tangy drops of man cream and then closed his mouth over the head of Phillip's cock, sucking it like a straw.

Unable to hold back any more, Phillip came, arching his back against his sofa and letting out a low groan. His copious load stippled his smooth belly. Then, with his jizz drying on his firm abdomen, he fell asleep.

Two days later Phillip was in Cranford Hills, a neighborhood of lavish, multi-million-dollar homes. He was at the gate of 512 Delsandro Way, the Sheppard residence, home of Clayton C. Sheppard, president of RTG, father of Channing.

Phillip sat in his car. The video was in his hands, in an envelope addressed to Channing's dad. Phillip had watched the video several times, jerking off each time. He and Channing even watched it together once, last night. Channing had trouble watching himself but liked how Phillip got turned on by it. He sucked Phillip's cock while Phillip watched.

And now, Phillip was going to put it in the Sheppard's mailbox. All he needed was the nerve to do so.

He took a deep breath. "Here goes," he whispered.

But then, he put the car into gear and drove away, the tape still resting on the passenger seat.

He wanted to watch the tape one more time.

T.M.I.

I was trying to sleep, except Tully had a hot new boyfriend and was doing his damnedest to make me jealous.

"Oh, yes, baby, take it *all!*" he moaned from his bedroom next door.

He was succeeding.

Another loud moan punched its way through the wall separating our rooms. I didn't need to look at my travel alarm clock to know it was too early in the morning to be kept awake. I sighed heavily and rolled over on the guest room's uncomfortable bed like that might improve matters. It didn't.

"My turn," Tully said as plain as if we were in the same room. "I wanna suck that hot cock of yours."

Jesus Christ!

When I'd called Tully last month to tell him I'd be in Tampa for a three-day marketing seminar, I'd only intended to get together for drinks, maybe dinner, catch up and reminisce about the days when we both worked together in Atlanta. But Tully insisted that I stay at his place. "You don't want to stay at the fucking *Sheraton*," he said. He was so insistent that I stay with him that I suspected he had an ulterior motive. I always thought Tully was attractive – no, that's an understatement. *Hot* is more like it. When we worked together, we didn't want to complicate things by fooling around. But, that was two years ago. Things weren't as complicated now. My excitement grew as I imagined what Tully had in mind for my weekend visit.

Tully's ulterior motive was, it turned out, showing off a twenty-six-year-old, dark-haired hunk so jaw-droppingly gorgeous that when we were first introduced I couldn't speak. His name was Devon, and I resisted asking if that was his stripper name. "Have you ever seen a finer ass?" Tully asked me, Devon standing only three feet away.

Devon did have a nice ass – high, round, the ideal bubble butt. In fact, from what I could see, Devon had a nice *everything*. And lest I had any doubts about the parts I couldn't see, Tully, who was forever being chastised for providing too much information, happily fleshed out the details. "Abs you could do your laundry on," he assured me. "And a *beautiful* cock."

That beautiful cock was now getting worshiped in the next room. Devon wasn't as big on giving a blow-by-blow (as it were) as Tully, but the way he moaned and groaned, made it plain that my friend was driving him wild.

I hated them both. The last time I had sex was nearly two months ago, a disastrous one-night stand with a guy who was so drunk he could barely remain conscious, let alone stay hard. Tully was forty-one, three years older than I, was having loud, fantastic sex with a twenty-something god and …

"Bring that ass up here. I'm gonna eat that hole until you beg for mercy," Tully growled next door.

… making me horny as hell.

A raging hard-on was straining against my briefs as Devon took over the lead vocals, moaning loudly as Tully presumably ate that hole. Even the most limited imagination could conjure the scene: Devon atop Tully, his superb ass in Tully's face, Tully spearing his asshole with his tongue. My right hand traveled over the pulsing mound in my underwear as I visualized Tully's face – I could just see his handsome face, even sexier now that Tully had grown a goatee – sinking between the smooth, muscled globes of Devon's ass, lustily tongue-fucking that hole (whether or not Devon shaved his asshole was one of the few details Tully hadn't divulged, but I imagined it was smooth).

"Oh yes oh yes oh yes," Devon gasped, filling out my mental picture.

My briefs were damp with pre-cum. I slid my hand beneath the waistband and touched myself. My cock pumped out another thick drop of juice.

"You want me fuck you?" Tully asked. I could practically hear the devilish grin in his face.

"*Yes!*"

My underwear came off then. I pulled back the top sheet and kicked my briefs onto the floor. I had a small bottle of lube in my shaving kit, but it wasn't necessary, not the way my dick was drooling. Things had quieted down in the next room, no doubt the couple concentrating on making the necessary preparations. I imagined Tully swabbing Devon's asshole with lubricant, working a finger inside. I had never seen Tully's cock, but I'd pictured it in my mind many, many times. He did have a nice package, especially noticeable when he wore jeans, so I always assumed he was well hung. I stroked myself as I imagined him lubing up his big, stiff pole then pushing that the plump cockhead against Devon's ass-lips.

The volume in Tully's bedroom picked up. I could deduce from Devon's whimpering gasps and Tully's deep grunts what was happening. The bedsprings squeaked. Devon moaned. Tully groaned. I panted.

"Oh, yeah," Devon cried out. "Hard and fast, hard and fast."

I spit in my palm and wrapped my hand around my cock, fucking my fist as I imagined Tully fucking that ass.

"I'm gonna come!" Tully practically shouted. "You ready for it? You ready for daddy's load?"

An electric current buzzed up my shaft hearing Tully's words. Even calling himself "daddy" – a line from a porn video if ever there was one – did it for me. My own heavy breathing drowned out Devon's response, but Tully's rumbling orgasm could be heard throughout the neighborhood. My cock erupted, my cum hitting my sternum as I imagined Tully's load filling my ass.

I meant: *Devon's* ass.

# # # # #

Daybreak arrived too soon. By the time I forced myself out of bed, I barely had enough time to shower and dress.

My horny hosts had gone jogging, sparing me the obnoxiously cheery company of the freshly laid. I might have made a clean break to my marketing seminar if I hadn't stopped to write a note for them, Tully and Devon returning as I was placing the note in front of the coffee maker.

Both men were covered with more perspiration than clothing. Tully pulled off his tank top and used it to wipe the sweat off his face. He may have had fifteen years on Devon, but time had barely touched his body, as tautly muscled as someone half his age. Only a few sprouts of gray in his chest hair suggested Tully was over thirty-five. My eyes dropped to Tully's crotch. He wore a pair of gray Spandex shorts, sans underwear. Not much imagination needed.

Devon wore only a pair of loose-fitting, red nylon gym shorts that hung off his delectable ass just so. He grabbed bottle of water from the fridge and gulped from it almost lustily, a few errant trickles escaping from the corners of his mouth. The bottle was half empty by the time Devon pulled it away from his mouth. "Guess I was thirsty," he chuckled.

"Aren't you always," Tully said. Leaning toward me and dropping his voice, he added: "He guzzles cum just like that."

My cock jumped. "Thanks for sharing," I said. "I'll leave on that note."

Tully still hadn't put on a shirt when I returned late that afternoon, though he had changed out of the dick-defining Spandex shorts in favor of a pair of tan cargo shorts. "It's casual day at the office," he joked. He was a freelance marketing consultant and usually worked from home. Devon was still at work but would be back in an hour, he said. I changed into a pair of shorts and a T-shirt and joined Tully on the patio for a beer.

"So, what do you think of Devon?" he asked. "Isn't he great?"

"You definitely got yourself a hottie," I said, grateful that I didn't have to lie.

Tully grinned. "You're jealous."

"What? No, I'm happy for you."

"Bullshit. But that's okay. I'd be jealous if the shoe were on the other foot – or the condom on the other cock." Tully laughed loudly at his own joke. "Don't worry, you'll find a young plaything soon enough."

"I knew I had a reason to live," I said, then changed the subject. But the subject soon changed back to Devon when he got home twenty minutes later. When we went out to dinner Devon offered to ride in the back seat. "Yeah, I might end up giving him a hand-job on the drive over if he sits next to me," Tully said. At the seafood café Tully leered at Devon over his entrée: "This blackened salmon is good, but not as tasty as your ass." He stuck out his tongue and wiggled it obscenely in Devon's direction.

"T.M.I.," I scolded, nervously looking around the restaurant to see if anyone else had heard.

"Especially when it's covered with my load," Tully added.

Just as drunks are irritating when you're sober, couples are insufferable when you are single. The last straw came when we were back at the house, out on the patio drinking beers as a hot day faded into a warm night. Devon stood up and announced he had to take a piss.

"Aw, just go out on the lawn," Tully said.

Devon and I thought he was joking. He wasn't.

He got out of his lawn chair and walked toward Devon. "Go ahead, I want you to and I want to watch."

Devon protested, and that's when Tully lunged. Devon hopped backwards, laughing as Tully grabbed at the air. He swiped again, snagging Devon's T-shirt in his strong hands, practically ripping it from his body. The couple tussled playfully, their laughter shattering the stillness of the evening. I looked away, pretending to be fascinated by the growth of a wisteria vine.

The giggling subsided. When I looked back at my hosts they were on the grass just beyond the patio. Tully was standing behind Devon, reaching around his narrow waist. Even though they had their backs to me I could tell what Tully's hands were doing. A second later,

Devon was pissing a steady stream as Tully purred appreciatively and kissed nape of his neck. They held that pose, even after Devon stopped peeing, Tully playing with his boyfriend's dick as he kissed his neck and whispered filthy nothings.

I grabbed my beer and stood up. "I'm going to bed," I called over my shoulder as I headed back into the house. I didn't care if it was only eight o'clock.

"Mark! Wait." Tully called after me. But I didn't turn around.

I should've stayed at the fucking Sheraton.

# # # # #

Low voices drifted through the wall. The tone was conversational, but then I heard a sharp groan, punctuated by Tully's throaty chuckle. *Here we go.* They hadn't awoken me, at least. I couldn't sleep.

Devon giggled, gasped and said something I couldn't make out but that made Tully chuckle some more. I heard lips smacking and waited for Tully to start announcing what they were doing – "*I wanna suck that hot cock of yours!*" – in case I was wondering. The couple was more reserved this night, however. Anything said was kept between them.

The door to the neighboring bedroom opened, and I heard soft footsteps on the hall carpet. The guest room door opened, and I sat bolt upright. It was Devon, his naked body backlit by the hall light.

He stepped into the room, not bothering to close the door behind him. He walked with a casual grace I envied, though not as much as I envied other things of his. Tully was right: Devon had a beautiful cock.

"Hey, Mark, you still mad?" Devon asked.

"I – I wasn't mad. Just... *uncomfortable.*"

Devon sat on the edge of the bed, which didn't exactly put me at ease. "Tully thought you might be jealous."

I swallowed hard and tried to keep my eyes on his.

He put a hand on my chest. "Tully also thought you should fuck me," Devon said.

The furious beat of my heart almost drowned out his words. "So I guess *he's* not jealous," I managed to say.

Devon's hand glided down my torso. "I want you to fuck me. You're pretty hot."

This was a joke. I was sure of it. Any minute Devon was going to burst out laughing, or Tully was going to barge into the room in mock rage. The top sheet was drawn up to my waist, and Devon's hand slipped beneath it, his fingers mapping the growing mound in my underwear.

"You're pretty hung, too." He squeezed my cock through my shorts as he said it. His cock, I noticed, was hard as steel.

Maybe this wasn't a joke.

He pulled the sheet down, telling me to just relax as he pulled at the waistband of my bulging briefs, cooing approvingly when my stiff dick was exposed. His fingers traced the engorged veins of my shaft, his touch so light as to make me question if he was touching me at all. But he was touching me, and it felt fucking great. Definitely *not* a joke.

Devon straddled my thighs, his bare skin on mine sparking a tingling heat that burned through my body. Then he surprised me with a kiss. My hands went to his waist and I kissed him back, harder than he kissed me. His balls rested on my throbbing hard-on. The delicate caress of his velvety nutsac against my cock made me shudder and moan.

"Hey, can you keep it down? People are trying to sleep."

Tully had arrived. He ambled into the room, shirtless but, surprisingly, still wearing those cargo shorts. Nevertheless, I found it difficult to look away – from his wolfish grin, from his muscled torso, from the tent pitched in his shorts. Only when Devon spoke did I take my eyes away from my friend.

"You want to suck my cock?"

Devon was now kneeling over my chest, pushing his rock hard dong toward my face. Moonlight cut through a gap in the curtains, hitting the oozing crown, making the piss-slit twinkle.

"It tastes as good as it looks," Tully said, standing by the bed now, close enough for me to see, even in the room's dim light, the few darkened spots on his shorts where his pre-cum had soaked through.

Devon's cock was right there for the taking, and I wanted to take it. But, gorgeous as Devon was, he wasn't my first choice.

"What're you waiting for?" Tully said. "Suck Devon's dick."

"I'm going to," I said, smiling at Tully. I reached out and hooked my hand between his legs. "After I suck yours."

Tully was visibly stunned. Devon broke out laughing, flopping beside me on the narrow bed. "C'mon, Tull, you heard the man."

Tully was still chuckling as I leaned over the edge of the bed and unbuttoned his shorts and unzipped the fly. His hard cock nearly hit me in the face. I took it in my hand and admired it. Tully was indeed well hung, his cock at least eight inches, maybe eight and a half, with a shaft so thick I couldn't close my fingers around it. He was cut and his cockhead throbbed enticingly.

I swallowed his pole down to the root and his chuckling stopped abruptly. He cried out as I slowly drew my mouth upward, my tongue tracing the engorged veins of the shaft. I swirled my tongue around the plump crown, tasting his salty juices, and then pulled my mouth away, a moist pop cracking the air as his cock broke free of my lips. I smiled up at him.

"Aw, man, I had no idea," Tully said breathlessly.

"Which, that I give good head or I that wanted to suck your cock?"

"Both."

I yanked Tully's shorts down until they fell in a heap at his feet and then cupped his balls, liking the way their weight felt in my hand. His sack was hairy, but not as much as I'd expected, like he'd shaved at one time and the hair was just starting to grow back. I cuffed his nutsac just below the base of his cock, and raised his balls to my mouth, tonguing the cum-swollen spheres.

A hand rested on my shoulder; Devon, leaning over me, whispering encouragement as I worshipped his lover's dick. He reached for Tully's hand, tugging it and telling him to join us on the bed.

We moved aside and Tully climbed onto the mattress. There was barely enough room on the guest room bed for the three of us. Tully and Devon's king sized bed would've been more accommodating, but I didn't want to interrupt the moment, waste time walking to the neighboring room when I could be slurping on Tully's cock. With Tully recumbent against the pillows, Devon and I worked on either side of his hard-on, our lips and tongues barely separated by Tully's drooling prick. Tully grabbed the tops of our heads, holding us in place as he thrust his dick between our wet lips.

Devon and I raised our heads from Tully's crotch to his face and our mouths converged in a sloppy three-way kiss. Tully's hand touched down on my shoulder and stroked my back. His affectionate caress excited me nearly as much as sucking his dick. Nearly.

The bed rocked as Devon rose up on his knees. He gripped his cock at the base and aimed it at Tully's lips, and Tully took it down his throat in one fluid gulp. I reached for Tully's dick, stroking while he sucked. I was prepared to do some more sucking myself, but before my mouth could travel back down Tully's torso Devon's cock had popped free from his mouth, as did Tully's ideas for how we should proceed.

"Sit on my face," he ordered Devon. "Mark can suck your cock while I eat your ass."

When we worked together Tully was known for his ability to take charge of a situation. He was a natural born leader – even during a three-way with his hot boyfriend and visiting friend.

After some scooting, rolling and straddling, we were in position, Devon astride Tully's face, me hovering over Tully's body, swallowing his young lover's cock. Devon rolled his hips, purring with delight as Tully tongue-fucked his hole, and I took his prick down my gullet. I sucked Devon's cock in long, lusty gulps, my spit dripping off his shaft onto Tully's chest.

At Devon's urging, I sat up on my haunches, between Tully's spread thighs. He eased himself down across Tully's body, clamping his lips around that fat, throbbing boner. My dick pulsed, dripping its juice onto the sheets, a sticky tribute to Devon's oral skill. I experienced that skill firsthand a moment later, when Devon's mouth jumped from Tully's cock to mine. Then my body shuddered.

His mouth alternated that way for a while, going from my dick to Tully's and back again, before taking them both at the same time. I moaned loudly and ran my fingers through Devon's short, brown hair. The sensation of my cock pressed against my friend's, held in Devon's hot mouth was pleasurable to the point of being unbearable.

A brief commotion followed as Tully extracted himself from beneath Devon's body. He stood beside the bed, his beard wet with spit, his eyes bleary with lust. The wolfish grin was still going strong. He told Devon to get on his hands and knees, told me to "eat that sweet ass." And then I was kneeling on the floor, behind Devon, now bent over the edge of the mattress, looking into his splayed butt cheeks. Devon's asshole was wet, rosy-pink and, as I'd suspected, shaved smooth. My fingertips toyed with his sphincter, a rubbery-lipped slit with delicate lines radiating outward like spokes on a wheel. The sphincter muscle contracted, Devon whimpered, and I dove in, stabbing it with my tongue. His whimpering became ecstatic yelps.

Tully stood over us, looking down at me as I tongued his twenty-six-year-old boyfriend's tender hole, jacking off and growling obscenities. I, unable to resist the temptation, pulled my face out of Devon's ass periodically to suck on Tully's fat cock and balls. Then I lifted my face from Devon's trench and Tully was gone.

"Where'd he go?" I asked.

Devon looked over his shoulder, his handsome face slack, his eyes drooping. He looked stoned. "What's it matter?" he gurgled. To prove his point, he slid off the bed, backwards, into my arms, his spit-lubed butt pressing up against my aching prick. He rocked his body against mine, expertly stroking my cock with his firm ass, and by the time Tully returned, I'd almost forgotten he ever left.

"Looks like we're on the same page," Tully said. He held up a bottle of lube and a couple of foil condom packets.

Devon hopped to his feet. He didn't say anything, but he was smiling excitedly, knowing his ass was going to get filled with cock.

I took a rubber from Tully, and asked him if he was using the other one. "I've never been the meat in the sandwich," I said suggestively. Truthfully, I'd never been in a sandwich, period, but Tully didn't need to know that.

"I've got something even more interesting in mind," he said.

Devon assisted in prepping my cock for his ass. "I can't wait," he whispered, drizzling lube on my sheathed hard-on. I tried to steer him back to the bed, where I planned to fuck him doggie style, but Devon clearly had other ideas. He grabbed the pillows off the bed and dropped them on the floor.

"Lie down here," he said. "I'll get on top."

Tully remained on the sidelines, fondling his stiff pole. His eyes were sparkling now; I could tell he had something planned, and whatever his plan was, he wanted it to be a surprise.

I grunted loudly as Devon lowered himself onto my cock. He sucked in his breath, his butt touching down on my thighs, my dick swallowed up by his asshole. I slowly pumped his ass and Devon rolled his hips. Looking at his taut sculpted physique; at the tense interplay of his muscles; at the sweat beading on his golden skin; at his rigid, weeping cock was almost as pleasurable as having my pole buried in his tight chute.

Tully circled us like he was taking in an exhibit at a museum: *Friend from Atlanta Fucking my Boyfriend, a live sculpture by Tully McCaul.* He paused beside Devon, hooked a hand behind his head and pushed Devon's face forward, toward his trembling cock. Devon sucked his dick in full, fluid strokes. Tully let out a low, raspy groan. From my vantage point I got a good view of Tully's muscled butt.

"Hey, Tull, you gonna let me eat that ass of yours?" I asked.

He looked over his shoulder, an odd look of amusement on his face. "You're just full of surprises."

But he didn't let me eat his ass. Instead, he pulled his cock from his boyfriend's insatiable mouth, picked up the bottle of lube from the floor and squirted some onto his hard-on. He smiled down at me as he rubbed his cock, making sure it was well coated in lube. A long, shiny strand of pre-cum hung from his cockhead, and I wanted to catch it on my tongue. Tully, his eyes trained on me, caught the slimy thread with his fingers and pushed those glazed digits into Devon's mouth.

He moved behind Devon, leaving me to wonder if I was about to be kicked to the side, jacking off while the two lovers fucked. Devon then fell forward, on top of me. "This is gonna be great," he panted. His tongue pushed into my mouth.

Devon's mouth jerked away from mine. His face was screwed into a mask of pain or extreme exertion. His cries seemed stuck in his throat, coming out in short harsh grunts. When I realized what was happening, I was surprised Devon's reaction wasn't more dramatic. Tully was pushing his cock into his hole, already occupied by mine. The pressure of our two pricks squeezed together in that hot, moist cave left me rapturous. For Devon, though, I worried the double penetration was far too painful to be pleasurable and was about to suggest as much out loud when Devon's tormented expression melted into one of bliss.

I pumped my cock into Devon's crowded chute, reveling in the friction between Tully's cock and mine. If I couldn't feel that fat monster in my own ass, this was the next best thing. I pumped harder, and so did Tully, our dicks practically fighting their way into Devon's stretched-out hole. Devon's body jerked and shuddered. Sweat dripped off his body and was grunting loudly. He rolled his hips forward, pushing his hard-on into my belly.

Tully and I fucked him harder.

I came suddenly and loudly, my orgasm hitting me like a thunderbolt. My body twitched spastically as my cock kept firing. I closed my eyes, for a moment only hearing my beating heart, frantically pumping blood while my cock was pumped jism.

My eyes opened when Tully announced he was coming: "*Aw, fuck, I'm gonna shoot! I'm gonna shoot!*" I could feel his cock pulsing with each spurt, and if I hadn't came already, that sensation would have pushed me over the edge.

We were all still for a moment, a breathing, sweating heap on the floor. Tully pulled out and stood up, shaking cum off his dick (he hadn't bothered with a rubber). Devon sat up, pushing his weight onto my still-hard cock. In his wake was a gooey puddle of jizz on my abdomen. He dragged a finger through his jizz and brought that finger to my lips. I sucked on it and he smiled. He fed me more of his load, and I happily ate every drop.

Tully knelt down beside us, leaning over my belly to lap up some of Devon's cream. His mouth moved up to mine and we kissed.

"I told you you'd like it better here than at the fucking Sheraton," he said.

Devon cut in, he and Tully kissing inches above my face. "Love you, baby," he said.

"You know I love you," Tully replied.

"T.M.I." I whispered.

Reborn in Vinyl

I got an instant hard-on the moment I put them on.

"C'mon out and let's see," said the salesman hovering outside the changing booth.

"Uh, in a minute," I said, turning to check out my ass in the mirror.

The black vinyl pants clung to every curve, the shiny fabric coating me like paint from the waist down. Only I didn't feel as if I were looking at myself. I was no longer Lane, with his uniform of khaki and Oxford shirts, whose most daring fashion choice in the past ten years was a pair of black jeans. In these pants, I was someone else.

But in the back of my mind, I heard the laughter. I heard Matt, my ex, telling me I looked ridiculous. Telling me the pants just weren't me. Then I heard the words he actually spoke, a month ago, when he said he was breaking up with me. "You're a great guy," he said, "but I need excitement." He said I'd make a great husband, but he wanted a lover.

"Well, do you like them?" the salesman pushed.

I turned back around to face myself in the mirror. The outline of my hard-on was plainly visible. "I think so."

"Then come out and show me."

I pulled my T-shirt down over my waist, only managing to conceal the top half of my boner. I took a deep breath and stepped outside the changing booth.

The salesman – a perpetually beaming, stick-thin twink – let out a whistle. "Oh, baby, yes!" he purred in his honey-thick Southern drawl.

"Not sure if it's exactly me," I blushed, voicing the doubts I imagined coming from my ex-boyfriend.

"Honey, you got nothin' to worry about. Turn around."

I did as he asked, simultaneously flattered and embarrassed to be putting on this private fashion show. The sales guy grabbed hold of my T-shirt, startling me. "Baby, you got to pull your shirt up! You don't get pants like this to hide the good stuff."

Holding my shirt above my waist, I stood in place while the salesman checked out my ass. He told me to turn back around. I hesitated. My cock had softened some, but not enough for the sake of my own modesty.

The salesman wasn't going to wait. Placing his hands on my waist, he steered me around, so I faced him. I could feel my face turning seven different shades of purple as he stepped back and inspected me.

He smiled and nodded. "Yeah, definitely," he said. "One suggestion, though: When you wear these out, don't wear underwear."

I took the salesman's suggestion that night. The erotic sensation of having my cock and balls in direct contact with their vinyl encasement was so intense I nearly came. I could barely keep my hands off myself, rubbing the mound at the front of my pants, feeling my dick pulse beneath as it pumped out pre-cum. The temptation to jack-off was strong, but I resisted, deciding to save my body for whoever might want it later.

I left my room an hour after putting the pants on – it took nearly that long to lose my erection. Though the salesman at the shop tried to sell me something equally shiny to complement the pants, I chose a simple white tee. Unlike my other T-shirts, however, this one hugged my body as tightly as the pants. Checking myself out in a mirror, I thought I cut a pretty nice figure. The appreciative stares I got as I sauntered through the hotel lobby confirmed my self-assessment, erasing the last of my lingering self-doubt.

The nightclub was called The Hole, tucked in a dark side street off the well-beaten path of Atlanta's gay midtown. Upon entering, I realized The Hole was short for Hole in the Wall. The club was crammed into a long, narrow space, and what little light there was illuminated walls the color of dried blood.

There wasn't much of a crowd. I checked my watch. Just after ten, still early yet. I walked up to the bar, surrounded by men who looked to have been occupying their stools since the club opened at six o'clock. When I ordered my beer, one of the barflies said to me, "Nice ass." I smiled at the compliment but made a hasty retreat with my beer lest he think my nice ass could be his.

More men came into the club. They were of different ages, sizes, races, and all very butch. It was clear that a drag queen wasn't going to feel at home at this bar. And for a moment, I wasn't sure I did, either. An attack of self-doubt had me feeling like an imposter. I wasn't some leather-clad daddy; I was Lane, the meek marketing rep from Charlotte, in Atlanta to pretend he was someone else. Sooner or later I'd get caught.

But then I felt a hand slide over the curve of my left butt cheek. "Nice looking pants," a voice rumbled in my ear.

On my left stood a man with ice-blue eyes and cheekbones as sharp as knives. When he smiled, his teeth nearly glowed, contrasting starkly with the black stubble darkening his face. I smiled back but said nothing.

Another hand touched my back. It belonged to a man standing on my right. Taller than either the man on my left or I, he looked down into my eyes, silently, but his expression loudly conveying his thoughts. This man was bald, with a triangular soul patch beneath his lower lip. Silver hoops adorned both ears.

"You should come downstairs," said the man on my left. He was practically leaning against me.

"Downstairs?"

He jerked his head toward the rear of the club. In the corner, I could see men heading down a staircase, disappearing beneath the floor.

Apprehension burned in my stomach. "What's down there?" I asked.

His hand slid down the front of my pants, giving my package a squeeze. His bald-headed friend leaned in and whispered, "Come down and see." He then flicked his tongue inside my ear.

I watched the two men – Blue Eyes and The Bald One – walk away, checking out their bodies. Blue Eyes wore a black tee with blue jeans, the ensemble fitting snugly against his muscular frame. The Bald One wore a black leather vest, showing off arms swollen with muscle and decorated with swirling, interlocking tattoos. His black pants fit like a pair of tights, accentuating his hard, muscled ass.

The two men stopped at the stairs, looking back at me and extending invitations with their smiles before heading down.

Once again, my cock was rock-hard.

Quickly, I went to the bar, got another beer and headed downstairs.

At the bottom of the stairs was a dance floor bathed in blue and red light. On the floor, a few men gyrated to the pounding beat of the music, but most stayed at the floor's outer edges, circling like wolves sizing up their prey.

The two wolves that cornered me upstairs moved in for the kill. Blue Eyes clamped a hand on my arm. He said something to me, but it was lost in the blaring music.

I took a big pull from my beer, hoping the alcohol would calm my nerves. I wanted another swallow, but The Bald One took the bottle from my hand. "We'll buy you another one. Later," he shouted above the din, dropping my beer into a trashcan.

They pulled me onto the dance floor. The two men – nameless, except for the nicknames I'd given them, still anonymous, as was I – fell into the rhythm easily, gyrating around me. My movements were less fluid, my body moving in stiff, uncertain jerks. Again, I heard the sneering voice of my ex-boyfriend, who told me I danced like I'd just broken a hip. At best, I managed to sway gently in a fashion that pantomimed real dancing.

My anonymous partners seemed unconcerned about my lack of grace. As they moved about me, I realized they were closing in, reducing my floor space until I could scarcely move at all.

The guy with the cheekbones ran his hands over my chest. My nipples, swelling to his touch, stabbed the cloth of my shirt. He leaned in to kiss me, and I accepted his tongue in my mouth without hesitation. Behind me, the other man ground his crotch against my vinyl-clad butt. I could feel his hardness, pressing against the crack of my ass. His lips rubbed against the back of my neck, sending a prickly sensation down my spine. His hands moved up my flanks, taking my shirt with it.

As my shirt was stripped from my body, so were the last of my inhibitions. The staid persona I clung to was as far away as my hometown.

Blue Eyes pushed his tongue deeper into my mouth, and The Bald One nuzzled the nape of my neck. Our hands groped wildly, pinching nipples, caressing rippling abs, grabbing asses. My hand gripped a cock. My eyes widened, showing my apprehension to the ice-blues in front of me. He urged me on with a smile.

I pulled at Blue Eyes' cock. Its length was average, but its girth considerable. The distinct rim beneath the plump cockhead told me he was circumcised. His dick drooled its own lubricant as I moved my hand up and down the shaft.

Blue Eyes' wasn't the only cock set free. As I stroked his prick, his fingers pulled at the front of my pants. My fly opened, and my dick jutted forward into Blue Eyes' waiting palm.

The Bald One's mouth was gliding over my shoulder now, the wet trail left by his tongue felt cool as it was exposed to the club's air-conditioning. That tongue continued down my spine, down to my ass. I felt The Bald One's face pressing against my butt crack, his tongue sliding between my vinyl-sheathed cheeks.

Blue Eyes backed away, and I fell forward, my face sliding down the soft material of his shirt, the hardness of the muscles beneath pressing against my cheek. My descent ended at his cock. I swallowed it whole, until the head pushed into my gullet and the musky, manly scent of his pubic hair filled my nostrils.

At this moment, the world outside was forgotten. The nightclub and its other patrons didn't exist. We were reminded of their existence, but rather than us being brought back to that outside world, they entered ours. Out of the corners of my eyes, I saw other men moving in, surrounding us. The lights seemed dimmer, and the music now had a slinkier, sexier groove, as if the club's management and DJ were in collusion with our debauchery.

The men circling us had their cocks out, too, jacking them as they watched me, bent at the waist, sucking Blue Eyes and getting my ass teased by The Bald One's prodding tongue. I sank to my knees, continuing to gulp down Blue Eyes' seeping dick, my arms encircling his waist, my hands kneading his firm butt, my fingers tracing the fuzzy crevice.

Then I was handed off, my mouth moving to another anonymous cock, this one more mysterious than Blue Eyes' for I didn't see its owner above the waist. This cock was longer, the pubes buzzed back to mere stubble, the balls shaved. Without a second thought, I gulped this one down my throat, its owner raking his fingers through my dark hair as his shaft disappeared between my lips.

My own cock ached, and I was sure a sizable puddle of pre-cum had collected on the scuffed floor beneath me. I reached between my legs, the urge to stroke my swollen prick so strong I was barely conscious of what my hand was doing. But another hand intercepted me, seizing my wrist and pulling my arm back behind me. A twinge wrenched through the muscles of my back, settling into mild discomfort. Rather than quelling my arousal, my excitement increased.

I felt the press of The Bald One's cock against the groove of my ass. He made no attempt to pull my pants down, to get at my pulsing asshole with his tongue and rod, preferring instead to rub his cock against the vinyl, using his own spit as lubricant.

My face got pushed toward another dick, this one dark brown, much darker than the rest of the man's skin. It was almost black, though the cockhead was much lighter, the color of milk chocolate with just a bit of cherry. I closed my lips around it, prepared to ease it into my mouth. Instead, the man grabbed a handful of my hair, held me in place and fucked my mouth. The music faded as my ears became filled with the sounds of my gagging throat and my desperate breaths. The only relief I got from the relentless stabbing of his cock was when he pulled it from my mouth to slap me in the face with it, its glistening black shaft smacking wetly against the sides of my nose.

The black man raised my mouth off his cock, picking my head up with my hair as if it were a suitcase and moving it to the spread cheeks of another man's ass. I was not allowed time to appreciate the fullness of those creamy-white globes or the pink lips of the hole. Rather, I was force-fed that ass, shoved between those cheeks and held there while my tongue worked its way into that twitching sphincter.

I'd lost track of my original seducers, though I was pretty sure The Bald One remained behind me, still keeping my hand away from myself, still keeping a layer of vinyl between his cock and my ass. Blue Eyes' whereabouts was anybody's guess. For all I knew, it was his ass I was eating.

The black man stayed with me, one hand clenching my hair in his fist, the other stroking his throbbing cock and batting it against the butt upended in my face. Another man joined him, jerking off over the other ass cheek. My head was lifted out of the anonymous ass, guided toward this new dick. This one was uncut, the cock's glazed tip blooming out of its foreskin sheath. Quickly, I covered the exposed cockhead with my mouth, my tongue licking off the sticky residue coating the crown.

A tight, burning pain rose beneath my scalp as two hands, each hand belonging to a different man, jerked me back by the hair. I was held at bay, my face kept a foot from the butt I'd been munching, the cheeks moist with my spit. The men holding me – the black one and the uncut one – pulled at their cocks. Seconds later they came. Jism, white and thick, splattered onto the small of the other man's back and slid downward into the channel of those anonymous butt cheeks. As their load sluiced down, my face was pushed forward. Without instruction, I knew what was expected and lapped up their mixing spooge as it dripped down the man's ass crack. Through the music and the moans, a few phrases made it to my ears: "Nasty little slut!" and "Horny little pig!" Not phrases ever used in reference to me, by past lovers or myself, and despite the snarling tones with which they were said, I found them as satisfying as the jizz I'd just eaten.

The ass moved away, its possessor standing and turning, presenting me with his fat, dripping dong. His dick was pierced, a small silver bar hooked through the skin at the base of the shaft. I brought my tongue to it, feeling the hard metal beneath the skin. From there I followed the rigid veins of his cock up the shaft, up to the engorged head with its silvery thread of pre-cum hanging from the slit. My mouth engulfed the organ, slurping on it loudly as if trying to suck the last drop of soda through a straw.

I sucked his cock until his body jerked and his cum flooded into my mouth. He pulled out, his cock still shooting, hitting me in the face. I looked up, finding a bearded face, mouth gasping in orgasm, looking down on me from atop a hairy torso and heaving chest. His eyes closed as his cock pumped the last of its load. When they opened, they focused on my cum-spackled face. The man smiled and wiped the last drop of jizz on the tip of my nose.

The hands that held my hair let go, and I fell forward, catching myself on my elbow. A man with a red buzz cut, a long narrow face and sleepy-looking eyes swooped down and licked my face clean. Standing astride my body was another man, getting his dick serviced by The Bald One as he continued to grind his dick against my slick pants.

Then Blue Eyes returned, reaching down and hooking his hands under my arms and lifting me to my feet. For a split second, I saw the faces of the horny men surrounding us. Some were cute, but more were average – men I wouldn't look twice at if I passed them on the street. Yet now I wanted all of them.

In the pack I thought I saw a familiar face, and it made my heart skip. It couldn't be …

Blue Eyes' face blocked my vision, and his tongue filled my mouth. I was willing to believe the familiar face was my imagination as the heat of Blue Eye's cock burned against my own aching member. When he pulled his mouth away, a dripping string of saliva hung between us. It snapped and hung from my lower lip.

He stepped away, and the other men moved in. Both my hands were pulled behind me, my upturned palms coming in contact with The Bald One's dick. I managed to curl my fingers around it, squeezing it, its juice leaking onto my hand. His head leaned over my shoulder and hissed into my ear: "We're gonna come all over you."

All the men seemed to hear this announcement, though it was only breathed into my ear. Surging forward, stroking their cocks, they fired their loads one by one. I don't know how many men there were –

seven, possibly ten. As they stepped up to me, I braced myself for an up-close encounter with the familiar face, wondering what I'd say, or would I be quiet and just smile. But I knew none of the men dumping their hot loads onto my thighs, my stomach, my shoes.

At the end of the line was Blue Eyes. He looking crazed: the corners of his mouth jerked downward spastically, and those ice blue eyes were now dark and wild. Standing inches from me, he pulled at his cock in frenzied strokes. Even in the club's dim light, I could see his face redden.

He came with a roar, his hot load splashing down on my quivering dick and my blue balls. Stray droplets were caught in the curls of my pubic hair. In my ear, I heard a sharp grunt. The Bald One came. Some of his slimy, warm wetness dripped onto my fingers, but most of it landed on my covered backside.

I had yet to get off. The need to do so was urgent, but no one was making an immediate move to relieve my swollen balls. The Bald One released my hands; however, before I could grab my throbbing hard-on, Blue Eyes intercepted, cuffing my wrists.

For a moment, no one did anything. I was on display, the crowd getting a chance to marvel at the white ribbons of man cream that streamed down my legs and butt, looking like white veins against the shiny black vinyl. Pre-cum dripped from the head of my cock and sweat oozed from my pores.

The two men got down on their knees, Blue Eyes in front, The Bald One behind. To my astonishment, they began lapping up the cooling rivulets of jism. The Bald One noisily slurped up his own load from the groove between my ass cheeks, while Blue Eyes held me in his gaze as he dragged his tongue up my cum-stippled thighs.

Their mouths met at my cock. The Bald One was wet with sweat, a rapturous expression on his face. The men pressed their lips against either side of my sticky shaft, their tongues massaging my dick. The Bald One dropped his mouth down to my balls, sucking my tight nut-sack into his parted lips. Blue Eyes wrapped a hand around my shaft, jerking it as he flicked his tongue at the head.

I came with such ferocity my legs nearly gave out beneath me. My load was heavy and copious, shooting over Blue Eyes' shoulder in a high arc. I thought I heard someone say, "Wow!" My final spurts grazed Blue Eyes' cheek and splashed down on his friend's gleaming skull.

A calm fell over me, and I felt I was already home in bed and all that happened was a wonderful, raunchy dream.

My eyes snapped open. The faces of strangers greeted me. Some gave me embarrassed smiles, others looked away, not meeting my eyes. I heard chuckling and the murmur of conversation. "You are too hot," Blue Eyes said to me, wiping his mouth with the back of his hand.

Then I saw the familiar face again, staring at me, his expression dazed.

"Matt?" My ex-lover's name came out a harsh whisper.

Panicked, I stuffed my shrinking dick back in my pants, zipped up and backed away from the crowd. Then I turned and ran. Like a kinky Cinderella, my sexy vinyl pants had lost their power. I stumbled up the stairs, chancing one final look back. Matt had disappeared once again, if I had actually seen him in the first place.

Upstairs, I pushed my way through the crowd until I burst out the door into the warm night air. I was no longer the "nasty little slut" or "horny little pig." I was now Lane, who wore khakis and held a steady job and took men to dinner before having sex and who would never *ever* consider offering himself as a sacrifice in a cum-soaked backroom orgy.

Until the next time I put on my vinyl pants and got that instant hard-on.

The Transformation

He was almost there. Across the ravine, through another wall of trees, and he would be in his special place, the clearing in the woods. This was Thomas's favorite spot, away from his family, basking in the summer sun and enjoying the privacy he could never find on the farm. Not when every moment was spent in company of his father, brothers and sisters.

Thomas discovered the place two years ago, when he was sixteen. He'd been wandering aimlessly in the forest when he came upon the clearing. In the midst of the field was a large stone. The stone was flat on top, like a table, a perfect place to sit and rest. The solitude and the warmth of the sun had a soothing effect. He had stripped off his shirt, letting the sun's rays dry the sweat off his lean, muscular chest.

It was while sitting here that Thomas had begun to indulge in what were considered "impure thoughts." That's what his father called them. He had said the thoughts were like inviting the devil to steal your soul. His older brother got a whipping once for having them, when his father caught him in the barn. Thomas didn't know what his brother had done until later. His older brother explained that if you rubbed your cock when it was hard it felt really good, but it was a sin, so you had to make sure no one else was around when you did it.

Thomas didn't understand until a few years later, when he had discovered the rock in the clearing. He had started thinking about something he'd seen earlier in the week, at the creek that ran near his house. He saw some men bathing, cooling down after working in the fields. Thomas hid behind the thick trunk of a tree and watched. The sight of their naked bodies had made him stiff. He didn't know why – he'd seen his brothers naked, and it never affected him that way. But, these men excited him. They were broad shouldered and muscular, their wet skin shimmering in the sunlight. Their dicks were long and thick, surrounded by a patch of bushy hair. Thomas spied on them for several minutes before he scurried away, fearing if he stayed much longer the men would catch him spying.

The image of the men in the creek had stuck with him, and he lingered over the memory as he sat on the flat rock. He wondered what would happen if the men had caught him. At the time, he knew little of the sexual possibilities that the world had to offer, so his fantasies about the men were simple: They'd grab him from behind the tree and drag him to the creek; they would strip him, their hands touching him all over, rubbing his cock and caressing his ass. His body would be sandwiched between them, and he could feel their dicks pressing against him.

Thomas's cock was as hard as the rock he rested upon. Almost without thinking about it, he reached between his legs, feeling his stiff rod through his pants. He unbuttoned his fly, eager to touch his own cock. It was red and twitching, the head oozing a clear liquid that Thomas at first thought was piss, but it was too thick and sticky to be that.

He took his cock in his hand. Instinctively, he stroked it. His brother was right: it felt *really* good. The pleasure urged him on. Thomas stroked his dick faster, until he became oblivious to his surroundings. All that mattered was the feeling crackling through his teenaged rod and radiating throughout his taut body.

Suddenly it was as if an explosion had ignited in his cock and balls. Thomas's entire body shook, and jets of heavy white juice fired out of his prick. In a few seconds, the tremors that gripped his body subsided. He felt spent and satisfied.

His hand was covered with the creamy liquid that shot out his cock. His brother hadn't told Thomas about this. Out of curiosity, he had sucked a drop of the white fluid off his finger. It had a tangy, almost metallic flavor Thomas found strangely intoxicating.

After that day, the clearing in the forest became Thomas's refuge, a place to indulge in his fantasies and explore his body, the surrounding woods shielding him from the eyes of others.

But today was different. As he stepped through the trees and into the clearing, he saw a man sitting on the flat rock – *his* rock. As

Thomas walked closer, the man called out. "Hello. Come to enjoy the sun as well?"

The man was old and withered. Practically a corpse, Thomas thought. His facial features were a collection of wrinkles and sagging skin. His hair – what remained of it – was a wispy, white ring around his skull. Although the weather was warm, the man wore a heavy cloak and dark suit. The material looked to be very fine, and the cane the man clutched in his hand was capped with an elaborate gold ornament. Thomas assumed he was wealthy, perhaps one of the businessmen who lived in town, which made his appearance in the forest that much more curious. The upper classes usually didn't come out to the country, not unless they were collecting debts from the farmers.

"Come, keep an old man company," the stranger said, patting the empty space beside him on the rock.

Thomas approached the man cautiously. He wanted to turn and flee, but years of being told to respect his elders compelled him to accept the old man's invitation.

"So what is your name, son?" the man asked, his voice reedy, like his next breath could be his last.

"Thomas, sir," the young man replied, looking down at the grass.

"Mine is Sir Benjamin Tallman, but you may dispense with formalities and call me Ben."

"Yes, sir," Thomas said, his voice barely audible.

The man smiled, and Thomas flinched; the man was missing most of his teeth. Ben turned his face up to the sun. "Beautiful day, isn't it?"

"Yes sir."

"I often like to come out here to the forest. I don't live far from here. My daughter doesn't like me to go wandering about. Says I could die out here and no one would know my whereabouts. I tell her if I'm going to die, I'd much rather do it out here than in that stuffy house."

At that Ben began to laugh – a surprisingly hearty laugh that quickly degenerated into spasmodic coughs. When the man regained his breath, he said to Thomas, "You like to come out here, too?"

"Yes," Thomas said. Ben was making him uneasy.

"I know, I've seen you," Ben said with a toothless grin.

Thomas's blood turned cold. All those times he thought he was alone – naked on the rock, touching himself in forbidden places – this hideous old man was watching.

"Don't feel ashamed," Ben said. "You're very beautiful. A pleasure to watch."

Thomas didn't respond. He couldn't look at the man, he felt so humiliated.

There was a moment of silence between them, and it was in that moment, the old man rested a gnarled hand on Thomas's thigh. The young man froze; he wanted to push Ben away, but the shock of the stranger's touch rendered him immobile.

"How old are you, Thomas?" Ben asked.

"Eighteen," Thomas replied, his voice sounding pinched. "Nineteen next month."

"Have you ever let another man touch you the way you touch yourself?"

Thomas couldn't speak. The man's hand was rubbing his thigh, moving further up with each stroke, until finally it came to a rest in Thomas's crotch. Although Thomas was in no way attracted to the man – Thomas found him repulsive, in fact – the feel of his hand between his legs caused his young cock to stir within his trousers.

Ben groped him, making Thomas's dick rigid. Once the old man was satisfied Thomas was fully erect, he began unbuttoning Thomas's pants, his swollen, aching joints making the process slow and clumsy. Thomas waited, now unable to tear himself away.

The elderly gentleman jumped slightly upon freeing Thomas's swollen cock, as if he hadn't expected it. He carefully wrapped a hand around it. Thomas shivered, amazed that Ben's hands, so bony and wrinkled, felt so good along the length of his cock.

"A beautiful boy," Ben whispered, fixing his twinkling grey eyes on the young man, admiring his long, sun-bleached hair, his handsome face and, most of all, his lean, muscular body. He began to pull Thomas's dick slowly.

Thomas tried to remain stone-faced; he didn't want the man to get any more encouragement beyond the hardness of his cock. Something as simple as a sigh or a moan could give Ben the idea that this meant something to Thomas, and Thomas did not want it to mean anything.

But, he could not keep his expression neutral for long. Ben was sliding off the rock, easing his weight onto his knees. Positioning himself between Thomas's legs, Ben grasped his sturdy thighs and leaned forward.

"I want to taste you," he said, his voice as light and fleeting as the summer breeze.

The feeling of Ben's mouth on his cock caused Thomas's whole body to shake. It was a sensation Thomas could not have imagined, and now that he was experiencing it, he didn't want it to stop.

Thomas leaned back on his elbows and closed his eyes. As much as he loved this new feeling that Ben was stirring within him, he could not bear to look at the old man. He was the antithesis of sex as far as Thomas was concerned, and he could only fully give himself to this experience if he filled his mind with fantasies of others.

He imagined other men – the men he saw bathing at the creek years ago, classmates, friends of his brother – in Ben's place. He tried to picture them with his dick in their mouths, with them licking and sucking it like Ben was doing. He fantasized of doing the same to these men, wondering what it would be like to have another man's cock in his mouth, to kiss his balls and taste his cum.

These thoughts combined with the sensations the old man's mouth aroused from his prick had Thomas groaning, his body gripped by a mounting pleasure. His muscles contracted, and his breathing became shallow. Unable to control himself any longer, Thomas succumbed to the ecstasy, letting it overtake him. In a sudden, almost violent, jolt, Thomas's cock shot its syrupy load down the elderly man's throat.

Ben lustily drank Thomas's jism, gulping it down as if it were his lifeblood.

In a way, it was.

Thomas slowly opened his eyes, willing to risk breaking the spell now that he'd been satisfied. Ben was still hunched between his legs, with only the top of his head visible. Yet it was different. The ring of white hair was becoming dark brown. It was covering the top of Ben's skull, growing before Thomas's eyes.

Ben's body shook beneath his cloak. His fingers dug into the flesh of Thomas' thighs, his grip becoming painful. Thomas noticed the old man's hands were changing, too, the skin becoming tight as flesh developed underneath. Soon, the hands of the decrepit old man were replaced with the hands of a man much younger and stronger.

Thomas remained motionless, watching Ben's transformation in both horror and fascination. Certainly he was still fantasizing. But, this was too clear, too real, to be in the realm of his imagination.

Then, suddenly, Ben was still. At least, Thomas assumed it was Ben, though from what he could see the man buried between his legs in no way resembled the man he first encountered.

Just when Thomas feared Ben might have died, the man looked up. Thomas jumped, scooting back on the rock.

"W-who are you?" he exclaimed.

Looking at him was a virile, handsome man no older than twenty-five. About the only feature he recognized from the old man were the eyes, still gray and sparkling.

The man stood up. The suit he wore was straining at the seams now that it housed a muscular young stud and not the shriveled figure it had originally been fitted for.

"Don't be afraid," the man said, his voice now deep and forceful. He untied the cloak. "It's still I, just an earlier incarnation."

Ben tossed the cloak on the ground and then began removing the suit. Thomas watched, spellbound by the young man who was Ben, yet *not* Ben. As the man stripped off his suit, he revealed a sculpted physique, each muscle defined beneath his smooth, tan skin. And when Ben stepped out of his trousers, Thomas's jaw went slack. His cock was long and thick, bigger than any he had ever seen. It stood straight up, quivering slightly.

Ben smiled, his mouth now full of straight, white teeth. "Would you like to touch it?"

Thomas gave Ben an astonished look, as if he didn't quite believe the invitation. He had never touched a dick other than his own and was now overwhelmed by the prospect, especially a cock as large as Ben's.

"Go ahead," Ben encouraged. "I want you to."

Thomas moved closer. As he reached out he noticed his hand was trembling. He gently wrapped his fingers around the engorged shaft of Ben's rod, his fingers unable to close around its circumference. Thomas began sliding his hand up and down the length of Ben's cock, just as he would his own.

"That's so nice," Ben sighed. "Would you like to put it in your mouth?"

This idea excited Thomas, for he had often wondered what it would be like to have a man's cock filling his mouth. However, he was embarrassed by his inexperience.

"I ... I've never done that before," he admitted.

"I'm confident you will learn quickly," Ben said, punctuating his reply with a wink.

Thomas lowered his head down to Ben's crotch, the idea of swallowing his enormous prick seeming more daunting as his face drew close. Yet he did not back away. Opening his mouth wide, he guided Ben's cock into his virgin mouth.

He circled his tongue around the crown of Ben's rod, pushing back the foreskin that covered it. He prodded the slit and recognized the flavor of pre-cum. The man's juices were salty, like his own, yet Ben's cock tasted sweeter than he could have ever imagined.

Ben moaned, clasping one of his large hands on top of Thomas's skull, pressing his head down. "Yes, lick my cock. Swallow it all."

Ben attempted to force the full length of his cock down Thomas's throat, but it was too much for the young man. He began to gag and pulled his head away, coughing and sputtering.

"Sorry," Ben apologized, patting Thomas on the back. "You were doing so well I forgot this was your first time."

When Thomas had regained his composure, he returned his mouth to Ben's cock, licking every inch of his rigid pole before sticking it back in his mouth.

Ben thrust his hips back and forth, making his cock slide over Thomas's tongue. Thomas relaxed his lower jaw, letting Ben fuck his mouth.

Thomas thought Ben would continue sliding his dick in and out of his mouth until he came, but he pulled away suddenly. His cock was dripping with Thomas's spit.

"You should get out of those clothes," Ben said calmly.

Thomas was still fully clothed, with only his fly unbuttoned and his dick exposed. He got undressed, peeling off his clothing in such haste he became tangled up in them. When he was out of his clothes, Thomas stretched, enjoying Ben's admiring gaze. Thomas's body was smooth and tan, with taut, sinewy muscles developed from years of helping his father on the farm.

Ben stepped up to the young man, placing his hands on his shoulders and gliding them down his muscular arms.

"Such a gorgeous creature," he whispered.

Thomas shivered from Ben's touch. The man pulled him closer, pressing his body against his. Their cocks touched, sending a pleasurable tingle through Thomas's body.

Ben's thick arms encircled him, his hands gliding down Thomas's back and seizing the firm globes of his butt. Thomas looked up at him, startled when Ben suddenly kissed him. It was a hard, passionate kiss. Thomas felt his tongue slither into his mouth, and he responded in kind, forcing his own tongue between Ben's lips.

Ben kissed Thomas all over his body, his mouth moving from his neck to his chest, to his abdomen, to his cock.

Thomas's prick was hard once again, and seemed to grow even harder when Ben took it in his hand. He stroked Thomas's cock with one hand while he played with his ass with the other.

"You have a lovely ass," Ben said softly, his fingers tracing the cleavage where Thomas' butt cheeks met. "Turn around."

Thomas did as he was told, curious as to what Ben had in mind.

He felt Ben's hands grasp his ass, spreading it open. He felt a light breeze caress his asshole. Then he felt Ben's fingers there, circling the tight ring. It was a strange, pleasurable sensation that made Thomas shiver and moan.

Ben lowered his mouth to Thomas's ass lips. Thomas closed his eyes and gasped, savoring the feel of Ben's warm, moist tongue as it lapped at his tender hole. Ben worked his tongue inside of Thomas's asshole, forcing the resistant muscle open. Thomas trembled; the sensation was heavenly.

Thomas then felt the invasion of one of Ben's fingers working its way into him, sliding into his warm insides. A second finger followed, stretching Thomas's sphincter wider.

Then, Ben withdrew his fingers.

Thomas turned to see Ben was now standing, stroking his turgid cock. "Suck it," he commanded. "Make it wet."

He kneeled before the lusty man and lowered his mouth onto his cock. It only *seemed* even larger than the first time he sucked it, stretching his lips as they closed around the thick shaft.

Thomas licked and sucked Ben's prick, coating it with his saliva. When Ben pulled his cock from Thomas's lips, it was dripping crystalline threads of spit.

"I want to be inside you, to fuck you," Ben said, his eyes boring into the young man. "Bend over that rock."

Thomas turned and bent over, placing his hands on the large boulder for support. Ben's wet fingers poked his hole in one final effort to loosen him up. Then, with his dick in his hand, he pushes his cock against Thomas's asshole, forcing his prick past Thomas's virgin ass ring.

At first, all Thomas felt was the head of Ben's cock nudging his puckered hole. Then, there was a sharp pain. Thomas yelped, then gnashed his teeth. As Ben eased his cock inside him, the pain became greater. He wanted to beg Ben to stop; he could not bear much more.

But once Ben's prick was all the way inside him, the pain leveled off, his ass acclimating itself to this new invasion.

Ben kissed Thomas between his shoulder blades. "You're doing very well," he purred. "Just relax."

Slowly, Ben thrust his cock into Thomas's ass. The agony Thomas felt when Ben first stabbed his dick into him became a memory. Now there was only pleasure.

Ben's hands gently glided over Thomas's body. He reached around the young man's torso and gripped his cock, pulling it in time to his rhythmic thrusts.

Thomas pushed his body backwards, meeting Ben's forward motion. His ass lips clamped down on Ben's meaty cock, refusing to let it go.

The two men were panting and grunting, their muscular bodies working against each other as they fucked beneath the blazing sun. An ecstatic crescendo enveloped them both, taking them ever closer to that final release.

Thomas's body began to buck and tremble; a series of whimpers and groans tumbled out his mouth.

"Yes," Ben whispered in his ear. "Oh, yes."

Sensing Thomas was nearing his climax, Ben stroked his cock faster until it fired jets of viscous, white cream onto the grass beneath him.

Ben placed his hands on Thomas's hips and stood upright. He continued to pound his cock into Thomas's ass, his thrusts quick and forceful. Suddenly, as if having a seizure, Ben froze. A growl seemed trapped in his throat as his body began to shake. Finally, releasing one loud groan, his hot load flooded Thomas's insides.

Ben slowly pulled his dick out of Thomas's ass. Thomas turned and threw his arms around the man, holding his naked body close. He kissed his neck. Ben placed a hand beneath his chin and raised his face, kissing Thomas's lips.

"Such a lovely boy," Ben sighed, and together the two men fell onto the grass in each other's arms.

The cool air awoke Thomas. The sun was sinking behind the trees. He was lying naked on the ground. Disoriented, he tried to remember what had happened to him before he nodded off.

It came back to him, in vivid detail: The old man. The transformation. His cock quivered at the memory.

He looked around him to see if the man was still there, but Thomas was alone.

Had anything happened, he wondered? Or had he become so lost in his fantasies that it seemed real?

As if to answer his question, Thomas suddenly became aware that he was not lying directly on the grass. Something was beneath him, like a blanket.

Thomas rolled off the cloth and picked it up. It was a heavy, dark cloak, the kind he remembered the old man wearing. He held it to his face inhaling the man's scent. He was recalling a memory, not a dream.

"Ben," he whispered. "Sir Benjamin Tallman."

The Jealousy Game

All I'd intended to do was rekindle my boyfriend's interest. That's why I went to the bar that night. I'd left a note for Trey to find when he got home: "At The Gilded Cage. Meet me there at 9:00 p.m. Love ya', Jack."

Of course, I'd be there at eight. I wanted to be there alone for a while. Wanted to see if I still had "it," and if so, I wanted Trey to be there to see.

Trey and I had been together for about a year. When we dated, every moment we spent together culminated in passionate sex. We'd try to surprise each other by initiating it in unlikely places: I'd give him a blowjob in the parking deck of a shopping mall; he'd give me a hand job in a movie theater; I'd suck him off in the men's room of a classy restaurant; he'd fuck me on the hood of my car on a little-traveled dirt road in the country.

We had been seeing each other for five months when we decided to move in together. That's when things started to change. The more months we lived together, the less sex we had. For the past couple of months, I was lucky if he even wanted to take a shower with me. Things had cooled to point that I was starting to grow icicles on my dick.

It's not like I let myself go after we moved in together. I'd often check myself out in the mirror after a shower: broad chest with just a small patch of dark hair in the center, rippling abs, sturdy legs, and a firm ass. I'd often do this self-inspection while Trey watched. Used to be he'd walk up behind me and start kissing the back of my neck, his lips traveling down my back until he reached my ass. He'd pull my butt cheeks apart and start tonguing my hole. He'd get me so hot my cock would be drooling like a bloodhound.

Last week he smacked me playfully on the butt and said, "C'mon, Miss America, put some clothes on. The movie starts in an hour."

That's why I was sitting at a table nursing a beer in some loud, trashy bar talking with Scott. I'd seen him at the bar when I first arrived. Tall, gym-built physique and short, wavy brown hair. He was dressed in the standard butch uniform of crotch-defining, faded blue jeans and a T-shirt that hugged every muscle. I made eye contact and smiled. He smiled back, and then I looked away. A minute later he was at my table asking, "Are you here by yourself?"

"For the time being. Why?"

He smiled. "'Cause I wanted to put a stop to that."

I smiled back and motioned toward the available stool across from me. "Feel free."

It was that simple. Scott was basically charming, and were it not for Trey, I could certainly see myself going home with him. But I wasn't here to cheat on Trey, just make him aware that he had a good thing and if he didn't start paying attention there would be others willing to take his place.

Trey arrived twenty minutes late. As frustrated as I had been with him for the past two months, I couldn't help but smile when I saw him. I could stare at his face for hours: His square jaw, the vague cleft in the chin, the full lips and piercing gray eyes, framed nicely by his tousled blond hair. His body was another marvel, every muscle defined perfectly beneath lightly tanned skin, with a huge cock to boot. My smile faded, though, as I remembered that I was being denied the pleasures of this incredibly sexy man. I turned my attention back to Scott.

"Hey, baby," Trey said breathlessly, kissing me on the cheek. "Sorry I'm a little late, but someone called just before ..." He stopped, noticing Scott. "I'm sorry, I don't think we've met."

I gave him my best Alexis Carrington smile. "Baby, this is Scott. Scott, this is my boyfriend, Trey."

Oblivious, Trey held out his hand. "Good to meet you. You work with Jack?"

Scott looked mortified. "Uh, no. We were just talking. Sorry, I ..." He looked at me. "You didn't say you were ..."

"I just met Scott tonight," I told Trey. "He's gorgeous, don't you think?"

Scott started to get up. "I think I'll let you two be alone."

At this point, things were going according to my plans. Scott would leave, I would let Trey know that Scott was trying to pick me up, and Trey would feel anxious enough to start tending to my much-neglected libido.

Trey, though, had to make things complicated. "No, no, no. *Stay.* I'm going to get something to drink. You guys want another beer?"

While Trey was at the bar, Scott looked at me intently and said: "Your boyfriend looks hot. Why do you want to cheat on him?"

I looked away. "Well, looking at him is about all I get to do these days. And for the record, I was not planning on cheating on him. I just wanted to make him jealous."

Scott was pissed. I could see it in the way he glared at me. When Trey returned with the drinks, I feared he might say or do something to cause a scene. Instead, he did something much worse. He turned his charm on Trey. Within five minutes, it was clear my plan had backfired. Trey and Scott were getting along famously, chatting non-stop while I sat there wishing I'd never thought of this dumb-ass scheme.

More surprises were in store, though. I nudged Trey, telling him I thought we should go. "Oh, sure," he said. "This place is a bit much. Say, Scott, what're your plans?"

"I don't have any."

"Why don't you stop by our place?"

Trey's sex drive apparently wasn't the only thing on the decline. He'd lost his mind, too.

Scott was no help. He quickly accepted the invitation, agreeing to follow us back to our apartment.

Before we got in our respective vehicles, Trey said to me, "Scott's a great guy."

"You do know he was trying to pick me up before you arrived, don't you?" I said icily.

"I know," Trey said with a knowing smile. "See you back at the apartment."

At the apartment, we all grabbed a beer and sat down in the living room. I sat on the sofa, expecting Trey to sit beside me. Instead, he sat in one of the chairs across the room and insisted Scott sit with me on the sofa.

Trey, never one to mince words, got the conversation rolling with: "Jack tells me you were trying to pick him up."

My heart seized up in my chest. The fucker was obviously trying to get back at me.

"Trey, don't do this."

Scott was visibly uncomfortable. He took a huge swallow from his beer and began to stammer. "It's okay," Trey encouraged. "You can be honest."

"Well, I was," he admitted. "That was before I knew about you."

"But, you still want to fuck him?" Trey asked pointedly. "I wouldn't blame you if you did. He's incredibly beautiful."

"Um, well, actually, I want to fuck *you*."

Trey chuckled, and then his mouth settled into a smug grin. "Really? What would you want to do with me?"

Scott looked down at the floor. "Well, you know ..."

"Come on, don't be shy."

In a low, monotone voice, Scott attempted to describe his sexual fantasy. "First, I'd ..."

"No," Trey interrupted. "Show me."

At that very moment, I hated my boyfriend. My original idea was selfish, sure, and certainly stupid, but Trey's revenge was cruel. I wanted to leave him right then, yet some sort of rage-induced paralysis made it impossible for me to get up from the sofa.

Scott looked up. "Are you going to get up, or should I come over there?"

"Demonstrate with Jack," Trey said. "I want to watch."

Okay, fine, I thought. I could play Trey's twisted game. If he wanted to watch, then by god I was going to give him a show.

Clamping a hand on Scott's muscular thigh, I set my beer down on the coffee table and said as seductively as I could, "C'mon, Scott, let's give him something to see."

Scott had a goofy grin on his face, as if he understood now. To him, Trey was just a voyeur who got his kicks watching me have sex with other guys. If that's what he wanted to believe, fine; it was much better than the truth.

Scott leaned over and kissed my cheek, his mouth quickly moving over to my ear. His tongue was hot and wet, tracing the outer edge of my earlobe. My pulse raced, my breath quickened. His hand slid down to my crotch, giving it a gentle squeeze.

"Stand up and take off your shirt," he whispered.

I did as he said, not even thinking about Trey's presence. I pulled my shirt off, tossing it onto the floor. I felt Scott's admiring gaze and smiled. My cock twitched in my jeans.

He reached up, lightly caressing my hard torso. "Very nice," he breathed.

His hands quickly moved lower down, unbuckling my belt and unzipping my fly. He pulled my jeans down forcefully. I stood before him with my pants around my knees, with only a pair of thin cotton briefs separating my swelling dick from his lips.

Scott buried his face in my crotch and gnawed at my cock through my underwear. I closed my eyes and undulated my hips, grinding my cock into Scott's face. The front of my briefs became soggy with pre-cum and saliva, causing the cloth to cling to my steel-hard prick.

"Suck it," I sighed. "Pull my underwear down and suck my cock."

Scott had his fingers hooked underneath the elastic waistband before I could complete my sentence. Freed from my underwear, my cock snapped upright, standing almost perpendicular against my belly.

He leaned back slightly, studying my thick, hard dick. Scott was breathing heavily, and I felt his warm breath swirl about my dripping cock. He gingerly cupped my balls with one hand and stroked my cock with the other. I shuddered as he touched me, longing for him to take me into that sexy mouth.

Scott prodded my nut-sack with his tongue. My body quivered as his tongue curled around my balls, then gradually moved upward. The tip of his tongue traced the thick vein on the underside of my cock until it reached the bulbous crown, whereupon he lapped up the heavy drop of pre-cum that hung there.

Then he swallowed me whole.

I cried out. My body convulsed as shockwaves of pleasure ripped through every muscle. I thrust my dick deep into his throat; he didn't gag once.

The feeling was incredible. As much as I was getting off on feeling the moist, warm interior of his mouth grip my dick, I was even more aroused by Trey watching. I threw my head back, the muscles in my back tensing up, and my ass clenching as this man – practically a stranger – sucked my cock. And Trey got to see every minute of it.

Scott slid a hand between my legs, plunging his fingers into my ass crack. I moaned as his fingers rubbed my puckered hole. Quickly, he removed his hand, moistened his fingers with his spit and returned them to my asshole, pushing his wet fingers against my ass ring, gently working one inside my hole.

"Oh, baby, *yes!*" I groaned. My cock was on the verge of exploding. Scott sensed it and sucked even harder. I didn't want to come yet, but I couldn't pull away. Overcome by the ecstasy, I thrust my dick in and out of his mouth until the inevitable happened.

"Oh, Jesus, I'm ... I'm ... I'm coming!" I warned in halting breaths.

There was barely enough time for Scott to pull his mouth away before I shot my load. Thick, molten jets of cream spurted out of my cock, splattering his face. "Oh, yeah," I grunted, pulling on my dick, milking out every last drop. "*Ooooh, yeah.*"

My orgasm left me dizzy. I wanted to collapse right then, but I was in no way finished for the evening.

Clumsily, I kicked off my shoes and stripped off my jeans and underwear, still bunched up around my knees. Completely naked now, I turned to look at Trey.

He was still in his seat across the room. He'd unzipped his pants and pulled out his cock, stroking it while he watched us. I flashed him an impish grin, though he didn't seem to notice. He looked like he was in a trance. He just kept staring and jacking off.

I turned back to Scott, who sat on the sofa grabbing his crotch. He had been so into sucking me off that he hadn't even bothered to pull his own cock out. I planned to change that real soon.

Facing him, I straddled his lap. I leaned forward and kissed his lips, our tongues sliding into each other's mouths. I could taste my cum on his lips, feel it wet my cheeks. I licked my load of his face, strangely enjoying the sharp taste of myself. I had never done this with Trey and wondered what he thought now that he was watching me do it with someone else.

My mouth moved lower, kissing Scott's neck and shoulders. I slid off his lap and, pushing the coffee table out of the way, knelt before him. I helped him out of his shirt, pleased with the flesh I'd exposed: a broad, smooth chest tapering down to a narrow, washboard stomach. A tiny trail of dark hairs started at his bellybutton and disappeared beneath his jeans. I followed that trail with my mouth, lightly circling his navel with my tongue then dragging it down the line of hairs until I reached the waist of his jeans.

Hastily, I unbuttoned the fly, pulling it open to reveal his undershorts: plaid boxers, with an enticing mound poking up in front. I raised an eyebrow and smiled mischievously as I slipped a hand into his shorts. I hooked my fingers around that pole and worked it through the fly. His dick was about eight inches long, almost two inches in diameter and uncut. The head peeked out from its collar of foreskin, trickling a syrupy stream of pre-cum.

Scott's cock was so beautiful; I wanted to devour it right away. I pounced on it, swallowing every inch.

"That feels soooo good," Scott moaned, thrusting his hips upward and running his fingers through my hair. The head of his dick was hitting the back of my throat; my nose was buried in his soft pubes.

I started tugging at his jeans; Scott got the hint quickly, stripping in ten seconds flat. Naked, Scott lay back on the sofa, waiting for me.

Without hesitation, I propped his legs up on my shoulders and lowered my face between his legs. I licked and sucked his balls, then tickled his groin with my tongue. I pushed Scott's legs back toward his chest, hoisting his ass into the air. His asshole was a tight, tan ring surrounded by dark, curly hairs. I pressed my lips against it, kissing his hole lightly before stabbing it with my tongue.

He writhed as I rimmed him, groaning loudly as I forced my tongue past his ass lips and into his chute. I reached for his dick, pulling on it as I licked his ass.

A shadow fell over us. Looking up, I saw Trey. He was out of his clothes now and clearly done with being the voyeur.

Trey flashed me a wicked grin, then knelt on the sofa, throwing his legs astride Scott's chest, stifling Scott's moans with his rigid cock.

I continued eating Scott's asshole and stroking his cock while Scott sucked my lover's dick. Trey raised his body over Scott's face and lowered his ass onto Scott's waiting mouth. Scott worked his tongue between Trey's tight butt cheeks, slurping away at his cleanly shaved asshole.

"I want to fuck you," Trey purred, riding our trick's beautiful face.

Trey suddenly dismounted and left the room. When he returned, he carried a bottle of lube and a few rubbers.

He tossed condom at me. "Put this on him," he said. He then told Scott to hold out his hand. Scott did this, and Trey promptly upended the bottle of lubricant, squeezing a small puddle into his palm. "You take care of him, and I'll take care of you," he said.

I tore open the condom packet with my teeth and extracted the thin rubber sheath, quickly rolling it over Scott's fat, throbbing cock. Standing up, I turned to face Trey. He leaned in to kiss me, but I stepped back so my ass was in front of Scott's face. Scott reached up with his lubricated hand and palmed my ass open, sliding his fingers into me easily.

Trey knelt between Scott's open thighs – and in front of me. He brushed his fingers over Scott's butthole and swabbed my semi-hard cock with his tongue. Then Trey took the bottle of lube and upended over Scott's asshole, drizzling it over his furry hole. With his other hand, Trey rubbed the slick fluid around Scott's ass-ring then poked an index finger inside. Scott gasped, and reflexively jabbed his fingers deeper into me.

Trey added more fingers, ultimately stretching Scott's sphincter with three fingers. Scott responded in kind, forcefully stuffing more digits into my quivering hole.

"I wanna fuck you now," Scott grunted.

I squatted, taking hold of his dick and guiding it into me until we were in a reverse cowboy position. My ass resisted at first, and I had to sit on Scott's cock with all my weight until it popped into me. The pain was sharp and sudden as his prick filled my ass, but that discomfort quickly melted into a tense, familiar pleasure.

Slowly, I rocked back and forth on Scott's cock. Trey had already covered his dick and was holding it, poised to plunge it deep into Scott. Which he did, suddenly. Scott cried out, digging his fingers into the flesh of my torso as Trey's rock-hard cock pierced his butt. Trey grabbed Scott's legs and raising them over his shoulders and causing Scott to fall backwards against the sofa cushions and me to fall back against Scott's chest. Not missing a beat, Scott crooked an arm around my waist and kissed the back of my neck.

I rode Scott's cock like a rodeo star, bouncing and bucking on that long, thick rod. Trey rammed Scott's ass with equal vigor, emitting terse grunts with each thrust. The excitement of having Scott's prick shoved up my ass and the sight of my lover fucking him at the same time had brought my cock back to life, hard as steel.

Trey grabbed my dick with a lube-slick hand, jacking me off as he plugged Scott's butt. He leaned forward and bit one of my hard, brown nipples. I felt as if I was experiencing more pleasure in one night than it had my entire adult life. Every thrust into my ass and every stroke of my cock brought me closer and closer to coming. As much as I tried to will myself to prolong the feeling, I knew I couldn't hold out much longer.

"Oh, baby, that feels so ... *Uuuuuuhhh!*"

Jizz erupted out of my cock in thin, watery streams, splashing onto Trey's chest. Trey, who always got off watching me come, fucked Scott harder, plowing into his ass so hard I thought for sure he was hurting the poor guy.

But pain was the last thing Scott was feeling. He was groaning and grunting, his body writhing beneath mine. Scott kept ramming his cock into my ass until, abruptly, his body froze. He came, his fingers digging into my skin and a choked, guttural sound rumbled in his throat, never quite leaving his lips.

Trey came about the same time. His body tensed, and he threw back his head, practically roaring as he shot his load. Trey shoved his hips forward a couple more times before he finally slumped forward against my chest, gasping for breath.

"Oh, baby, that was so fucking hot," he panted. "Glad you thought of it."

I smiled and ran my fingers through his sweaty blond hair.

# # # # #

Trey waited at the other end of the bar, watching me at the corner table. Five minutes later he approached.

"Hey," he said, a smile stretching across his face. He had an even bigger smile for the guy sitting across from me: Buddy, a hunky ex-military man whose hormones were seething after years of not telling when asked. "What'cha been up to?"

"Not much," I said, returning his smile. "Let me introduce you. Trey, this is Buddy; Buddy, this is Trey."

I didn't mention that Trey was my boyfriend. Some guys were frightened off by that revelation.

"Maybe you'd like to join us," I said suggestively.

The rising bulge in the crotch of Trey's khakis told me he'd love to.

Swann Dive

Win didn't want to jump from the cliff, even if it wasn't any higher than an Olympic high dive. He contemplated continuing his walk, ignoring the two men bobbing in the water below. The afternoon sky was darkening and thunder rumbled in the distance. He wanted to get back to the house before the rain started.

"C'mon! We jumped, and we lived!" one of the two men called out. He had a Spanish accent; "jumped" came out *joompt*. He was dark-haired, tan, muscular; his handsome face shaded by stubble. Win thought he'd seen him somewhere before but didn't know where. The other man in the water – blond hair buzzed down to the scalp, thick arms covered with tattoos – said nothing.

Then the dark-haired man rolled over to swim away, revealing the perfectly shaped globes of his bare butt as he kicked his way toward his silent buddy.

"Fuck it," Win said. He kicked off his sandals but didn't remove his orange and blue board shorts. He'd risk diving off the cliff, but he wouldn't do it naked. He stepped several feet back from the edge, took a deep breath and made a running leap over the edge. Win soared, midair, arms outstretched. But what started as a graceful dive ended as a belly flop, Win hitting the water like a sack of flour dropped from a rooftop.

He surfaced to mocking applause. The tattooed man spoke for the first time: "Damn!" He had an accent, too – a deep Southern drawl.

Win couldn't say anything; he was breathless from the impact, and his chest stung like hell. The dark-haired man, the one who urged him to *joomp*, laughed. "Worst swan dive *ever*."

"I didn't know that's what I was doing," Win said gaspingly, rubbing his hands over his chest as if that would ease the pain. "But I guess any dive I do is a swan dive. That's my last name: Swann, with two n's."

The dark-haired man cocked his head. "Mr. Swann's son?" His smile broadened. "I work for him, at his house."

Win remembered now. The dark-haired man was working at his father's villa the other day. He had watched the man from the sunroom clearing away the bamboo that threatened to overtake the pool house, admiring his bare, sweaty torso glistening in the sun as he swung his machete. When his father walked into the room Win reacted as if he'd been caught jacking off. He asked who the new gardener was, and his father, Winton Junior, told him the man wasn't a gardener. "Just a local guy who's helping out with a few odd jobs," his father said vaguely.

"I'm Manuel. That's my friend, Dallas."

Dallas nodded and pantomimed tipping a hat. Win didn't think Dallas was as cute as Manuel – his features were a little too blunt and meaty – but he found him just as sexy. The two friends were in their mid-twenties, he guessed. Win was twenty.

"I'm Win, short for Winton."

Lighting pulsed through the gathering clouds, and thunder cracked angrily. Choppy waves pushed them around like bullies on a playground. "Better head back," Dallas said. In a lunging sidestroke, Manuel's tattooed friend confirmed he was naked, too, Win catching a glimpse of his dick as he swam back to land.

The rain was falling in hard, heavy drops as they reached the scabby patch of sand and rock at the base of the cliff. Win hung back as Manuel and Dallas scurried onto shore, his eyes glued to their bare asses – Manuel's the ideal bubble butt; Dallas's not as round but solid muscle, with a small tattoo on the left cheek that Win couldn't make out. They snatched their clothes up from where they lay piled atop a boulder and hastily dressed: Manuel in loose-fitting workout shorts, Dallas in tight-fitting jeans cut off above the knee. They had shirts but neither bothered to put them on.

Once Manuel and Dallas had put on their shoes they took off into a maze of trees and brush, Manuel motioning for Win to follow.

Win took off after them, not bothering to collect his sandals from the top of the cliff.

They ran until they reached a narrow dirt road where a small, rusty pickup truck was parked. Dallas got behind the wheel; Manuel held the passenger door open and waved Win inside the cab then climbed in after him. Win was straddling the center hump – "riding bitch," as one of his college friends called it – sandwiched between the two men, the cab so cramped that their shoulders and knees touched. The truck had a standard transmission, and Dallas's arm would brush the inside of Win's thigh when he shifted gears. When he put the truck into fourth his wrist pressed into Win's crotch, staying there a bit too long to be accidental. Manuel gripped on Win's right thigh to steady himself as the truck bounced along the muddy road. "There's no room," he giggled. Win chanced a look down at Manuel's crotch. The rain-soaked shorts clung to his body, his cock in sharp relief beneath the wet fabric. Win swallowed hard and looked away.

The rain had slacked off by the time they'd reached their destination, a small, flat-roofed bungalow a few miles inland. Though Manuel helped maintain the pristine grounds of the Swann's summer villa, this house, by contrast, was nearly swallowed up by the wild foliage surrounding it. Inside, Manuel switched on a lamp with its dim light illuminating walls of flaking plaster and floors covered by pockmarked linoleum. The house seemed more of a hideout than a home, and in that context, the shabby surroundings seemed exotic.

They dried themselves with threadbare towels Dallas supplied. Win went to the bathroom to wash his bare feet, caked in mud and sand from his run to the truck. The bathroom was as dreary as the rest of the house. Instead of a bathtub, Win found an open shower stall with a glazed cement floor, like one would find at a public pool. When he returned to the living room, Dallas was sitting on quilt-covered sofa, taking a deep drag off a joint. He was leaning back in the cushions with his legs spread, giving Win a good eyeful of his bulging basket.

"You smoke?" Manuel asked, appearing beside him with three cans of beer.

"Sure," Win said, taking one of the beers from Manuel. He sat down on a futon mattress tossed on the floor. Manuel sat down beside Dallas.

They passed the joint around. Dallas put on a CD, some indie rock band Win never heard of, and danced his way back to the sofa, undulating suggestively but smirking like he was just being silly. They finished their beers quickly, and Manuel got fresh cans with equal speed.

Manuel said, "You look like your father."

Though he'd have to wait until his father's death to inherit his money, Win had already inherited his father's good looks: deep blue eyes set in handsome features, chestnut brown hair and an athletic build. But Win bristled at comparisons to his father. "We only look alike," he said, taking another hit off the joint.

"You don't like your father?" Manuel asked.

"We just don't … he doesn't understand." Win said without elaboration.

The pot and beer made Win feel heavy and weightless simultaneously. Dallas, wearing a dreamy smile on his thick lips, fairly melted into the sofa. He slid a hand between his legs and scratched himself, his smile broadening when he caught Win looking.

"Wanna scratch it for me?" It was one of the few times he'd uttered more than three words since they met.

"He's just teasing," Manuel chuckled, exchanging a glance with Dallas that belied that statement.

Win said he was tired, and before he knew it, he was lying down on the futon watching the room float away. He closed his eyes.

# # # # #

He was alone when he opened his eyes. The weak rays of the setting sun seeped into the room through dingy windows. Music still played – a twangy ballad now – but music wasn't all he heard. Grunts and gasps came from another room. He took a swig from what remained of his beer and retched. It was warm and foul tasting. Win stood up unsteadily; he still wasn't sober. A loud groan emanated from the bathroom, followed by husky-voiced whispers.

Win started down the hall. Even before he reached the bathroom door, he knew what he'd find; his heart pounded and his cock twitched in anticipation. The bathroom door was wide open, but he stopped at the threshold as if blocked by an invisible force field.

They were in the shower. Dallas stood feeding his cock to Manuel, kneeling before him. He thrust his hips, sending his dick deeper into Manuel's mouth. Manuel gripped the base of Dallas's cock; his other hand disappeared between his tattooed friend's corded thighs. Neither appeared to notice Win standing at the door.

Dallas said something, his words unintelligible but their obscenity plain. He pulled his dick from Manuel's mouth, taking thick ropes of saliva with it. Dallas's cock was formidable in both length and girth; it was easy to see why Manuel chased after it with his tongue. Dallas teasingly pulled his cock away then batted it against his friend's open mouth. Only when Manuel encircled his fingers around his brutish buddy's ball sac and squeezed did Dallas relinquish his cock, shoving it forcefully down his throat until Manuel gagged.

Win remained frozen at the doorway. He'd watched men have sex before – the Internet had long become an integral part of his masturbation routine – but watching paid performers on a computer screen paled in comparison to seeing two men live. He felt as if he were spying, even though the men had made no pretense of wanting privacy, and that made the moment all the more thrilling. Win's cock was like granite and his whole body tingled. It was an excitement akin to when he'd first discovered sex.

Manuel swallowed Dallas's cock and tongued his balls in lusty abandon. Manuel's uncut cock, a shade darker than the rest of him, the foreskin rolled back to reveal a mauve-colored crown, stood ramrod straight between his thighs. He reached down to pull on it a few times, but couldn't seem to keep his hands off Dallas's body long enough to devote much time to jacking off.

Dallas again pulled his cock away from Manuel's mouth. "You ready for it?" he rasped.

Win held his breath, thinking Dallas was about to come. The thought of Dallas spraying his load all over Manuel's beautiful face made Win's cock jump.

Manuel nodded. "*Sí.*"

Dallas gripped the base of his stiff cock, bent it as much as he was able so it pointed at Manuel's hairy chest, and let loose with a stream of piss.

Manuel leaned back onto his hands and received the golden shower with a beatific smile on his face. He bent forward, getting his dark, curly hair doused. Then he tilted his head back, opened wide and Dallas pissed directly into his mouth, the stream splashing off his tongue. When his mouth was full, Dallas jabbed his cock between his lips, the displaced urine gushing out Manuel's mouth and streaming down his chin and chest.

Win was stunned. His sexual experiences were few, and then his fear of getting discovered was so great that he wanted to get off quickly to ensure a fast getaway. Now he was being exposed to sexual realms he'd never wanted to explore. More shocking than the couple's kinky display, however, was Win's physical reaction to it: He was so turned on, it was almost painful. His cock ached, pumping out so much pre-cum a wet spot formed on the front of his shorts.

Dallas looked toward the bathroom door and his face contorted into a lopsided smile. Manuel also turned his gaze to Win, his grin making it clear they knew he was there all along.

Dallas said, "Get outta those shorts."

For a moment, Win didn't move. He was again at the top of the cliff and they were goading him into jumping, only this time he was even less sure of what he was diving into. His dick, however, had already made up its mind, and Win was stepping out of his shorts before he'd realized he was doing so.

He approached the couple cautiously.

Dallas grabbed Win and pulled him close, seizing his mouth in a forceful kiss. Win felt the heat of his cock pressing against his own. He awkwardly placed his hands on Dallas's narrow hips. Dallas cupped his ass and squeezed.

"You ready to play, rich boy?" Without waiting for an answer, Dallas said, "Get down there and suck my dick."

Win sank to his knees. The floor was hard and uncomfortable, but he was so horny he didn't care. Manuel was now behind his friend, fingering his asshole.

Dallas made a ring with his hands around his cock and balls, dripping wet with piss and spit, and shook them. "Go on, suck it," he chuckled. "Don't worry, I won't piss on you 'less you ask for it."

He hesitantly brought his mouth to Dallas's cock, flicking his tongue around the salty-tasting head. Win couldn't swallow it as wholly as Manuel, but he tried, managing to take two-thirds of the fat pole into his inexperienced mouth before he choked.

While Win worked on Dallas's cock, Manuel ate his asshole. Dallas let out a low, raspy moan, rolling his hips so that he alternately ground his ass into Manuel's face and thrust is dick deeper into Win's mouth.

Then Dallas pushed Win's face away and stuck two fingers into his mouth. Win sucked on them, like he'd seen it done by the guys in the porn videos – like he was sucking a cock. The fingers were withdrawn, replaced by Dallas's dick. As Win slurped on his throbbing pole, Dallas bent over him, placing one hand on Win's shoulder while the other reached down to his ass. Win felt Dallas's fingers – moistened by Win's spit – gently press against his ass lips. He applied more pressure, until his index finger slipped into Win's asshole. Dallas slowly worked that finger deeper into his chute. He added a second finger, and Win's sphincter contracted in protest.

"Good an' tight," Dallas said.

Dallas pulled Win to his feet and kissed him so hard he almost came. He grabbed Win's cock, and Win thought he really would bust a nut. "We're gonna suck *you* now." Dallas made it sound like a threat.

He knelt on the shower stall floor beside Manuel. The two shared a wet, sloppy kiss before attacking their guest's quivering hard-on. Dallas sucked his cock in full, lusty gulps while Manuel sucked Win's balls. Manuel cut in on the blowjob, his tongue working over every inch of Win's shaft until his mouth finally closed over the drooling tip.

"I'm about to … I'm gonna *shoot*," Win panted.

Dallas pumped Win's cock with his fist. "Oh, yeah, give us that load." Manuel hovered nearby, poised to catch the spray. "Shoot it all over us."

Pleasure burned throughout Win's trembling body, increasing with each pull of his stiff prick until a final, ecstatic explosion overtook him. Win let out a howling moan, spraying his load all over Dallas and Manuel's faces. The two men fought to catch the flying drops of jizz. Dallas stuffed Win's cock into his mouth, greedily swallowing the remaining spurts. Manuel lapped up the splat of cum clinging to Dallas's right cheek.

Dallas and Manuel stood and circled their arms around Win, kissing either side of his face. Dallas scooped up a dollop of jizz off Manuel's chin and fed it to Win, commanding him to lick his fingers clean. Manuel moved in to give Win a kiss on the lips. The sour stench of piss clung faintly to his body, but Win didn't resist, holding Manuel tight as he accepted his probing tongue in his mouth.

Win said, "Man, that was awesome," wincing as the words left his mouth. He sounded like a total dork. He realized the other two men hadn't gotten off and added: "I didn't mean to come so quick. It just sort of ... happened."

"Don't worry 'bout it," Dallas said, switching on the shower. "Now clean up. We're not done with you yet."

They emerged from the bathroom clean and damp. Just outside the door, Manuel pushed Win against the hallway's rough wall, putting his whole body into a kiss that left Win lightheaded. Manuel's cock throbbed against Win's lower abdomen, smearing its sticky residue onto his skin. Win had gone soft earlier, but Manuel's fierce kiss teased his dick back to life.

Manuel pulled his mouth away smiled. "It's easier now that I've washed, no?" He took Win's cock in his hand and fondled it lovingly. "It turns Dallas on, the pissing. I'm turned on when my man is turned on." He toyed with Win's swelling cockhead. "You turn me on."

He took Win's hand and they entered the living room, where Dallas waited. He lay on the futon, a big smile on his face as he played with his hard-on. Manuel joined his man on the futon, climbing onto

Dallas and kissing him as passionately as he'd kissed Win. Seeing the two men wrapped in each other's arms, tongues pushing into each other's mouths, further aroused Win – his boner had almost fully returned – but this time he felt a sting of jealousy.

Before he could dwell on being a third wheel, Dallas motioned for Win to join them.

"Sit on my face. I wanna eat that cute ass of yers."

Manuel was already kissing his way down Dallas's washboard stomach to allow room for their guest. Win started to ease down so he'd be facing the wall behind Dallas's head, but he was quickly told to reverse his position. He squatted until his ass hovered above Dallas's face. Dallas hooked his arms around Win's thighs and pulled him down, tearing into Win's asshole like a hog at a trough.

Win let out a startled yelp, nearly toppling over from the sudden rush. Dallas's tongue plunged into his chute in hard stabs; his teeth gnawed at Win's quivering ass ring. Win felt Dalllas's nose pressing into his crack and his bristly soul patch scratching his taint.

Manuel was at Dallas's cock, swallowing it in full gulps. His mouth moved down to his friend's balls, sucking one of the engorged spheres all the way into his mouth, pulling it until the nutsac tightened and Dallas flinched. He repeated the action with the other nut, giggling as he released it from his lips.

Dallas brought his legs up and urged Win to lean forward until they were in a sixty-nine position. Though Dallas's meaty cock was just inches away from his lips, Win bypassed it to kiss Manuel. Dallas's dick wasn't ignored for long, however. Manuel quickly inserted it between their slithering tongues. Then, surrendering his muscular buddy's cock to Win's mouth and flashing a conspiratorial smile, Manuel's mouth moved down, over Dallas's balls and into the valley between his spread thighs.

They remained in that position for several minutes, Dallas eating Win's ass while Win sucked his cock and Manuel tongued his hole. Win felt Dallas jerk beneath him and was quickly pushed off onto the mattress.

"I was getting close," Dallas said, his voice a husky rasp. "Why don't you *eat my ass* for a while?"

When his request wasn't heeded right away, Dallas repeated it as an order: "Get down there and eat my ass."

Manuel got out of the way so Win to take over where he left off, but Win was slow to move. Although he didn't think twice about sitting on Dallas's face – he easily enjoyed that – he didn't want to return the favor. He'd never rimmed a guy before and wasn't eager to learn. But he didn't want to appear prudish, either. He knelt between Dallas's open legs and steeled himself to lick his asshole.

Dallas brought his knees to his chest, raising his ass to greet Win's face. Win could finally get a good look at the tattoo on his left cheek: the head of a cartoon pig, winking. A strangely whimsical yet wholly appropriate choice, he thought.

"Go ahead – that's all for you," Dallas said. Win stalled, gently tracing the outer edges of the brute's rosebud. Dallas's ass was smooth, a detail that surprised him. (He couldn't see this tattooed roughneck going in for Brazilian wax.) His fingertips moved to the tan, creased lips of his hole, pressing against the pucker. Dallas's winked his asshole at him.

"It won't bite," he said.

Win brought his mouth to that twitching sphincter with the same enthusiasm a child accepts a forkful of broccoli. He flicked his tongue around Dallas's butthole, only to have a hand clamp down on top of his head and press his face into his splayed ass.

"Don't lick it – *eat it*," Dallas commanded.

Win sputtered and tried to pull back, but that only got a chuckle from Dallas. "What is it, rich boy? My ass not good enough for you?"

Manuel leaned in, whispering, "Don't be nervous. It felt good when he did it to you." He kissed the back of Win's neck. "You'll make Dallas feel just as good."

Closing his eyes, Win prodded Dallas's hole with his tongue. "That's it, keep goin'" Dallas encouraged. Before he knew it, Win's tongue pushed through the rubbery sphincter into Dallas's anus. He mimicked what he'd seen done in porno videos – and what he'd felt being done to him: jabbing, gnawing, licking, slurping.

"Oh, yeah, that's what I'm talkin' 'bout," Dallas purred, resting his legs on Win's shoulders.

To his surprise, Win was turned-on as much by eating ass as by getting his eaten. His cock fairly vibrated, and it was drooling onto the floor. The louder Dallas groaned, the deeper into his chute Win tried to force his tongue.

Manuel's mouth had traveled down Win's back to his ass. There he kissed, licked and prodded. He gripped Win's cock, pulling it back to slurp up its nectar, then returned to munching his butt. Manuel slipped a finger into Win's hole, and then a second. He shoved them in deep, hitting Win's prostate and sending a bolt of pleasure through his body.

Win felt a cool wetness on his ass crack and turned, startled. His first thought was Manuel was peeing on him. Instead he discovered the handsome Latin holding an upended bottle of lube, squirting it onto his hole. Manuel met his gaze, smiled and inserted his fingers – three this time – back into his asshole, working the lubricant inside him. Win didn't need to be told what Manuel had in mind.

Only it was Dallas who fucked him. Manuel tossed Dallas the bottle of lube and a wrapped condom ("I may be a freak but I'm safe," Dallas said when he caught Win's look of relief). The tattooed hunk prepped himself quickly; within seconds he was coaxing Win to sit on his sheathed cock. Win held his breath and slowly lowered himself onto Dallas's pole. He'd only attempted bottoming once before in his life, with some grad student who'd cruised him at the student union. He hadn't enjoyed it – the grad student forced his cock inside Win with one brutal push; the pain was shocking. But Dallas ceded the control to Win, allowing him to ease his ass down inch by inch. This time, the pain was minimal. The tension of his sphincter stretching to accommodate Dallas's cock was pleasurable in a way Win had never imagined. When the full length of that rock-hard prick was buried inside him, a feeling was nothing short of exhilarating.

Dallas gripped Win's hips and thrust upward. Win threw his head back and moaned, his body rocking as the burly stud bucked beneath him. "Ride my cock," Dallas growled as he drove his dick into Win's chute.

Manuel appeared at Win's right, holding his engorged dick. He whispered something in Spanish that Win didn't understand, but he could easily interpret Manuel's body language. He opened wide, accepting a mouthful of Manuel's dark tool. As Dallas fucked Win's ass, Manuel fucked his face.

They changed positions, Dallas abruptly sitting up and causing Win to tilt backward onto the mattress. And then Win as on his back and Dallas was on top, ramming his ass in full, decisive thrusts. Win gripped Dallas's shoulders and wrapped his legs around his waist, holding on tight and grinding his cock against Dallas's abs as the brawny stud fucked him hard and fast.

Manuel crouched at Win's head, his cock and balls in easy reach. Dallas sucked Manuel's dick and Win licked his engorged balls. Ultimately, however, Manuel had to be satisfied by his own hand, stroking his cock while Dallas and Win vocalized their mounting ecstasy.

"That ass is good and tight," Dallas grunted, driving his cock all the way in to the hilt.

"*Ohyesohyesohyes*," Win gasped.

"I'm gonna come," Manuel announced, a millisecond before his cock erupted, his warm jizz splattering Win's face and neck. Dallas leaned in, opening wide to catch the second spurt, drinking down Manuel's thick juice with obvious relish.

Dallas still had his mouth on Manuel's dick when he came. His body shook; his cries – muffled by Manuel's swollen cock – became urgent. He breathed loudly through his nose, like a bull about to charge. His cock plowed into Win's ass in one final, hard thrust and came with a violent shudder. Win could feel the shaft of Dallas's cock pulsing against the walls of his chute, pumping out a copious load.

Dallas had barely caught his breath when he grabbed Win's cock and started stroking. Manuel lay down beside Win, kissing him while tweaking one of Win's stiff, brown nipples. "You're so hot," he sighed.

A bone-rattling orgasm overtook Win. His body twitched as his cock fired out jets of spooge onto his flat belly. A soothing buzz that no drug could ever replicate hummed beneath his skin.

Dallas raked a splotch of jizz off Win's abdomen and brought it to his lips, glossing them with Win's cum. He was sucking Win's load off his fingers when something beyond the mattress caught his attention.

"Got a sweet tasting boy here, boss," Dallas said. He scooped up another dollop of cum from Win's abs. "Wanna try it?"

Winton Swann, Jr.'s, well-muscled frame filled the bungalow's front door. His bearded face was like stone, but rage burned in his eyes.

Win felt sick and hoped death would soon follow. How did his father even know to look for him here, at this house in the middle of nowhere?

"Get dressed and get in the car. Now." Winton, Jr., didn't raise his voice. He didn't have to.

Neither father nor son looked at each other on the drive home. A suffocating silence filled his father's luxury SUV as Win waited to be disowned for being a worthless faggot. When his father did speak, he simply said: "Maybe you should've spent the summer with your mother." There was a tone of defeat in his voice.

The next few days were spent in self-imposed exile at the villa, Win and his father careful to avoid each other – so much so that half the time Win didn't know when, or if, his father was home. At the very least, Win expected his father to put him on the first flight to Spain to join his mother and her new boyfriend in Majorca. But, Winton Swann, Jr., couldn't even look at his son long enough to tell him he had to go.

While shame had crushed Win's spirit, it had not killed his libido. His thoughts returned often to the evening spent with Manuel and Dallas. The memories – Manuel writhing beneath a shower of piss, sucking Dallas's cock, sitting on his face, getting fucked – produced intense hard-ons. Win jacked-off frequently. As he stroked his dick, he'd think about returning to that grubby little bungalow, plotting what he wanted to try with the couple (he'd eat Manuel's ass; he'd be the meat in a Manuel and Dallas sandwich; he'd let Dallas pee on him).

But after he came, he'd recall his father's face, glaring at him from the door of the bungalow. Guilt and shame had Win vowing to never see Dallas and Manuel again.

But his desire was too strong to stay away.

A week had passed when he snuck out of the villa after sunset and returned to the bungalow. Though it was dark and he had only been to the house once, he had little trouble finding the place; his cock led the way. The rusty pickup was parked in front and a light shone in the front window. Win was already pitching a tent in his shorts when he got out of his Z4 and bounded up to the front steps. He didn't notice the second vehicle, parked up the road in the shadows.

The front door was ajar, and he could hear grunting and groaning. Manuel and Dallas were already going at it. He pushed the door open, prepared to sneak inside, strip and join the couple.

But, another man had already joined them.

Winston Swann, Jr., was on the sofa, Manuel astride his burly thighs, taking his cock deep into his shapely ass. Dallas stood on the sofa's seat, squatting slightly to feed his cock into the older man's mouth. Win's father swallowed his dick greedily.

Unasked questions were suddenly answered: Win's father hadn't come to the bungalow that night looking for his son; he'd come for Manuel and Dallas. He wasn't disgusted by the discovery of his son having sex with two men; he was jealous.

Dallas noticed Win by the door. His mouth curled into a devilish grin. "I've got a big load saved up for you, boss. But you may have to share."

Win turned and ran. He kept running, running until his lungs hurt. He fell to the ground, gulping in air. His heart was pounding against his sternum and tears streamed down his face. The bungalow was just a tiny glow in the distance now, no bigger than a firefly.

Beyond a scraggly forest edging the road, he could hear the surf. He walked toward the ocean, stepping carefully through the trees and brush until he found himself standing at the edge of a rocky cliff.

Winton Swann III kicked off his shoes and removed his clothes. He stood there, looking out at the ocean, the crashing waves drowned out by his beating heart. Then he jumped, the moonlight bouncing off his naked body as it arced toward the water.

It was a perfect swan dive.

Pagan Moon

The sun was starting to set when Paul was forced to admit what he had suspected for some time: he was lost.

Lost in the middle of fucking nowhere.

"It just gets better and better!" he said to the trees.

He should've known the weekend would be a disaster. As soon as he'd accepted the invitation to join Doug and his "friend" Dean for a weekend up in the hills, Paul began having his doubts. He wasn't much for wilderness, and even less for being a third wheel. But Dean had a cabin, and Doug said Paul was welcome to bring a friend of his own, so Paul accepted the invitation.

The guy Paul invited – not exactly a friend but a guy he desperately wanted to fuck – broke things off before anything had really begun. The "cabin" turned out to be a three-room shack in the Tennessee hills. It smelled of mildew and the only form of air conditioning was a small box fan that was perfectly suitable as long as one sat naked in front of it.

"Isn't this great!" Doug beamed when they stepped inside.

"At least it has indoor plumbing," Paul said dryly. "It *does* have indoor plumbing, doesn't it?"

The absolute worst, though, was feeling as if he was always in the way. Paul was constantly excusing himself from Doug and Dean's presence whenever they starting making out, which was about every thirty minutes. The first night they were in the cabin, he tried to fall asleep to the sounds of them fucking. By the afternoon of the second day, when Doug and Dean locked themselves in the bathroom after skinny-dipping in nearby lake (Paul excused himself from that, too), he had had enough. When the grunting and groaning started, Paul headed for the door.

"I'm going to take a walk," he called out, though he doubted either of them heard him.

And now, he was lost.

He didn't know how far he had hiked. Two miles, maybe? Possibly more. There were no trails, just spots where the brush wasn't as thick. Initially he thought he could just turn around and head back the way he came, except he didn't know which way that was.

He didn't know if there was anyone else up here. Dean's cabin was the only sign of civilization he knew, and he'd left that long ago.

Paul thought he heard something and stopped walking. He listened, perplexed by what he heard.

Sounded like drums.

Hoping he could get some help and more than a little curious as to what was going on, Paul walked toward the drumming until the sound became overpowering. He heard voices accompanying the drums. People were chanting, though what they were saying was indecipherable. Paul smelled smoke, and through the trees, he could see the glow of a fire.

He walked further until he came to a meadow. Remaining in the shadows of the forest, he took in the bizarre scene. There were about forty people – a few women, but mostly men – gathered around a bonfire. Five men were furiously pounding drums while everyone else danced and chanted around the fire. Some even jumped over the flames. Many of them were nude. Those who weren't wore loose-fitting, gauzy clothing. Quite a few people had painted their bodies.

"What in Christ's name *is* this shit?" he muttered to himself.

"It's worship," said a voice behind him.

Paul's heart nearly leapt out of his throat.

He spun toward the voice. Standing behind him was a man about six feet tall, and every foot was solid muscle. His dark, wavy hair cascaded down his back. His features were sharp and angular. A closely trimmed beard framed his mouth. If it weren't for his friendly, inviting eyes, Paul would describe him as demonic.

The man was one of the people from the meadow. A burgundy vest, adorned with elaborate gold embroidery, was laced tight around his torso. He wore several bracelets on each arm, and a delicate, silver belly chain circled his midriff. A thin, muslin skirt flowed down to the man's legs, the hem meeting the top lacing of his gladiator sandals. Though the sun was descending quickly, enough light shined through the skirt to illuminate the fact that the stranger wore nothing beneath it.

"Goddamn, you scared me," Paul gasped.

"Sorry. I didn't mean to frighten you." The man stepped closer, offering a hand. "I'm Kiron."

Paul took the hand, letting Kiron grip it firmly. "I'm Paul. Kiron's an unusual name."

"It's not my birth name. It's my coven name."

"Coven?"

Kiron nodded. "It's a pagan ceremony."

"*Pagan?* Like devil worship?" Paul asked, not masking his alarm. Being slaughtered in a sacrifice to Satan would be the cherry on top of this awful weekend.

A deep laugh rumbled within Kiron's broad chest. "Far from it. We worship the spirits of nature, like the ancients did. It's actually a very beautiful and empowering religion."

Paul wasn't sure whether to laugh or run. He was not particularly religious in general, but this was so alien from anything he had ever encountered that he found the concept both silly and scary.

"I grew up Methodist myself," he said.

Kiron changed the subject. "So what brings you out this way? Are you lost?"

"Very," Paul replied. "I'm staying in a cabin about two miles or so from here. I just kept walking, and now I don't know north and south from my ass."

"You must be thirsty," Kiron said, unhooking a canteen strapped over his shoulder. "Have some water."

Paul gratefully accepted the offer. He hadn't realized how thirsty he was until the cool water washed down his throat.

"Sorry, didn't mean to drink you dry," Paul said, handing back the half-empty canteen. "Thanks."

"You're welcome," Kiron smiled, sliding the canteen strap over his shoulder. "And you're welcome to stay here if you like. There's room in my tent. In the morning, we could help you return to your friends."

"Uh, I don't know ..."

Kiron stepped even closer. His scent, a mixture of patchouli and his own natural musk, wafted up Paul's nostrils. "Why are you so nervous?"

"This isn't really ... uh, it – it's not my scene."

That was only part of the reason for his nervousness. Kiron was a powerfully sexy man, emitting a seductive vibe that simultaneously excited and frightened Paul.

"You don't have to convert," Kiron chuckled. "I'm just offering you a place to sleep. However, there are some aspects to our worship that may appeal to you."

Kiron's chest brushed up against Paul's. The pounding of Paul's heart drowned out the drums. His cock swelled uncomfortably in his shorts. "Like what?" he asked.

Kiron reached up and stroked Paul's light brown hair. "Sexuality is a very strong expression of our spirituality. We don't view it as a sin, like many Christian religions do. To us, it's a celebration."

Paul's breathing became fast and shallow. When Kiron wrapped his thick arms around him, Paul could feel the thickness of Kiron's cock pressing against him. Kiron then placed his mouth on Paul's, kissing him deeply.

"Then let's celebrate," Paul said breathlessly,

Smiling, Kiron ran his hands down Paul's body. "First, we need to do something about your clothes."

Kiron pulled at Paul's T-shirt, lifting it over his head and tossing it aside. Though he did not have Kiron's bulk, Paul's body was well defined, every muscle on his slender frame standing out firmly beneath his smooth skin. Kiron's hands glided over Paul's bare chest admiringly.

"You're very beautiful," he whispered, gently pinching one of Paul's erect nipples.

They kissed again. Paul's trepidation quickly dissolved into lust. He plunged his tongue into Kiron's mouth; his hands clutched Kiron's firm ass.

Kiron planted kisses on Paul's cheek, then bit him lightly up and down the side of his neck. Paul gasped, unprepared for the wave of erotic feelings conjured by Kiron's mouth. His cock was like iron and his underwear damp with pre-cum.

The kisses and bites continued down Paul's chest. Kiron's tongue circled a nipple and his hands kneaded Paul's ass. Paul pulled at Kiron's vest, eager to strip him of his ritual attire. As much as he was enjoying what Kiron was doing to him, Paul wanted him naked, so he could give it back tenfold.

Kiron, though, had slipped from his grasp. He sank to his knees and removed Paul's khaki shorts. His hand reached between his legs, his fingers slipping underneath the briefs and grazing his asshole.

Then, his hands suddenly gripping the waistband of his underwear, Kiron literally tore the underwear from Paul's body. The designer briefs, now reduced to rags, were flung to the forest floor.

There was a sensual thrill in feeling the warm summer air against his nude body, but Paul had only seconds to savor it. Kiron's strong hand gripped his rigid prick, stroking its length as he lapped the glaze of pre-cum from the swollen head.

Paul fell forward, clamping his hands down on Kiron's wide shoulders for support. He shuddered as his cock slid between Kiron's wet lips.

"Oooh, that feels sooo ... maybe you should ... maybe ..."

Paul's body shook and his head spun as Kiron swallowed his cock. He knew he wouldn't be able to control himself if Kiron didn't stop. He tried to pull away, but could not force his body to move.

He tried to warn Kiron, tell him to ease up. But, the all he managed was a sharp cry as he fired his load.

Kiron pulled his mouth away just in time to catch the first spurt of Paul's cream as it splashed against his chin. The rest of his load splattered his forearm as he milked Paul's cock with his fist. "Oh, yeah, man," Kiron sighed. "Come all over me."

As satisfying as his orgasm was, Paul felt cheated. He wanted to do more with Kiron than just get a quick blowjob.

"That was beautiful, man," Kiron said, standing up. A glob of cum clung to his beard, but he made no move to wipe it off. He wrapped his arms around Paul, pulling him close and kissing him.

"You got me so hot," Kiron rasped, standing back and unlacing the front of his vest. He removed it and the canteen, dropping both on the forest floor. The sun had disappeared from the sky, but the moon was full. Moonlight bounced off Kiron's rippling muscles and shimmered in the thatch of hair sprawling across his chest.

The pagan was pitching a tent in the front of his skirt, which would've struck Paul as funny were it not for the fact that it was a pretty big tent.

"What do you want to do to me?" he asked seductively.

Paul wanted to do so much with Kiron's ravishing body that he couldn't think of where to begin. He stepped forward and ran his hands over Kiron's furry chest, down his rigid abs. Paul leaned forward to nibble at Kiron's neck while his hand strayed to Kiron's dick, grasping it through the soft material of his skirt.

Kiron sucked in his breath. He gripped Paul's ass and forced Paul's body against his. "I want to feel your mouth on my cock," he whispered, thrusting his hips forward for emphasis.

Paul smiled and kneeled, dragging his tongue down Kiron's torso as he sank down. Once on his knees, Paul slowly raised the skirt, giving a teasing kiss to each of Kiron's muscular thighs. *It's like unveiling the bride*, Paul thought as he lifted the skirt over Kiron's cock, *only much, much better.*

Kiron's cock was long, thick and cut. The swollen head glistened in the moonlight.

Paul's pulse raced as he lowered his mouth onto Kiron's throbbing dick, his tongue caressing every inch as it slid down his throat. Kiron cupped the back of his head and pushed Paul's face forward, grunting sharply as he drove his cock deeper. Amazingly, Paul did not gag as the swollen head of Kiron's cock hit the back of his throat and his nose rested in the cushion of Kiron's pubic hair.

He pulled back slowly, his tongue tracing the raised veins of Kiron's shaft. His fingers curled around the hard phallus, and his lips brushed the tip of the crown. The taste of Kiron's pre-cum was intoxicating.

While his mouth teased the head of Kiron's cock, Paul reached up between Kiron's legs with his free hand, tracing the hairy crack of Kiron's ass until he found his hot hole.

Kiron pushed his ass back against Paul's fingers. "Play with my ass," he hissed.

Paul didn't want to abandon Kiron's cock entirely. He jerked it a few more times, running his tongue over his balls as he handled the pagan stud's dick. Then, grabbing Kiron's upper thighs, Paul directed him to turn around.

Kiron turned, taking a few steps away and leaning forward, supporting himself against the trunk of a small tree. He pushed his ass toward Paul's face, inviting him to take advantage.

Except that damned skirt covered his ass. Paul considered removing it altogether, but to his surprise he found it kind of sexy. Being able to just lift it and do whatever he wanted was an incredible turn-on.

He raised the skirt and folded it over on Kiron's back. Kiron's butt was as perfectly formed as the rest of him: firm and round, with slight dimples on the sides of his cheeks. Though Kiron was amply covered in body hair, his buttcheeks were relatively smooth.

Paul kissed both cheeks then slowly ran his tongue down the furry divide. Kiron spread his legs further apart, encouraging Paul to move deeper. But Paul wasn't going to be rushed. He teased Kiron's ass-lips, his tongue slowly spiraling toward the puckered center. Then, in a swift and sudden move, he speared Kiron's asshole with his pointed tongue.

Kiron cried out and his body trembled. "Oh, gods, yes," he moaned, grinding his ass into Paul's face. "Eat that ass."

Paul clamped his hands onto Kiron's butt, pulling his asscheeks apart. He drove his tongue into his splayed ass, gnawing at the tender sphincter. The pagan whimpered when Paul's tongue snaked up his chute.

"Stand up," Kiron commanded hoarsely. "I want to have some fun with your ass, too."

He obeyed, reluctantly pulling his mouth away from Kiron's moist hole. Kiron turned around and kissed him, his tongue swirling around Paul's mouth. Kiron reached for Paul's cock and that's when Paul realized he was hard again. Paul had been so into eating Kiron's ass he hadn't even noticed.

Kiron ordered Paul to turn around. Paul leaned against the tree as Kiron had done, and within seconds Kiron's mouth was on his ass, his tongue digging into his hole. Paul howled and his cock quivered and drooled as Kiron's tongue burrowed deep into his ass. Even the sensation of Kiron's beard scraping the smooth skin of his ass was a turn-on.

Kiron pulled his butt cheeks apart, licking Paul's hole with savage intensity. He reached between Paul's legs and pulled at his hard cock while stabbing Paul's quivering hole. Paul writhed and moaned, his body buzzing with erotic pleasure.

Then Kiron abruptly took his mouth away from Paul's ass. Seconds later Paul felt Kiron's thick, hard dick pressing against his spit-lubed butt crack.

Paul became anxious. Much as he wanted Kiron to fuck him, Paul wasn't sure he could handle his endowment. He was sure he'd be split in half if Kiron entered him.

Except Kiron didn't enter him. Instead, he ground his cock against Paul's asshole, humping his ass without actually entering it. Paul had never really bothered with frottage, not considering it to be "real sex." But Kiron's cock grinding against his butthole felt good. Fan-*fucking*-tastic, in fact. He pushed his ass back, creating a delicious friction between their bodies.

The sexy pagan leaned over Paul, planting a kiss between his shoulder blades. He reached around Paul's waist, gripping his cock and pulling it while his own dick slid up and down the crevice of Paul's ass crack.

The pleasure became so intense Paul grew lightheaded. He groaned loudly. Kiron jerked him off at a faster pace.

"Come in my hand, man," Kiron grunted. "Shoot your load."

Just keep doing what you're doing, Paul thought. The pressure of Kiron's cock against his ass, his hand hammering up and down his dick had already taken him past the point of self-control. His body convulsed as an orgasm ignited within his cock, the shockwaves exploding through his body.

Kiron made appreciative noises as Paul's jism splashed into his palm and dripped between his fingers.

When the last drop of cum has dribbled out of Paul's cock, Kiron took his hand away and wrapped it around his own throbbing prick. Using Paul's cum as lube, he jacked off.

"I'm gonna cum all over your back," he panted

Aiming his cock toward the center of Paul's back, his balls resting in Paul's butt crack, Kiron stroked his dick in long, deliberate strokes. But his controlled handling of his cock could not prolong the moment any longer. Letting out a growl that sounded not unlike a wolf about to pounce, Kiron fired his generous load all over Paul's back. Paul felt the warm, heavy splats of cum rain down upon his bare skin and turned to watch as the last spurt of juice shot out of Kiron's cock.

Then all was calm.

Paul turned to face Kiron. The bearded hunk stood there panting, his expression dazed.

Paul broke the spell by falling into his arms. Kiron pulled him close, his hands running up and down Paul's cum-soaked back, massaging his thick juice into Paul's skin.

The drums in the meadow beat louder. The celebration continued.

#

Doug and Dean were driving down the main road in the early hours of the morning, continuing their search for Paul, when two men in a dusty pickup flagged them down. The driver of the truck was a bearded, longhaired guy in a vest and jeans. Paul got out on the passenger side.

"Where the hell have you been?" Doug shouted. "We spent half the fucking night looking for you!"

Paul looked disheveled and spent, but he also looked happy. A satisfied smile seemed permanently fixed on his face. He looked at the good-looking hippie guy, then at Doug.

"I was at church," he said.

Crossing the Line

"This is nice," Jason said, smiling, sinking down into the hot tub until only his head was above the steaming, bubbling water.

I took the towel from around my waist and slid into the tub, so quickly my embarrassment didn't have time to catch up with me. The sun was setting, but the heat hung in the Florida air, stirred only by a soft breeze churned by the rolling surf, the Gulf a little more than a stone's throw from the house we'd rented. It was nice, I agreed – as long as no one found us bare-ass naked in the hot tub.

"We should've bought some wine," I said, settling in the tub across from Jason and looking over my shoulder at the neighboring bungalow, reassuring myself it was still vacant. The building was identical to ours, and the two properties shared a central courtyard as well as the hot tub. But, all the lights were off at the house next door. *Good.*

"Maybe tomorrow," Jason said. Then: "Why are you all the way over there?"

"So we can see each other when we talk."

"Maybe I don't want to talk," he said, grinning.

I smiled. "Here?"

"*Relax.* We've got this place to ourselves."

Though still wary, I moved next to him. "Hey, there," he said softly, playfully. We kissed – a quick smack on the lips, first, then deeper. Jason's hand moved down my shoulder to my chest. He pinched my right nipple, and I felt a bite of pleasurable pain.

My hands began to wander as well: down his arms then jumping one of his to his muscular thighs and traveling upward. His cock was hard. My hand curled around it and squeezed. A soft moan tumbled from Jason's lips. His mouth moved to my ear, his tongue gliding along its outer edges. I felt his hot breath on the side of my neck. Then came the dirty suggestions, whispered so softly I only heard a few select words above the roar of the bubbling water: "I'm ... cock ... lick your."

I shifted my position, climbing on top of Jason and straddling his lap. We ground our hard-ons together as we kissed, our tongues fighting their way down each other's throats. It was feeling like it used to, when we were first together and couldn't keep our hands off each other. Back before we fell into a pattern, only fucking on the same days of the week, same time of day, same place, doing the same things – something to cross off our "to do" list.

The outdoor light of the neighboring bungalow flashed on, falling on us like a bucket of ice water. We both froze.

"When did ...?" I started to ask.

"I don't know," he said.

Our eyes fixated on the building, watching as interior lights switched on and shadows moved around inside. "That's a mood killer," I said, getting off Jason.

"We could finish up inside," he said.

"Definitely," I said, poised to climb out of the tub.

The opening of a sliding glass door stopped me in my tracks. Our neighbors stepped into the shared courtyard, both wearing swimsuits, with brightly colored beach towels draped around their necks. They were an older couple – older than us, anyway. We guessed early-to mid-forties, though the additional years barely left a mark on them. One had shocks of silver and white threading through his closely cropped hair and neatly groomed goatee. He was tall, maybe six feet four. The other was shorter, with dark hair – no gray, but his hairline was making a fast retreat. Both were muscular, tight and tan, and their suits were well packed.

"Mind if we join you?" asked the taller, gray-haired one.

Yes, we do, I thought. Instead, Jason said, "C'mon in. May have to reset the timer, though."

The shorter one padded over to the timer switch and turned it back to the maximum amount of time. His partner pulled his beach towel from around his neck and dropped it on the cement deck. He started to get into the tub then stopped. "Oh, you're naked."

I felt my face grow hot with embarrassment and started to apologize. "We thought ..."

"Babe, they're naked," the taller one called to his partner, hooking his thumbs in the waistband of his electric blue boxcut. "We can lose the suits."

Off came the swimsuit, and "wow" went our eyes. His cock had to be seven inches flaccid. It was a thick one, too. He was cut, but a generous collar of foreskin framed the head like a fleshy turtleneck. A set of low-hangers dangled below like a ripe fruit. Jason and I tried not to stare as he stepped into the hot water.

"I'm Richard," he introduced himself, presenting his hand across the water. "Just Richard, not Dick." Though Dick would've been quite appropriate.

Jason shook his hand and introduced himself, and then Richard turned to me.

"Keith," I said. His handshake was firm.

Richard's partner appeared at the hot tub's edge, having lost his suit while we were exchanging introductions. His torso was blanketed with curly, dark hair. He was well endowed like Richard-not-Dick, though his cock looked closer to six inches than seven, soft. His balls didn't hang as low, propping up his dick, so it looked like as if it was resting on two pink, fuzzy pillows.

"This guy here is Lawrence," Richard announced as his other half eased into the tub.

"Please, don't call me Larry," he said as he shook our hands. "I don't even let my mother call me that anymore."

"He had her killed," Richard said, following the comment with a loud *har-dee-har-har* type laugh. Jason and I laughed along, though not as boisterously.

Small talk followed. They were vacationing from Houston, came here every year, sometimes twice a year. They had been together for fifteen years. Our turn: Vacationing from Charlotte, North Carolina, our first time here – we practically had to sell pints of blood to afford our four-day stay. We had been together for six years. Jason is thirty-four, I'm thirty-two. They didn't volunteer their ages, and we thought it would be rude to ask.

Then Lawrence asked: "So, are you two monogamous?"

Jason and I answered quickly, in unison: "*Yes.*" We weren't shocked by the question so much as we were the tone, like the hoped-for answer was no.

"We are, too. Now," said Lawrence, sounding mournful of that fact. "For eight years now."

"Seven," corrected Richard. "Don't you remember those two guys in Italy."

"Oh, yeah. Angelo was so fucking hot ..."

I quickly steered the conversation toward a more innocuous topic, like how beautiful it was outside. The sun was down now, and Richard tilted his head back, looking up into the dark sky. "You can see every star. So relaxing out here."

Lawrence leaned against him. "Love it out here, away from everything ..."

Jason started to speak, but he instantly stifled whatever it was he was going to say as Lawrence-please-don't-call-me-Larry leaned in to kiss his lover of fifteen years, seven monogamous ones. At first, it was an affectionate peck on the lips, but mouths soon opened, and tongues slid to and fro. Richard's hands cupped Lawrence's face. Richard's hands were beneath the water, doing I-could-only-imagine what.

These guys, neighbors but strangers, asked Jason and I if we were monogamous, then, minutes later, start making out hot and heavy in front of us, like we're not there. Was this our cue to leave – or to watch and join in?

Truth was, if we weren't monogamous, I wouldn't mind playing with these two. I found them attractive, and seeing them kiss so hotly, Lawrence's hand no doubt pulling at Richard's cock under the cover of bubbling water, made my own dick stiffen. My hand sought out Jason's cock. These guys were having the same effect on him, too. We exchanged a questioning glance, one that asked: *What do we do now?*

Just as they started getting heated, Richard and Lawrence immediately pulled away from each other, giggling. "Sorry," Lawrence said sheepishly. "We sometimes get carried away. Didn't mean to embarrass you."

"Not a bit," I said, a smile frozen on my face, the kind of smile I wear when Jason's parents visit. I started to take my hand away from Jason's cock, but he grabbed my wrist, holding it there.

"Our vacations are just an excuse to dedicate time to fucking non-stop," Richard volunteered. "Like, one time, early in our relationship, we went to Paris, and I think we spent most of our visit picking up guys and bringing them back to our hotel room. Didn't even make it to the goddamn Eiffel Tower!"

"The *Elysées Matignon* was a beautiful place to play," Lawrence added.

My hand moved to Jason's balls, fondling them as the churning water batted them around. Chuckling, he said, "Yeah, know what you mean. Keith and I, we always treat our getaways like second honeymoons. I mean, who wants to take a tour of historic sites when you could be fucking?"

Lawrence settled back against Richard, resting his head against the side of his partner's face. "Fortunately, there are no historic sites around here to distract you."

He smiled at us, in a way that told me he knew what I was doing to Jason under the water. I tried once again to move my hand away, and again Jason wouldn't let me. Instead, he guided my hand to the head of his cock.

"No, they just have two old farts interrupting them," Richard said.

I circled my fingers around Jason's shaft. "You're not interrupting," he said, a small quaver in his voice giving away the pleasure he was feeling.

The hot tub's timer ran its course and the water instantly went still. "I'll reset it," Richard volunteered, hoisting himself out of the water. Very nice ass, at any age: Firm, as tan as the rest of him, the crack darkened by hair sprouting from it. A Yin-Yang symbol was tattooed on his left cheek. I hoped Lawrence didn't catch me licking my lips.

Richard set the timer, and once again we were like vegetables simmering in a stew. Richard turned and headed back for the tub, and mine and Jason's jaws dropped simultaneously. His seven-inch cock had hardened into an eight-and-a-half inch boner. I'm not sure if we were embarrassed or impressed. It wasn't an etiquette dilemma I'd seen handled in the lifestyles section of our local paper. Though I could think of more enjoyable ways to handle Richard's hard-on, I decided to deal with it as one deals with breast-feeding mothers or a loud fart in public: I tried to ignore it.

Lawrence, however, couldn't refrain from comment. "Now I think you can call him Dick."

Jason and I responded with uneasy chuckles.

"Like none of you have hard-ons," Richard said sarcastically, sitting down on the edge of the tub, his legs dangling in the hot water, his stiff cock directly in our line of sight. I wasn't sure if Richard would consider it rude if I continued staring or be insulted if I looked away.

"You'll have to forgive Richard. He's handicapped," Lawrence giggled. "He has no sense of decency."

"If you're that embarrassed, make it soft," Richard challenged, gripping his cock and shaking it. His mouth pulled into a lecherous grin.

"We could talk about your irritating sister."

Richard gave Lawrence's shoulder a squeeze. "*You know* what I mean."

We all knew what he meant.

Lawrence's mouth settled into a conspiratorial smile. He stood up, the water hitting him just below his navel. Beneath the surface I could see his hard prick, its details blurred beneath the fighting bubbles. He turned and positioned himself between Richard's knees, then, kneeling on the cement bench that encircled the tub's interior, he hoisted himself up, so he was eye-to-eye with Richard and his firm, full ass above the water.

We heard them speaking in hushed voices, then heard the loud, wet smacks of their lips.

Lawrence's body slowly sank into the steaming water, his tongue sliding down his lover's toned torso. It kept sliding, not stopping until it reached Richard's crotch. Jason and I turned to each other, our mouths gaping. *Were they really ...? In front of us?*

Both men chuckled, then Richard let out a gasp. His eyes closed and his lips went slack as Lawrence's head bobbed between his legs.

Yes they were.

To make sure we knew what was going on (as if there was any doubt), Richard spread his legs wider, and Lawrence turned sideways, so we could see his tongue flick the engorged head of Richard's cock.

I could hear my heart pounding in my chest. The situation was shocking for its uncertainty (what was expected of us?) and exciting for obvious reasons. My dick was so hard it ached. I fondled it compulsively, my fingers gliding lightly along the shaft and over the head – teasing myself, not really jacking off. Jason's cock vibrated in my other hand. Neither of us spoke, but we both wondered how to proceed. I wanted to mimic our neighbors and suck Jason's cock. I also wondered about sucking Richard's cock, or licking Lawrence's ass. And I wondered if Jason was thinking about the same thing.

Jason's hand sought out my dick. His firm grip sent an electric jolt through me. I inhaled sharply. My eyes briefly met Richard's, and he grinned at me. His crotch was hidden from view once again by the back of Lawrence's head. He supported his weight with one hand while the other was hooked around Lawrence's skull, keeping his lover's head in place between his legs. By the movement of his thighs, I could tell Richard was thrusting his hips forward, fucking Lawrence's mouth.

My eyes returned to Jason. He was staring straight ahead at our neighbors, his lips parted, his eyes dreamy, like he was stoned or hypnotized. I leaned over and nibbled on his earlobe. "What do you want to do," I whispered.

Before Jason could answer, Richard called out, "Hey, just 'cause you guys are monogamous doesn't mean you have to be shy." Looking at me he said, "Go ahead, suck his dick. I know you want to."

I felt like the losing contestant on a game show. As much as I wanted to suck Jason's cock, I wasn't sure about doing it with people watching. Hell, I was wary about just being *naked* in front of other people. I looked at Jason, not liking the mischievous smile on his face.

"C'mon," he said, getting out of the tub and sitting back down on the edge, dangling his legs in the water. I gave him a you-can't-be-serious look. Yet, the sight of him – his torso with the arrow of chestnut hair jutting upward between his hard pecks and his thick cock, standing up between his thighs – defeated any arguments I might have made. Horniness trumped self-consciousness.

I moved in between Jason's legs and took his dick in my pruned hands. The purplish head pulsed visibly, and more than just water dripped off it. Roughly, Jason pushed my face down to his crotch. "Suck it," he hissed.

His cock filled my mouth, its veiny contours pressing against my tongue. Jason pushed his dick deeper, to the back of my throat.

Richard said, "Oh, *yeah!*" Whether he was groaning about my sucking Jason's cock or Lawrence sucking his, I didn't know – or care.

I circled Jason's cockhead with my tongue as my lips massaged the shaft. The tip of my nose brushed against his pubes, wet and smelling of chlorine. I put my arms around his waist, squeezing his body as I sucked his dick, feeling him writhe in my arms.

There was splashing behind me. Seconds later, I could feel the presence of Richard and Lawrence on either side of us. I looked up to my left to see Lawrence staring down at me with Jason's dick in my mouth, wearing that glazed expression men have when their cocks take control of their minds. His prick was hidden just beneath the water's surface, as was his right hand.

"Get up there," Richard instructed. I looked to my right to see if he was talking to me, but his eyes were on Lawrence.

Jason's hands steered me back to his cock. I resumed my sucking as Lawrence climbed out of the tub and Richard moved around me. As much as I enjoyed the feel of my lover's dick buried in my mouth, I also wanted to watch our neighbors' impromptu sex show.

It was Jason who gave me the opportunity to indulge my voyeuristic tendencies. "I'm... I'm getting close." His voice was tense. Gently, he pushed me back, his cock popping out of my mouth and snapping against his torso. His face was flushed, and his lower lip trembling as he stifled an orgasm through sheer force of will.

"Sure you don't just want to come in my mouth?" I asked playfully, my hand gently stroking his shaft.

"Not yet," he said, slapping my hand away.

Our eyes traveled to our left. Lawrence was on his elbows and knees on the deck, ass in the air – and in Richard's face. Richard, crouched in the steamy water, speared his hole, his hands gripping his muscular thighs as his tongue bore into Lawrence's chute. Lawrence rolled his hips, rubbing his ass against his lover's face. Supporting his weight on one elbow, he reached between his legs with his other hand to stroke his cock – a cock, first hidden under water and now obscured by Lawrence's crouched position, that I had yet to see in its erect glory,

I also had been hidden under water for most of our time outdoors and decided it was time to step out. My fingertips resembled raisins and any misgivings I had about strangers seeing me naked were dashed a while ago. Besides, Richard and Lawrence acted as if they'd forgotten we were still present.

Though the temperature couldn't have fallen below 80 degrees, I felt a slight chill from the contrasting temperatures of the water and air as I stepped out of the hot tub. My tan nipples got harder; my ballsac tightened.

I leaned over Jason, my hands resting on his shoulders, and kissed him. Before I knew it, I was on top of him, our pulsing dicks pressed together, one of his hands running through my damp, wavy brown hair, the other sliding down my back. "I think you owe me something," I said, my voice low and husky.

"Like what?"

I moved off him with all the grace of an elephant seal. I planned on straddling Jason's chest and saying: "A blow job or a rim job: take your pick." Instead, I flopped onto the cement deck, flat on my back and nearly toppling Lawrence. Lawrence let out a startled yelp before resuming his grunts and groans as Richard resumed his rim job.

Before I could get on top of Jason, however, he got on top of me, confronting me with his winking butthole. Not part of my plan, but I could hardly argue.

As I raised my face to Jason's rosy-tan sphincter, my cock was engulfed by Jason's warm, wet mouth. A shudder went through me, and I gasped as his tongue swirled around my much-neglected hard-on. I allowed a few moments to enjoy the buzzing pleasure that shot through me each time Jason swallowed my cock; then I tore into his gorgeous ass.

Jason's hole contracted and pulsed as I prodded it with my tongue. His body twisted atop mine, his cock rubbing against my sternum, leaving its slimy snail-trail of pre-cum. I pushed my hips upward, stabbing Jason's hot mouth. He took the full length of my cock, all the way down to the root, while he caressed my balls with a free hand.

He lifted my legs, curling them back, so my butt was raised up, giving him easy access to my asshole. Fingers, wet with spit, teased the outer edge of my hole, pushing against the tightly closed ring. His tongue gingerly licked around my hole, making me squirm in anticipation of the moment he speared my ass. Jason's ass was now pushed into my face, my nose pressed into his ass-crack. My tongue slithered inside him, twitching just beyond his ass-lips.

Jason cried out, and I felt his mouth on my butthole once again, lapping at it hungrily. He pried my hole open with his fingers and then, like a hunter going in for the kill, pierced my sphincter with a quick, sharp jab. His tongue dove inside my chute, his bristly facial hair scraping against the tender skin of my open trench.

But Jason was clean-shaven.

I don't know which surprised me more: Richard brazenly helping himself to my asshole or Jason's allowing him to. Jason, who still had my thighs under his arms, actually encouraged him, breathily repeating porn-video *bon mots* like: "Yeah, eat that hot hole. Shove your tongue up there, all the way."

Shocked as I was, I was also very, *very* turned on. Just knowing someone other than my boyfriend was eating my ass – and that my boyfriend was watching – excited me so much that I feared I might spontaneously shoot my load.

I was about to attack Jason's ass with renewed vigor when Lawrence knelt down above my head, his dick hovering just over my face. Finally, I got to see his cock: Nearly eight inches hard, and fat, too. His nut-sack was tight, making his balls look like some sort of fuzzy, exotic fruit, ripe and ready for picking.

Lawrence pulled on his dick in slow, even strokes. Pausing, he let a thick gob of saliva ooze out his lips and fall onto his extended rod – and onto my forehead. With this new dollop of natural lube on his cock, he resumed stroking with one hand. His other hand admiringly traced the curves of Jason's ass.

"Keep eating." Lawrence's voice was soft, almost distant. "I just want to watch."

My tongue pushed its way past Jason's ass-lips once again, snaking into his tight hole. It was difficult to concentrate, what with Lawrence's juicy cock over my face and his lover's tongue plunging into my twitching asshole.

A prolonged moan forced its way out of Lawrence's mouth, ending with a short, loud, grunt. Seconds later, I tasted his load, thick and tangy, as it ran down the channel of Jason's ass and onto my lapping tongue.

"Jesus, that's so hot," Lawrence gasped. In one swift move, he lowered his body further, the head of his dick touching down on my tongue. Just as swiftly, without a second thought, my lips closed over its engorged head and sucked the remaining drops of jizz from the slit.

Suddenly, Jason moved backwards, forcing Lawrence to step aside. "Wanna show these guys how much you love cum?" he practically growled, kneeling over my face, pumping his hard, drooling dick. "'Cause I'm about to blow a huge load all ... over ... *your face!*"

He came, ribbons of jizz splattering my face, hair and the deck. I caught a few drops in my open mouth, noting that Jason's spooge tasted sweeter than Lawrence's.

Jason leaned down to kiss me. I wondered if he realized those were Lawrence's juices he tasted on my lips as well as his own? This thought was fleeting, though. I was more interested in getting off. When I grabbed my cock, and it vibrated in my hands. I jacked off frantically, my legs pushing against Richard's shoulders as his tongue dug into my butt. Within seconds, I was spraying jism all over my smooth, flat stomach.

Richard's tongue quickly traveled upward, from my ass, over my balls and up to my spurting cock. He licked the cum-frosted head then slurped up the glistening white stripes of cream crisscrossing my belly. For a brief moment, I placed a hand on top of his head, but pulled it away quickly, thinking this might be too affectionate a gesture.

Richard's eyes met mine. He wore a cat-ate-the-canary grin (or would that be a horny-homo-who-ate-the-jizz grin?) as he slowly raised himself up from my body, standing in the now-still waters of the hot tub. Seconds later, he joined us on the deck, his naked body dripping onto the concrete. One hand stroked his pulsing dick; the other pointed at Jason, now sitting on his haunches by my head. "You, suck my balls while I shoot my load."

Jason's eyes went from Richard down to me, as if asking permission. I nodded, and he moved closer to Richard, leaning in to chew on his shaved ball sack while Richard jerked off. Lawrence stood up and moved in behind his partner of fifteen years, his arms circling Richard's chest and pinching his engorged nipples.

Richard leaned back against Lawrence and roared as cum erupted from his cock like champagne from a bottle. Jason kept licking and sucking Richard's balls as the heavy drops of man cream landed on the side of his face and shoulder.

The distant gleeful shouts of a child on the shore, followed by the concerned warnings of his mother, snapped us all out of our post-orgasmic reverie. Richard and Lawrence laughed heartily.

"That was fun," Richard chuckled, licking the spooge off his fingertips.

Lawrence busied himself gathering their swimsuits and towels. Jason and I laughed along, but our laughter was not very convincing, especially to ourselves.

Richard and Lawrence gave us hugs and suggested we get together the next day.

"I know some secluded places on this beach," Richard said. "We could do some nude sunbathing." His tone was heavy with innuendo.

Jason and I exchanged a look. We'd jumped over a line in our relationship we never even planned to go near. Dare we risk crossing that line again?

We answered in unison: "Maybe."

Forbidden Forest

Pa told Peter never to go into the woods alone. He hadn't planned to disobey his father, but the maze of trees and brush seemed to beckon him, and he wanted to explore the dense woods without his father and little brother in tow. Privacy was a luxury Peter wasn't afforded at home, where his family seemed to intrude on his every waking moment. The forest promised solitude.

Still, it was time to head back. If he hiked much longer, his father would come looking for him. If Pa found him in the forest, Peter knew he'd get a whipping, no questions asked.

Then he heard a noise.

At first, Peter dismissed it as just an animal, maybe a raccoon or deer. He stood still and listened. He heard the noise again and tried to identify the animal. It was a low, grunting noise. Perhaps it was a bear, Peter thought, both excited and frightened by the prospect. When he heard the noise again there were voices accompanying it. Men's voices.

Peter walked toward the noises. They sounded as if they were coming from the other side of the creek. Maybe it was some hunters who trapped an animal and were now surrounding it. He quickened his pace.

He crept up to the wall of shrubs that lined the creek bank and peeked through the leaves.

His eyes widened in shock and amazement. On the opposite bank, beneath a large pine tree, were three men, naked. One was tall and slender, with long brown hair. He looked to be around Peter's age, eighteen or nineteen. An older man, about thirty Peter guessed, with a more substantial build – a deep chest and hard, flat stomach – reclined on a smooth bolder beneath the tall, slender one, swallowing his cock.

A third man was crouched on all fours before the older man, his head bobbing at the man's lap and his naked ass undulating in Peter's direction.

Peter watched silently as the man seated on the rock swallowed the prick of the younger man, fondling his balls as he took his cock down his throat. The younger man's head was tossed back, his eyes closed. He let out a low, guttural moan. Perhaps he was the one Peter had mistaken for a bear.

Occasionally, the older man would run his fingers through the dark blond hair of the man kneeling between his legs. The kneeling man stroked his own cock, pleasuring himself as he pleasured the man on the rock.

The whole scene fascinated Peter – and aroused him tremendously. His rod had swollen and now twitched inside his pants; a pleasing, tingling sensation radiated throughout his body. Almost without thinking about it, he unbuttoned his pants and pulled out his cock. He stroked his dick as he watched the men on the other side of the creek, wondering what it would feel like to have someone suck his prick or to have a cock inside his own mouth.

The tall, long-haired man cried out. His body jerked, as if he were having a spasm. The man sitting on the rock licked his balls as streams of white juice shot out the tall man's dick and rained down upon the older man's face and shoulders. Soon thereafter, the older man had a similar spasm. He groaned and threw his head back, then looked down at the man on his knees before him.

"That's right. Drink it all," he purred in a deep, seductive voice.

Finally, the man on the ground stood up. He sat on the older man's lap and they kissed. Peter was shocked. It wasn't a kiss like Pa used to give him when he was a little boy, a quick peck on the lips or forehead; this was a slow passionate kiss, like he'd seen men give women. Seeing two men kiss this way made his cock throb in his hand.

He got a better view of the man who'd been on his knees. He was young, too, though his muscles were more pronounced than the long-haired man's. The older man massaged his cock until he, too, was shot thick, white jets of cream. They kept on kissing, with the older man periodically turning to kiss the tip of the tall man's still-pulsing cock.

Peter flogged his rod at a furious pace. He'd jacked off before, even though Pa told him it was a sin, but it had never felt like this. Not this intense. Forgetting that he wasn't alone and that he was supposed to be hiding, he grunted loudly as he came, shooting his load into the wet dirt.

The older man looked up suddenly. Peter froze as the man looked in his direction. He seemed to look right at Peter. A smile crept across his lips and leaned over and whispered into the blond man's ear.

The man was crossing the creek before Peter could even think to run. He was reaching to pull up his pants when the man climbed through the bushes.

They were silent for what seemed like a long time, Peter looking frightened and the man looking amused. "You don't need to be afraid," the man finally said. Peter didn't reply.

"My name's Jacob. What's yours?"

"Uh, Peter, sir," Peter mumbled.

The man smiled. "You liked what you saw."

Peter remained silent.

Jacob reached forward, touching Peter's chin. His fingers were wet with semen. "Such a pretty boy," he said. Then, leaning down, he whispered, "Let's hope we see each other again."

Jacob then put his lips on Peter's. Peter stood motionless as Jacob's tongue filled his mouth and his hands stroked his face. Then, abruptly, he pulled his mouth away.

"You'll be like us, now," Jacob said, putting a finger to Peter's lips.

He backed away, disappearing through the bushes.

Peter licked his lips, tasting the man juice from Jacob's fingers. When he looked through the bushes again, all three men were gone.

# # # # #

Peter lay on his bed, wearing only his underpants. His hands were tied to the headboard. "That oughta' keep you from abusin' yerself," Pa had said.

In the days since he had seen the men in the forest, Peter had been consumed with desire. Every nerve ending in his body seemed to come alive, as if anticipating – no, craving – erotic sensation. Peter's cock was perpetually hard. Pre-cum seeped from the head in a never-ending stream. Fueling his arousal were the images of the three men in the forest, the sight them freely devouring each other's cocks playing over and over in his mind.

His mother was the first to see the change. Peter had been jacking off in the barn, rubbing his cock and fingering his asshole, when his mother stepped in. Even when she screamed, he could not stop. His father had taken a belt to his ass, saying it was nothing compared to the punishment the Lord would give him if he didn't "respect" his body. But Peter was lost to his parents' demands. When he was supposed to be helping his father out in the fields, Peter ran away, stripping off his clothes as he went. Pa caught Peter as he was about to enter the forest in search of the three men.

They took him to the preacher, convinced he was possessed by a demon. The preacher agreed, shouting warnings of eternal damnation and begging Peter to pray for his own soul. "Suck my cock," Peter had whispered, grabbing his bulging crotch. The preacher's head looked as if it might explode. Pa swung his hand down hard across Peter's face.

Now they kept him in his bedroom, away from the rest of the family. Only his father entered the room, to feed him and take him to the outhouse. Still, the desire he felt – longing to take a cock into his mouth, to have a man's mouth on his dick, to feel a prick inside his ass – did not go away. It only got stronger.

It was such agonizing arousal that kept him awake now while the rest of the house slept. Peter pulled on the ropes that bound his wrists and shifted his weight, though he already knew any attempts to get comfortable were futile. He closed his eyes. When he opened them a man was standing there, the moonlight shining on his long hair. It was the man from the forest, the tall, slender one. The one who – Peter shivered at the memory – fed his long, stiff dick into Jacob's mouth.

Now he was in Peter's room, dressed in a billowing cotton shirt and dark trousers. He was smiling at Peter.

"So this is why we haven't seen you," he said, his voice soft and light. He approached the bed. "Jacob said we might have to come to you."

Peter wanted the man to strip off his clothes and let him suck his cock and tongue his ass. He wanted the man to spread his legs apart and fuck him. But before Peter could voice his desires his visitor placed a finger on his lips, urging Peter to be silent.

"I'm John," he said. "I'm here to take you home."

He pulled a small bottle out of his pocket and removed the cork. "Drink this before I untie you. It'll help you relax."

John held the bottle to his lips, and Peter drank. The bitter elixir affected him immediately. Peter felt his body go limp. The arousal that tormented him was fading.

"I've got a horse outside," John explained, untying the ropes around Peter's wrists. "Just keep quiet and we can be out of here without anyone knowing you're gone 'til morning."

They crept out of Peter's room and downstairs. The slightest sound seemed amplified. Peter paused after each step he took, expecting to see his father's angry face. But his family remained asleep.

Outside, John hopped on his horse and motioned for Peter to climb on behind him. Peter mounted the horse, though it was with some difficulty; he was suddenly very sleepy and lacked coordination. He wrapped his hands around John's waist and pressed his body against his back. John kicked the horse, and it started off in a quick trot across the fields, toward the forest and away from the house Peter had shared with his family.

Peter didn't look back.

When he awoke, Peter felt the warmth of the sun on his body and an even greater heat in his loins. His eyes opened and saw that he lay on a ratty quilt thrown on the ground near a pond. The splashing of water nearby prompted him to sit up, resting his weight on his elbows.

John and another man – the blond – climbed out of the pond and heading toward Peter. They were naked, their semi-hard cocks bouncing as they walked. Peter reached down and stroked his dick through the thin cloth of his underwear.

"Sleep well?" John asked as they approached. Both men were smiling.

"Where am I?" Peter asked, barely lifting his gaze from their pricks to John's face.

John knelt down beside him. "You're free," he said, reaching out and stroking Peter's long, honey-colored locks. Peter looked at him longingly.

The blond man sat on the other side of him. He touched Peter's shoulder, and then rubbed his hands across Peter's smooth, firm chest. Peter reached out, clumsily grabbing at the blond's torso, his fingers running over the cords of muscle that bulged beneath his tan skin. The blond giggled.

"I think he likes you, Ian," John said, looking into the young man's eyes as he said it. He leaned in, opened his mouth and clasped his moist mouth over the Peter's.

Peter embraced John, pulling him closer. He felt Ian's mouth on one of his hard nipples, and his hands pulling at his underwear. Peter kissed John all the more urgently.

Ian shucked off Peter's underwear and took hold of Peter's cock, his fingers tracing its length. His touch was light and delicate, handling Peter's dick as though it were fragile. Ian's mouth moved down Peter's torso, his tongue playfully flicking his bellybutton as it glided down. Soon, Peter felt Ian's breath on his aching cock. Then ...

"Oh, YES!" Peter nearly shrieked as Ian's mouth closed over his dick. The feeling was beyond his imagination. Ian's mouth was wet and warm. His tongue lapped at the crown of his cock then slid down the shaft.

Nearly frantic with desire, Peter reached for John's rod, now fully erect and wanting attention. He curled his fist around the throbbing shaft and sighed contentedly, savoring the feel of the organ in his hand.

John rose to his knees. "Suck it," he said, aiming his cock at Peter's lips.

Peter carefully took John's dick between his lips. It filled his mouth completely. He nudged the tip with his tongue. It tasted faintly of salt.

"That's it," John sighed, running his fingers though Peter's hair. "Try and swallow it all."

He tried, nearly gagging. His attention to John's prick began to waver, though, as the pleasurable feelings humming through his own cock grew more intense. Ian sucked his dick in full strokes, taking it deeper and deeper down his throat. Each time he dove down on his cock, a stronger wave of pleasure shoot through Peter's body until he could hold back no longer.

His small, muscular body was wracked by involuntary contractions. He leaned back, letting John's prick slide out of his mouth. In a series of small, quick spasms, he emptied his load into Ian's mouth. He looked down and saw his cream splashing onto Ian's tongue and face, gasping at the sight. Ian closed his mouth over Peter's hypersensitive cock and sucked on it, making the young man squirm. Then his body relaxed.

Yet he still was not satisfied.

Ian stretched out beside Peter, giving him a kiss. Peter could taste himself on Ian's lips. John leaned down, and his and Ian's tongues danced before Peter's eyes, touching and curling like two pink little snakes.

Ian got up on his knees and John did likewise. The two men hovered over Peter, their cocks arching over his face like drawn swords. Peter raised his head and, taking hold of each rod in each of his hands, steered them into his mouth one at a time. They moaned and thrust their hips, delighting in the feel of Peter's eager, hot tongue.

"Keep that up, and he'll be worn out before noon," said a familiar voice.

Jacob was in center of the pond, leisurely swimming toward them, his sly smile visible from the shore. As he reached the shallow part of the pond, Jacob began to walk toward them, his body rising from the water's surface with each step. Peter was transfixed by the sight of him, and moistened his lips when Jacob's enormous cock came into view.

He stopped several feet from the bank, the water at his knees. Looking directly at Peter, he motioned for him to come forward. Peter rose and stepped into the cool water, walking toward Jacob in an almost dreamlike state.

When Peter stopped, inches away, Jacob seized him, drawing Peter into his massive arms. He kissed him roughly, his hands cupping Peter's ass and pressing Peter's body against his. Peter ran his hands down Jacob's back; he ground his hips against Jacob's body, feeling his cock rub against the older man's.

Jacob pulled away, looking into Peter's eyes. His piercing gaze told Peter what was expected of him, and he sank obediently to his knees.

His cock was longer and thicker than John's or Ian's. Peter tried to close his hand around it, but his fingers would not touch, and he had to stretch his lips wide to fit it into his mouth. Slowly, Peter sucked Jacob's dick in long, deliberate gulps, eager to swallow as much of his fleshy tool as he was able.

A low, rumbling groan leaked from Jacob's lips. He closed his eyes and he tilted his head back while thrusting his hips forward, sending his cock deeper into Peter's throat. Peter played with Jacob's balls, occasionally letting the heavy orbs roll over his tongue. Jacob's groans grew louder.

"Get ready, boy," Jacob growled. "Daddy's gonna feed you ..."

Making a noise that sounded like the roar of an angry bear, Jacob unleashed his load, his warm spunk spilling over Peter's lips and dribbling down his chin. Peter lapped it up, enjoying the bittersweet taste of the older man's juice.

Jacob helped Peter to his feet, wrapping him in a tight embrace. Jacob's hands fell on Peter's ass, kneading his pert butt cheeks as the kissed. Then, swept away by a need that he could neither explain nor deny, Peter hopped up and locked his legs around the man's waist. Jacob cupped Peter's ass in his big hands and carried him to the bank.

John and Ian cleared a space on the quilt for them. Jacob set Peter down and stood back up, looking down at the horny young man. John and Jacob exchanged a long, probing kiss that Ian interrupted with a kiss of his own. But Jacob wanted Peter, and he quickly brushed the two other men aside and joined their newest family member on the quilt.

As Ian had done earlier, Jacob's mouth wandered down the length of Peter's body, exploring his bare skin with his tongue. A warm pleasure flowed through Peter's body, turning white-hot when Jacob swallowed his cock. He sucked it in leisurely gulps, his tongue swirling around the shaft and crown. Peter's body trembled with raw excitement.

But Jacob didn't stop at Peter's cock. He forced Peter's legs up in the air and apart. Suddenly, Peter felt Jacob's wet tongue diving between his ass cheeks, burrowing deeper with each plunge. He nearly passed out when Jacob's tongue forced its way past his anal ring and into his virgin hole.

"That oughta' loosen you up," Jacob said wryly, sitting up. "Now turn over."

Peter did as he was told, getting on his hands and knees in front of big, brutish man. Jacob swabbed his asshole a few more times before sliding a finger inside. Peter gasped as the man's index finger twitched inside his chute. Then there were two fingers, then three.

John and Ian knelt in front of him, holding their rigid cocks to his lips. "Let's finish what we started," John said. Peter opened his mouth and John inched his rod past his lips and over his tongue.

Suddenly, Peter stiffened and let out a muffled cry. Jacob was entering his ass, his huge dick stretching his asshole to its very limits. Jacob slowly eased his cock inside Peter's hole, but his delicacy did little to lessen the initial pain.

"Stop, please," Peter sobbed, his plea not making it past the man-meat filling his mouth.

Jacob had worked the entire length of his cock into Peter's ass, until Peter could feel Jacob's bristly pubic hair brush against his butt cheeks. Jacob began to thrust his hips back and forth, sliding his dick in and out of Peter's chute in careful, controlled movements.

The excruciating pain gave way to excruciating pleasure. As Jacob pounded his ass, Peter once again concentrated on sucking John's cock. Ian cut in, his throbbing dick demanding attention. Then both men had their dongs in Peter's hungry mouth.

Jacob fucked him harder. He punctuated each thrust with a quick slap on Peter's tender butt. The sharp sting of his hand against his skin heightened his arousal, strangely, making Peter writhe as the rapturous sensations radiated throughout his body. He reached between his legs and pulled at his swollen cock, working himself into an even greater state of lusty pleasure.

With a final shove, Jacob shot his second load. Peter felt Jacob's warm jism filling his gut as his ass muscles milked the man's dick dry.

John's and Ian's grunts and groans became more insistent. Soon, their cocks erupted, filling his mouth and splattering his face.

Jacob pulled his massive rod out of Peter's asshole, leaving a gaping emptiness in his wake. For all the pain he endured initially Peter was surprised that he missed having Jacob's fat cock buried deep inside him. He couldn't wait for the older man to fuck him again. And again.

Jacob rolled him over on his back, the young man resting his head against John's knees.

He took Peter's cock in one of his big hands and began jacking him off briskly. The young man was soon gasping for air, breathless with ecstasy. John stroked Peter's hair and Ian rubbed his chest.

The high-pitched squeal that emanated from his mouth seemed to be made by someone else. Peter's body shuddered and convulsed as his thick, syrupy, load exploded from his cock and fell onto his torso in shiny white ribbons.

Then all was still.

The four of them stretched out on the quilt, their bodies pressed against one another as the sun shot its rays through the trees and onto their satiated flesh.

"Glad to have you in the family," Jacob whispered in Peter's ear, and Peter knew he'd never leave the forest again.

Shared Secrets

"Oh, *yeah!*" Clem moaned, his body arching backward above Lang's. His arms stretched taut behind him in two thick, muscled columns. His ass hovered above Lang's lips, awaiting another invasion by his lover's enthusiastic tongue.

The tip of Lang's tongue lightly grazed Clem's hole, then ferociously stabbed into his chute. Clem cried out, grinding his butt into Lang's face. Lang clamped his hands onto the fleshy globes of Clem's ass, prying his buttcheeks apart and lapping his tender rosebud.

Carefully Clem shifted, so his knees bore his weight. His hard cock was dripping pre-cum like a leaky faucet. He began to stroke it, waves of pleasure making him light-headed. "Oh baby," he groaned, "you got me so hot. Don't think I can hold back any longer."

Usually, this was Lang's signal to ease up and let Clem lavish some attention on him. But Lang continued gnawing Clem's asshole, refusing, this time, to let his lover choreograph their sex. If he was on the verge of shooting his load, so be it.

Clem took his hand away from his dick, hoping to prolong the moment by eliminating the extra stimulus. Lang, though, was not going to let that happen. He quickly reached around Clem's waist and grabbed his cock, picking up where his lover left off. Clem tried to think non-sexual thoughts – he needed to clean the apartment, the McGraw project at work was due next week – but to no avail. How could he not think about sex with Lang licking his ass and pulling his cock?

Trying to stave off an orgasm soon became futile. Clem's muscular body trembled as he let out a guttural cry, his face contorted into a mask of extreme exertion, like he was trying to bench-press a refrigerator. Thick streams of jism splattered Lang's torso and the sheets. His skin tingled and he felt dizzy. His position above Lang became precarious as his arms began to shake. Quickly, he rolled off onto the bed before he lost his balance and fell on Lang's face and broke his nose.

Lang quickly got up on his knees and straddled his boyfriend's torso. Clem smiled, admiring Lang's physique: the bulging biceps, pecs that were two slabs of solid muscle, the carpet of dark hair covering his chest and abs, and that huge cock jutting up from between his legs.

Lang dragged his fingers through the pools of cum that collected in the valleys between the hard muscles of Clem's stomach. Using Clem's juice as lubricant, Lang jacked off, his hand moving up and down the thick shaft of his cock in long, luxurious strokes. "I'm ... gonna ... shoot. I'm ... gonna ... *shoot!*" Lang chanted between short breaths, his eyes closed and his head thrown back.

Spiraling ribbons of cream erupted from Lang's swollen dick, raining down on Clem's shoulder and chin. Lang's body jerked as the last few drops of jism splashed down on Clem's torso.

He collapsed on top of Clem. The lovers shared a deep kiss before Lang rolled over to the vacant side of the bed. They lay still, enjoying the heady afterglow of truly satisfying sex before they headed to the shower to wash away the sweat and cum that glazed their bodies.

The ringing phone interrupted their post-coital languor, startling them back to reality. Clem let out an annoyed groan and picked up the receiver of the bedside phone. "Hello," he said impatiently. Then, in a lighter tone, "*Oh, hi!* How're you doing? No, you didn't wake me up ..."

Lang listened to Clem's side of the conversation, trying to figure out whom he was talking to, until his attention returned to Clem's body. Their relationship was relatively young – they'd been together scarcely six months and had only lived together for two – but Lang couldn't imagine ever growing tired of looking at Clem. He admired the rounded contours of Clem's chest, how the modest patch of brown hair between his pecs tapered to a thin line of fur that guided the eye down the firm ridges of his abdomen, flowering out around his cock and balls. Usually, Lang's eyes stopped at the crotch, but when he allowed them to continue their tour of his boyfriend's body, he had to appreciate the tight, muscular legs that were in perfectly proportion to the rest of his well-built body.

"Uh, sure. When? Um, that's fine. How long will you be staying?"

Lang snapped out of his reverie. Sounded like they were going to have a houseguest.

"Okay. Do you remember how to get here?" Lang watched Clem as he spoke into the phone, giving directions to whoever was on the other end of the line. He smiled, noticing a small drop of coagulating cum clinging to his lover's clean-shaven chin, just below his lower lip.

"All right, then. We'll see you next week. Take care." Clem hung up the phone.

"So, who's our houseguest?" Lang asked immediately.

"My brother. He'll be visiting us next week for spring break."

"For how long?" Lang asked, irritation creeping into his voice. A houseguest would undoubtedly put a damper on their sex life.

Clem let out a defeated sigh. "The *full* week."

"Does he ...?"

"No, he doesn't. So as far as he's concerned, we're just roommates."

Lang scowled. "Roommates who share the same bed?"

"It's a two-bedroom apartment," Clem replied flatly. "I'll take the spare bedroom, and Cliff can sleep on the sofa."

"Cliff and Clem? How precious. I hope he's worth my going back into the closet for," Lang sneered.

"Don't make this any more difficult than it needs to be. I'll tell him, just not ... now."

Lang sighed. "I'll play along this time, for you. But don't think I'm okay with it."

"Look, for what it's worth, we don't have to be *celibate* for a week," Clem said, leaning over to give Lang a quick peck on the cheek. "After all, he's got to sleep sometime."

Cliff arrived at their cramped midtown apartment the following weekend. As Clem headed for the front door to let his brother in, he made one last visual sweep of the apartment, making sure he hadn't overlooked any "incriminating" evidence when he "straightened up" the apartment. No gay porn DVDs lying on top of the TV, no rainbow paraphernalia, no posters of scantily clad men on the walls. Satisfied, he opened the door.

Clem's brother strode in, dressed in a Florida State T-shirt and loose-fitting khaki shorts, topping the ensemble off with a baseball cap. He immediately dropped an overstuffed gym back and large canvas suitcase onto the floor. "Hey, how're ya' doin'?" Cliff drawled, giving Clem a quick, brotherly hug.

Lang stood in the background, watching as the brothers greeted each other. He couldn't help but appraise Cliff's appearance. The brothers had similar facial features – same deep-set eyes, same full lips, same squared chin – but these features were softened on the younger brother. Cliff was cute rather than handsome. Still, cute was very nice to look at, and Lang would be looking at him for a full week. Yet there was something about Cliff's appearance that gave Lang an eerie feeling of *déjà vu*.

"Cliff, this is my *roommate*, Lang," Clem introduced them.

Clem's brother stepped forward, offering his hand.

"Nice to meet ya … *Lang*?"

"Short for Langston. My parents are kind of pretentious," Lang joked as they shook hands. Then their eyes met and Lang saw the same flash of recognition in Cliff's eyes that he knew was mirrored in his own.

"You look awfully familiar," he said. "You ever been down to Florida?"

"Um, not in quite a while," Lang answered slowly, beginning to realize where their paths had crossed …

It was eight months ago, while he was attending that marketing seminar in Tallahassee, at the queer bar next to the hotel. He was sitting at the bar nursing a gin and tonic when this cute young man took the stool next to him. *Has to be at least twenty-one to be in here, but this guy's twenty-first birthday couldn't have been too long ago. Must be a college student*, Lang surmised. Lang was twenty-six, and he felt like a dirty old man when he lustily regarded the boy's lean, athletic physique, displayed to its best advantage in a tight T-shirt and even tighter jeans.

They sat next to one another for several minutes, not speaking, though Lang sneaked glances at the college kid when he thought he wasn't looking. Then the guy tapped him on the arm. "'Scuse me. I need to use the rest room. I'll buy you a drink if you save my seat for me." Lang agreed, saying no drink was necessary. He watched as the guy wove his way through the growing crowd, admiring the guy's firm ass in those faded blue jeans.

When the student returned, they began a conversation. The guy was a junior who didn't come the bar much at all for fear his classmates might find out. Lang asked him to dance, and they undulated on the dance floor together, their bodies getting closer and closer. Lang embraced the young man and kissed him. The college kid was resistant at first, but soon opened his mouth to let Lang's tongue inside. They ended up making out in a dark corner of the bar for some time before Lang asked if the guy wanted to go back to his hotel room. The invitation was accepted quickly, as if it might be rescinded if he pondered it too long.

Their sex was urgent. The young guy was obviously inexperienced but eager to please, trying to take as much of Lang's cock as his virgin mouth would allow. Lang could feel the man's body shaking anxiously as he kissed and licked and nibbled every square inch of it. "Don't be nervous. Just relax," Lang had said several times. He asked the college kid if he could fuck him, and the guy said yes. Lang tried to be gentle, but could tell that his young trick was unprepared for the initial shock of a stiff prick invading his ass. He cried out in pain as Lang buried his cock inside him. Still, he didn't ask Lang to stop.

The student lay on his back, his feet resting on Lang's shoulders as Lang rammed his dick into that tight hole. Lang stroked the guy's swollen cock as he fucked him, and they came almost simultaneously.

And then their night together ended. The kid got dressed quickly, saying he had to be up early the next morning. They parted with a brief but probing kiss, their shared experience to become nothing more than a fine, faded memory ...

Until now, when it all came flooding back, that trick from Lang's past standing in his living room. His boyfriend's brother; what were the odds? Neither of them had changed much in appearance. Cliff's hair was shorter, and Lang had grown a Van Dyke, but these changes weren't enough to disguise the past they shared. Suddenly, pretending to be Clem's roommate seemed the least of Lang's problems.

The first couple days of Cliff's visit were uneventful. On the night of Cliff's arrival, the two brothers stayed up late talking about old times and complaining about their parents. The second day, Lang and Clem drove Cliff around Atlanta, pointing out various clubs he might want to go to while he was in town. Of course, Clem was only pointing out straight clubs, but neither Cliff nor Lang dared correct him. They went out to dinner then returned to the apartment where the brothers talked some more. Again, it was late when they all went to bed. Clem and Lang managed to sneak a conversation while Cliff was in the bathroom brushing his teeth.

"I'm really too tired to do anything tonight," Clem whispered. "Maybe he'll do some club hopping during the week, give us some privacy."

Yet the next day, it was Lang and Cliff who got the privacy. Lang came home from work to find a message on the answering machine from Clem, asking Lang to call him at the office.

"What is it?" Lang asked when Clem picked up the phone.

"Look, I'm really sorry, but I've got to work late on this damned McGraw project if it's going to be ready by deadline. Do you mind entertaining Cliff for me?"

"Um, no problem."

"Is he there?" Clem asked.

"No, I just walked in. He must be out or something." Just then, he heard the bathroom door open. Cliff appeared in the living room wrapped in a towel. Lang immediately averted his eyes, focusing intently on an end table.

"Well, I'll see you later this evening, probably around eight. You two have fun. Love you."

This was Lang's cue to say, "Love you, too." But with Cliff standing there, he said: "Okay, see you tonight."

Lang looked over at Cliff, now standing next to his luggage at the opposite end of the sofa from where Lang sat. Cliff ran a comb through his light brown hair, a seemingly unnecessary gesture given that his hair was clipped close to his skull, with only enough length on top to allow for a few wisps to fall across his forehead.

"How's it goin'?" Cliff asked casually.

"Uh, okay. 'Fraid Clem has to work late, so it's just me. You want to go out to dinner?"

Lang was trying to be nonchalant, trying not to stare. Cliff, however, was hard to ignore, especially when he was only wearing a towel. Lang let his eyes drift from Cliff's face to his taut, muscular chest, down his compact torso, following the trail of silky, brown hairs that started at his navel and disappeared beneath the towel.

"Sounds good," Cliff said, dropping his comb onto the coffee table. "Where're we going?"

"Hmmm? You like Chinese?"

Cliff made a face. "How 'bout Mexican instead?"

Lang agreed, even though he wasn't in the mood for Mexican, not to mention that there was a dearth of good Mexican restaurants in their neighborhood.

"Just give me a few minutes to get dressed," Cliff said, pulling some clothes out of his suitcase.

And then the towel came off.

Lang looked away, but not without first getting a good eyeful. Cliff's flaccid dick was about six inches long, curving slightly to the left. His balls were nearly hairless, dangling low between his legs. The sight, though brief, was enough to cause Lang's own cock to stir. Standing up from the sofa, he announced: "Well, I'll give you some privacy."

"Doesn't matter," Cliff said, stepping into a pair of olive green boxers. "I've got nothing you haven't seen before."

Lang left the room, anyway, wondering if "nothing you haven't seen before" was meant to be as suggestive as he was taking it.

Dinner went smoothly enough, though Lang felt nervous without Clem along as a buffer. Every time Clem's brother opened his mouth to speak, Lang expected him to mention that night in Tallahassee. But the topic didn't come up – until they went to The Duke for drinks afterwards.

"I think I remember where I met *you*," Cliff said as they settled into a booth near the back of the dimly lit bar. He had an impish grin on his face. "Do you?"

Lang's heart seized up in his chest. At first he considered feigning ignorance, but thought better of it. "Yes," he answered softly. "That bar in Tallahassee, next to the hotel I was staying at."

Cliff's grin became a full smile. "You remembered!" Then, in a flash of panic: "You didn't tell my brother, did you?"

"Jesus Christ, *no!*"

A sigh of relief. "Good. He doesn't need to know about … what I am. I know I should tell him, but every time I plan to do it I chicken out."

"He might be more accepting than you think," Lang offered.

"Does he know about you?"

"I think he has a good idea," Lang answered carefully. "We've never really discussed it, though."

They were silent for a moment. Then Cliff leaned forward. "So, when do you think Clem's gonna get home?" he asked, his eyes brimming with lascivious intentions.

This was no longer the nervous closet case he'd deflowered less than a year ago, Lang thought, feeling his face grow hot. That Cliff was coming on to him was unnerving enough, but even more unsettling was that Lang realized he might not be strong enough to fight the temptation.

"I'm glad you reminded me," Lang answered quickly, gulping down his cocktail. "Cliff is going to be home any minute, and I'm sure he'll want to see you. No need for me to monopolize all your time."

When they got back to the apartment, Clem was there scarfing down a microwave dinner. "You guys have fun?" he asked through a mouthful of Salisbury steak.

"Oh, yeah," Lang replied breezily. "Dinner and some drinks afterwards."

Cliff, who had grown quiet after Lang ignored his advance, excused himself to use the bathroom.

The moment Cliff was out of the room Clem winked and said: "Tonight."

Lang responded with a wan smile, too preoccupied with Cliff to get worked up over sex with his boyfriend.

When Cliff came out of the bathroom, his brother did his best to persuade him to experience Atlanta's nightlife, even offering to let his younger brother use his car. But Cliff was less than enthused. "Maybe tomorrow," he said. "Think I'll just hang out here tonight."

The three of them stayed up until eleven o'clock. Clem was the first to announce he was going to bed. Not trusting himself alone with Cliff, Lang also excused himself.

In the privacy of "his" bedroom, Lang stripped and settled in beneath the covers. He tried to pass the time reading a horror novel, but he couldn't concentrate. He wondered how long Cliff would be awake. He was really getting horny, only it was Cliff, not Clem, who had him worked up. His cock grew rock-hard as he remembered that night in

Tallahassee. Then seeing Cliff naked earlier this evening … Lang hoped Cliff went to sleep soon so Clem could sneak across the hall.

He was about to give up waiting for Clem when he heard a light tapping at his door. It was nearly midnight. He hopped out from beneath the covers, fluffed the pillows and arranged himself on the bed, naked and ready for sex. "Come in," he said seductively.

The door opened. It wasn't his boyfriend.

"Oh, hi!" Lang said, trying to sound pleasantly surprised rather than mortified. He quickly grabbed the sheet and pulled it over his naked body. "I was just getting ready to go to sleep," he added, though no one with a functioning brain stem would believe that line.

Cliff stood at the foot of the bed. He wore only the olive green boxers Lang saw him stepping into earlier. He could tell by the tent Cliff was pitching in his shorts that Clem's brother wasn't just here to say goodnight. Finding Lang reclining nude in bed with a raging hard-on did little to discourage him.

"Hey," Cliff said sheepishly. There was a partial grin on his face. "Couldn't sleep."

"There's still some wine in the fridge," Lang suggested in a tone so artificial it could cause cancer in lab rats. "Couple glasses should relax you."

Cliff, though, would not be dissuaded. He walked over to the side of the bed and sat down next to Lang. "I had something else in mind." To bring his point home, he picked up Lang's hand and guided it to his crotch.

Lang got a good feel of Cliff's stiffening cock beneath his boxers before pulling his hand away.

"Um, well, I …" His face grew warm. He needed to tell Cliff he was in a relationship. No need to mention that relationship was with Clem, he reasoned. But, god, he was so tempted. He desperately wanted to rip those boxers off Cliff's taut body, bury his face between his firm legs and suck that hot cock. Then he wanted to slide his own dick between those high, round ass-cheeks, like he did back in Tallahassee.

Yet, he felt as if he were cheating on Clem for merely *thinking* these things. He certainly couldn't act on them.

"Don't worry about Clem," Cliff said softly, leaning forward. "We'll be real quiet. He'll never know."

At that, Cliff kissed him. His tongue darted inside his mouth, dueling with Lang's. Lang knew he should push him away, but couldn't summon the necessary will power. Cliff pulled at the bed covers, exposing Lang's muscular body. He ran his hand down the furry terrain of Lang's torso, coming to a stop at Lang's cock. Cliff's fingers circled the throbbing organ, massaging it roughly. His thumb rubbed across the slit, toying with the beads of pre-cum oozing from it.

Lang was unable to resist. He put his hands on Cliff's back, letting his fingers gently glide over his smooth skin, down to Cliff's waist. He tugged at Cliff's boxers, pulling them down and exposing that pert butt, tracing the crack with his fingers, nudging his tight asshole. Cliff moaned softly.

Cliff stood and kicked off his boxers. His cock jutted forward, fully erect. He hopped on top of Lang, grinding his butt against Lang's aching prick. "You're so hot," he whispered, pressing his lips against Lang's mouth.

Lang's heart beat furiously. *I shouldn't be doing this*, he told himself as he reached for Cliff's dick. *We've gone too far already*, he thought, his hand still gliding up and down Cliff's cock. *Got to stop it!* his inner voice shouted as he rubbed his prick against the crack of Cliff's ass.

"Look," Lang gasped, trying to push Cliff away. "We shouldn't be ... oh, yeah ... doing this. I'm in ... I'm in a relation ..."

As if on cue, there was a soft rapping on the door.

For a fraction of a second, Cliff and Lang froze. They looked at one another, their expressions saying the same thing: *Oh, shit!*

Lang finally pushed Cliff away. "Closet!" he hissed. Cliff was across the room in three bounding steps, opening the closet just as the doorknob turned. Clem entered the bedroom only a millisecond after Cliff sequestered himself.

Clem wore only a pair of white cotton briefs, the outline of his semi-hard dick clearly visible. "You sure know how to make a guy feel welcome," he said, a devious grin on his face as he eyed Lang's naked body.

Lang covered his panic with a smile. "I was beginning to think you fell asleep."

"Can't sleep when I'm horny," Clem purred, walking toward the bed.

Your brother has the same problem, Lang thought. "Speaking of sleep, are you sure our house guest is dozing?"

"Living room light is out. Unless he's just sitting in the dark, I think we're safe," Clem said, sitting down on the mattress. "We'll try to be quiet, just in case."

Clem leaned forward and placed a soft kiss on Lang's lips. Lang was hesitant to respond. How could he go through with this knowing Clem's brother was hiding in the closet? It was one thing for Cliff to find out that he and Clem were more than roommates, but finding out like *this*? But he couldn't very well tell Clem he was too tired or not in the mood or had a headache. Not when he was reclining naked on the bed, his cock hard as steel and dripping pre-cum. He was just going to have to risk damaging Cliff's psyche.

Lang's lips parted and Clem's tongue slid inside. He ran his hands down Clem's back, going directly to his ass. Clem nibbled the side of Lang's neck then traced his ear with his tongue. Lang slipped his hands beneath the waistband of Clem's briefs, kneading his muscled butt. Clem pinched one of Lang's hard, distended nipples, whispering, "I want you so bad."

Clem's mouth traveled south, kissing and biting Lang's body on the way down, until he reached Lang's dick. He nibbled at the insides of Lang's thighs and then kissed his hard, flat belly on either side of his pulsing cock. He was fond of teasing Lang this way, sometimes asking playfully: "Am I missing anything?" This both aroused and annoyed Lang, lying there wondering when Clem would finally plant those kisses on his dick. Sometimes Clem stretched his patience so thin Lang would snap: "Just suck it, already!" He suspected this turned Clem on, hearing Lang demand a sex act.

"Suck my cock," Lang grunted tersely, grabbing the base of his dick and batting it against Clem's chin.

Clem chuckled. "Are you horny, baby?" he asked mockingly.

Lang wondered what Cliff was thinking, hearing this exchange. Then Clem took Lang's cock into his mouth, and he forgot all about Cliff hiding in the closet. Clem swirled his tongue around the cockhead, then eased the entire length of his rod into the warm, moist depths of his throat. Lang ran his fingers through Clem's soft, brown hair, holding his head in place while he thrust his cock deep into his mouth.

Clem's tongue prodded the plump head of Lang's prick. He then dragged his tongue down the length of the shaft, to Lang's balls. His tongue swirled around the plump spheres, hanging low in their fuzzy sac. His mouth moved lower still, toward the dark valley of Lang's ass.

Lang hoisted his legs up in the air, raising his asshole to Clem's face. No verbal prompting was necessary this time. Clem dove right in, lapping at Lang's pink hole. Lang moaned softly, then a sharp grunt escaped his lips as Clem forced the tip of his tongue past his tight sphincter.

"Ssshhhh! He'll hear us," Clem scolded.

If only you knew, Lang thought.

Clem continued eating Lang's ass, sliding his tongue deep inside his chute. He briefly returned to Lang's balls then moved back to his cock, swallowing it in quick, fierce gulps. Lang bit his lower lip to keep from crying out.

The cocksucking came to an abrupt stop, Clem sliding his body on top of Lang's. They kissed urgently, Clem grinding his crotch against Lang's dick. Lang tugged at Clem's briefs. "You're over-dressed," he whispered in his lover's ear.

Clem pushed himself up on his knees so that he was straddling his boyfriend. "What're you going to do about it?"

Lang knew precisely what to do about it. He scooted down the bed, sliding between Clem's legs, until his head was positioned beneath the swell of Clem's crotch. He raised his head to it, pressing his face against the soft mound of his balls and getting a whiff of his manly scent. Resting on one elbow, he was able to get his mouth on the tubular bulge of Clem's cock, prodding it with his tongue and tasting the salty pre-cum that had soaked through the cloth. He tugged at the waistband of Clem's underwear, eager to free the hard cock beneath.

"Let me help you," Clem offered, pulling his briefs down until they were stretched tight around his thighs. His cock leapt out as if spring-loaded. Lang went right to work, hungrily gulping down Clem's dick. It had only been three days since they last had sex, but Lang sucked Clem's dick as if they'd been abstinent for months.

Clem flopped down on the mattress and pulled off his briefs. The couple got into a sixty-nine position. Lang continued sucking his lover's cock, while Clem bowed his head between Lang's thighs and, once again, started licking his asshole.

Lang curled his fingers around Clem's prick, stroking the shaft as his tongue circled the head. He felt Clem's fingers against his hole, working a fingertip inside him, sliding the digit in and out of his ass.

"I want to fuck you," Clem said in a low voice. "Do you want me to fuck you?" He shoved his finger in deep.

"Yes," Lang whimpered.

"What?" Now he was thrusting two fingers into Lang's ass.

"You want me to shout it? I thought we were trying to be quiet."

Clem stretched his arm over to the bedside table, opening a drawer and blindly fumbling for lube and condoms. Lang rolled over on his back and watched as Clem tore open the condom's plastic wrapper with his teeth. He squirted a few drops of lubricant into the rubber and quickly rolled it over his throbbing cock. Clem squirted more lube into his hand and slid his fingers between Lang's buttcheeks.

"Ready for me?" Clem asked, his finger probing Lang's lubricated asshole.

Lang nodded, bringing his knees to his chest.

Gripping his sheathed cock, Clem pressed the head against Lang's puckered sphincter. Lang gritted his teeth as his boyfriend's dick pierced him. Slowly, Clem eased the length of his rod into Lang until his balls were resting against Lang's upturned ass. He started thrusting – gently at first, then picking up the pace as the pleasure increased. Lang put his hands on Clem's ass, digging his fingers into those muscular globes as Clem fucked him.

"Harder," Lang grunted between clenched teeth. "Fuck me hard!"

Clem fell forward, his body hovering over Lang's, his cock plowing Lang's ass at full throttle. The bed shook violently, the sound of creaking bedsprings filling the room. Clem seemed past worrying whether they would wake Cliff just as Lang was well past worrying about what psychological damage Cliff might suffer. They soon forgot about Cliff entirely, their grunts and groans growing loud enough to be heard throughout the apartment.

Clem spit into the palm of his hand and reached between Lang's thighs, curling his fingers around Lang's cock and jacking him off while fucking him.

"*Oh-God-oh-God-I'm gonna come!*" Lang panted, his body trembling.

Clem pounded his ass harder.

"I'm sooo – *oh!*" A pearly-white missile of jism hit Lang in the face, followed by less forceful spurts that splattered his chest and abdomen.

Clem immediately bent down to lick his boyfriend's syrupy cream off his face. Leaning back, he gripped Lang's thighs and pumped his cock in and out of Lang's hole at a furious pace. His body became rigid. His dug his fingers into Lang's thighs as he came, his copious load filling the condom. Once his balls were drained, he fell on top of Lang's in a heaving, sweaty heap. They lay there, silently, Clem's dick still buried in Lang's ass, their bodies tingling.

Lang looked over at the digital clock on the bedside table. The glowing red numbers read 1:26.

"Jesus Christ," he groaned, "seven thirty is going to come early."

Clem looked over at the clock as well. "Guess it's time to go to sleep." Ordinarily, this would just mean a hasty clean up and rolling into each other's arms. Now, with Cliff staying with them, it meant Clem had to return to the guestroom. Clem slid his softening cock out of Lang's ass and pulled off the cum-filled rubber, dropping it in a nearby wastebasket as he stepped off the bed.

He bent down to pick his underwear off the floor. "When did you get these?" Clem asked. He held up Cliff's olive green boxers.

"Uh, I forget. Last time I went shopping for clothes, I think," Lang answered, hoping Clem wouldn't grill him for more details or wonder why Lang had a pair of boxers when he preferred briefs.

He shrugged and dropped the boxers on the bed. "You'll have to wear them for me sometime. Boxers can be kind of sexy."

Clem stepped into his briefs then leaned down to give Lang one final goodnight kiss. "Love you," he whispered before backing toward the door.

"I love you, too."

Once Clem was out of the room, Lang grabbed a washcloth from a drawer in the bedside table, glad that he had made it a practice to keep a supply of cum rags handy. ("But do they have to be our *good* washcloths?" Clem had once complained.) He mopped up the drying jizz glazing his face and torso. Once cleaned up, he took a deep breath and walked over to the closet door.

Cliff didn't look at him when the door opened. "Look," Lang said consolingly, "Clem wasn't ready to tell …"

The younger man nodded, stepping out of the closet with his shoulders hunched, his eyes downcast. "Sorry," he mumbled before shuffling out of the bedroom, not even bothering to retrieve his boxers.

Lang felt like a class-A shit. Here Clem and Lang had played the charade of being roommates to spare Cliff's feelings, when ultimately it did more harm than good. He was about to shut the closet door, then hesitated. Something was streaming down the inside of the door, barely noticeable against the white paint. Was it…?

Holy shit! Cliff had jacked off in the closet, listening to Lang have sex with his brother. Maybe he had watched, too. The idea was simultaneously nauseating and arousing. He tried to visualize Cliff, in the closet stroking that mouth-watering cock of his. Lang came very close to sucking that cock tonight, and he wondered how far he'd have gone if Clem hadn't knocked on the door when he did.

The important thing, he told himself, *was he'd done nothing*. He was still the faithful boyfriend. However, he'd be having his way with Cliff's hard body in his fantasies for quite some time.

For the next few days of his visit, Cliff spent more time out of the apartment. He finally went club hopping, first consulting with Lang to learn which were the choicest gay clubs in town. On Friday, when Lang returned home from work, he found the brothers sitting at the kitchen table, drinking beer. Both wore broad smiles.

"Guess what?" Clem beamed.

"Can't imagine. What?" Lang asked shortly. He hated dealing with cheerful people when he'd been at work all day.

"I came out to Cliff. He *knows*: About me. About us."

"Good for you," Lang said, managing a smile.

"Wanna know what else? This is too funny."

"Doubt Mom and Dad will think so," Cliff said.

"Cliff's queer too!" Clem burst out laughing. "Guess the pressure's on Chloe to provide grandchildren."

"Chloe?" Lang asked.

"Our sister," Cliff explained.

Cliff, Clem and Chloe? What kind of sick fucks were their parents?

"I got home early from work," Clem said, "and Cliff says he has something to tell me. And all I could do was laugh. He gets pissed, but then I explain it's okay, 'cause I'm a homo, too. We've been sharing secrets all afternoon."

Sharing? Lang's heart skipped a beat. Exactly what all was shared? He looked over at Cliff. Cliff caught his gaze and smiled, giving him a wink to let him know *their* secret is safe.

"That's great," Lang said, this time with genuine enthusiasm. "We should celebrate."

"Yeah, we should," Clem said loudly. Obviously, he was not drinking his first beer of the evening. "How 'bout a three-way?"

Clem roared with laughter, but Cliff and Lang looked at each other in horror. For a split second, Lang thought about explaining they had come close enough to that already. But he didn't. Some secrets were best kept.

Lang said: "How about dinner instead."

The Catch

"You wanna fuck me?"

Noisy as the bar was, we heard the question clear as day. Still, Darren said, "What?"

The guy repeated the question: "You want to fuck me?"

Cary asked, "Which one of us you interested in?"

The guy wore the sly grin of a soap opera vixen. "All three of you."

Darren might as well have been speaking for the three of us when he tossed back the remainder of his cocktail and whooped, "Hell, yeah!" Before the guy invited himself to join our table, Darren had been lamenting his recent dry spell, telling us he wanted to break off the relationship he'd developed with his left hand. (Cary said, "I didn't know you're a lefty.") But we'd have taken the guy up on his offer even if we were all getting laid seven nights a week. The guy – think he said his name was Tim – was nothing short of stunning, possessing the face and physique you stared at, so you could commit every detail to memory for when you jacked-off later. And you were content to beat off to the memory because the fantasy was all he'd allow you to have.

Yet here he was, offering himself to us.

It wasn't until we were following him out of the bar that I had second thoughts. Darren, Cary and I are not trolls, but we don't have guys in Tim's league (or age group – he was in his mid-twenties while we were all clinging to thirty-something) throwing themselves at us, certainly not within ten minutes of introductions. With Darren and our shared trick a few paces ahead, I asked Cary, "Do you think this is a set up? You know, like he gets us somewhere and then some big guys jump out and rob us?"

"Been watching a lot of crime shows lately, Graham?"

"I just think it's too good to be true. There's got to be a catch. By the way, what's his name? Is it Tim?"

Cary said, "I thought he said Jim."

Tim/Jim told us he lived nearby, and he wasn't kidding. He lived in the condos across the street from the bar, his place on the fourth floor. He's either got a rich family, a sugar daddy, or deals drugs, I thought as I checked out the living room, the décor on the colder side of chic. I saw some photos displayed on a glass shelf, but Tim/Jim intercepted me before I could get a closer look. "I'll start the tour in the bedroom," he said, taking my hand and leading me down the hall. Darren and Cary followed.

The bedroom was on the small side, dominated by a large platform bed. Lube and condoms sat out on a night table; Tim – I'm sure that's what he said his name was – confident he wouldn't return home alone. A large window facing the west afforded a great view of the city, but we were too enraptured by the view less than five feet in front of us. Tim stripped off his shirt, stretching his arms out wide and puffing out his chest, letting us admire the tight muscles that girded his slim torso. Darren, squeezing his own crotch, whistled and said, "Oh, yeah, baby." Cary and I, though less vocal about it, shared Darren's sentiment. Tim stood there, one hand lazily tracing the ridges of his hard abs while the three of us waited for his designer jeans to come off.

He said, "I'd have an easier time deciding whose cock I wanted to suck first if you guys were naked."

Darren, Cary and I undressed like our clothes were on fire. Once nude, we stood before Tim, letting him inspect our goods. I felt self-conscious, this being the first time Darren, Cary and I had ever been naked in front of each other. We gave each other sideways glances, but mostly, we kept our eyes on our host, wondering whose cock would get the honor of the first blowjob. Darren was fully hard, his cock vibrating in the air, and for this reason alone I thought he'd be the first blessed with Tim's favors; Cary and I only had semis.

Instead, Tim went to me.

"You seem kind of nervous," he said, curling a hand around my dick. "I'm going to relax you."

Tim leaned in, pressing his lips to mine. His kiss was surprisingly delicate – sweet, almost. Even the way his tongue skimmed my lower lip was more playful than lusty.

That changed when he got on his knees. My prick turned to stone the moment it was enveloped by Tim's velvety mouth. I looked down, watching him take my cock in hungry gulps, then closed my eyes and tilted my head back, enjoying how his tongue massaged my shaft, telling him if felt so good.

I felt the nearness of other bodies and opened my eyes. Cary and Darren standing on either side of me, the three of us making a tight semi-circle around Tim. Cary put a hand on my butt, giving me a mischievous look. Funny, but until Cary put his hand on my ass, I didn't consider the possibility that I'd be messing around with my two friends as well. After all, if we'd been interested in each other "that way" wouldn't we have played together sooner?

I looked over at Darren, engrossed in watching Tim suck my cock. My eyes traveled down his furry, muscled torso, down to his thick, drooling dong. Before the night is over, I thought, I wanted to suck Darren's dick, while I had the opportunity. Then I felt my cockhead hit the back of Tim's throat and my eyes were closed again, me groaning, "Oh, yeah."

Tim moved from my cock to Cary's. I swear, it was like he was intentionally torturing Darren, who'd only been with his left hand the past month. Cary removed his hand from my ass, putting both his hands on top of Tim's head, holding it steady while he fucked Tim's mouth, Tim taking the sharp thrusts with ease. Cary, always so cool and even-tempered, got aggressive, grunting, "Take it all, man. Take it *all*."

Darren had that stupid slack-jawed look you get when you're cock's doing all the thinking. I looked down at his dick, thinking, *grab it now*, but Darren beat me to it, sighing as he squeezed his rigid shaft. So I rested my hand on the high ridge of his muscled ass instead, my fingers touching down lightly as if I were afraid of getting burned. Darren didn't respond to my touch, just kept watching Tim blow Cary.

Cary pulled his dick out of Tim's mouth – big, bubbling ropes of saliva hanging off the head – and ordered the young guy to tongue his balls. Tim sucked on the pendulous spheres one at a time, stretching

Cary's silky pink nutsac tight as he pulled them between his lips. That's when it struck me that Cary shaved his balls, like a porn star. I wondered if he shaved his asshole, too, and if I'd get an opportunity to see it.

I turned my attention back to Darren. Since he hadn't protested when I touched his butt, and since Tim was in no apparent hurry to pay him any attention, I removed my hand from his ass and reached for his dick. Darren closed his eyes, whimpering a little. I massaged the crown of his cock with my thumb, smearing his pre-cum around the tip. I was going to tell him that if Tim wouldn't suck his dick, I would. That's when Tim pulled my hand off Darren's prick. "Let *me* do that," he said, as if I didn't know he was the designated cocksucker.

Whatever irritation I felt quickly melted away as I watched Darren's pole disappear between Tim's hungry lips. The guy definitely enjoyed sucking dick and was pretty damn good at it. Darren looked as if he was going to cry, he was so happy to have Tim working on his cock. Cary slid his arm around me, his fingers tracing the crack of my ass. He leaned over and said, "Still worried?"

Darren jerked his hips forward, fucking Tim's mouth but not has hard as Cary had done. Tim lunged into each thrust, trying to swallow every last inch of Darren's cock. "Wait," Darren moaned, trying to push him away. "Better – oh, yeah – better ease up. I'm too close."

That got Tim to sucking his cock harder. Darren started breathing hard, shallow breaths. Cary and I looked at each other, thinking: *Any second now.*

"*I'mgonnacomeI'mgonnacome!*" Darren cried; his face all scrunched up. Again, he tried to push Tim away, this time so he wouldn't come in his mouth, trying to adhere to post-1980s sexual etiquette. But Tim was having none of it, grabbing onto Darren's thighs, making sure he didn't get away. Darren's body tensed, a gasp fighting its way out of his mouth as he pumped his load into Tim's mouth.

Tim released Darren's cock then, tilting back his head and sticking out his tongue, letting us see the pool of jizz resting on it while Darren shot another splat onto his face, just missing Tim's eye. Tim pulled Darren's cockhead down into the load collected on his tongue, rubbing it back and forth in the thick white puddle, then drawing his tongue and Darren's dick back into his mouth.

Cary and I exchanged another look, both of us thinking: *We've got a total freak on our hands.*

Tim stood up and next thing I knew, he was thrusting his tongue into my mouth, giving me a taste of Darren's cum. Seconds later, he was snowballing with Cary, the two of them slurping loudly as their tongues fought between their mouths.

"I didn't want to come so soon," Darren said. His cock was sagging at half-mast, but still looking tasty.

"You can eat my ass, help get you back in the mood," Tim said, smiling, splats of Darren's spooge still on his cheek.

He took a few steps back, undoing the top button of those designer jeans, the bulge in front big and inviting now. We watched with the anticipation of an eight-year-old on Christmas morning as Tim unzipped his jeans. Even Darren, in his premature ejaculation funk, perked up.

Tim's jeans came off, but the jockstrap he wore stayed on. It was one of those designer numbers meant to be sexy, not an actual athletic supporter, Tim's hard-on barely caged in the thin pouch. Pre-cum had soaked through the silky cloth, making me lick my lips at the thought of that cock going down my throat. Darren, Cary and I might start throwing punches when Tim took off his jock, fighting to see who got first dibs on his dick.

Except the jock didn't come off. Instead, Tim backed up to the bed, raising a leg up onto the mattress while keeping his eyes on us. The three of us stepped forward, predators closing in on their prey.

Tim sat on the bed and scooted to the center. Then he turned over and got on all fours, wiggling that perfect round butt of his. He might as well have shouted, "Come and get it!" We all climbed onto the bed and scrambled toward him, Cary getting there first. Cary pried Tim's ass cheeks apart with his thumbs, staring at the pink rosebud as if it were a holy relic. Darren and I, leaning in on either side of Cary, were equally entranced by Tim's butthole.

Then Cary dove in. Again, I was surprised by his ferocity, the way he dug his tongue into that little pink pucker, the way he smothered his face between those succulent ass cheeks. I always had an easier time picturing Cary in a tuxedo than naked, but after tonight, I was pretty sure that whenever Cary and I saw each other my mind would flash back to this moment, of my friend eating ass like some crazed sex pig.

I was feeling like a crazed sex pig myself, my cock agonizingly engorged with desire. I stroked my dick; it felt so good I didn't want to stop. Yet I had to or else I'd end up shooting too soon like Darren, and not even in Tim's mouth. No, I needed someone else's cock to play with, so I reached under Tim's body, cupped my hand over the damp, filled-to-capacity jock and gave it a firm squeeze. Tim pulled my hand away.

"Just my ass," he gasped, grinding his butt into Cary's face.

Fine, then. "Hey, Cary, how 'bout letting me and Darren get a taste?"

Cary looked up at me, his face glazed with his own spit, eyes glazed with lust. "If you insist."

Still, he took his time moving away from Tim's ass. Darren, sitting on the other side of Cary, watched us as he pulled on his cock, looking like he was back in the mood.

I lowered my face to Tim's butt, delicately tracing his ass-lips with my tongue, feeling the muscled ring pulse beneath his skin. My tongue darted into his hole, and Tim moaned softly, rolling his hips.

A pair of wet fingers slid down my ass-crack. Looking over my shoulder I saw Cary, kneeling on the bed beside me, one hand on his boner, the other playing with my butt. "Anyone tell you you've got a nice ass?" he said, grinning.

"My turn," Darren said, pushing his head in front of mine to get at Tim's butt. Before he could dive into the deep valley of that gorgeous ass, however, Tim rolled over on his back.

"Wanna sit on my face?" he asked no one in particular. I wanted to, and crawled across the bed to cover his handsome visage with my butt.

He pushed his tongue inside me, digging into my hole. Darren burrowed between Tim's legs, his forehead, red and beaded with sweat, rising over the throbbing mound of Tim's jock. Darren made an attempt to free Tim's neglected hard-on, but his hands were slapped away as mine had been. Tim said something, but his words were muffled in my splayed ass.

Cary was at the night table, his eyes focused on the action on the bed as he rolled a rubber over his dick. He walked up behind Darren, stroking his sheathed cock with one hand, holding a bottle of lube in the other. "Ready for that fuck now?" Cary asked.

Darren got out of Cary's way. His cock was as hard as it was when we all first got undressed, and he delicately fondled it as Cary positioned himself between Tim's spread thighs. Cary pulled the horny trick's legs up, hoisting his ass off the bed. The mattress rocked, and I almost lost my balance atop Tim's face. Cary lubed Tim up quickly, then, holding his cock at the base, eased himself into the younger man's chute.

Cary fucked Tim in slow, easy thrusts at first. I rode the movements of Tim's body beneath me, grinding my ass into his face as Cary pounded his butt. I stroked my weeping cock, biting the inside of my cheek as hot, tingling pleasure hummed throughout my body. I had to force myself to let go of my dick lest I come all over Tim's chest. It took all my will power to do so. Tim's jock was soaked, his stiff dong pulsing beneath the thin fabric. *It must be torture*, I thought, yet he hadn't touched himself once, nor had he allowed anyone else to do so.

The bed shook as Cary started really pounding Tim's butt, his lips drawn back exposing his gnashed teeth, his brow furrowed, his eyes wild. Darren had since readied for his turn and now stood behind Cary, his dick covered and lubed.

Cary let out a harsh grunt each time he rammed his cock into Tim's chute, getting louder and louder with each push. Then he froze, closing his eyes and holding his breath as he came. Seconds later, he let out a loud, contented sigh.

Darren barely allowed Cary enough time to pull out before he was taking his place, plowing Tim's hot hole in full, savage thrusts. I climbed off Tim's face then, intending to go over to the night table and put a condom on, but Tim grabbed my wrist before I could get off the bed.

"Let me suck your cock," he whispered. "I want you to come all over my face."

"But I ... but I want to fuck you," I practically whined.

"All over my face," Tim said, reaching for my cock. "He likes it when there's cum all over my face."

He? Christ, did he have some sort of multiple personality disorder, referring to himself as a third person? It was not a debate my cock had time for, so I turned and straddled Tim's face once again, this time so my dripping dick jutted over his open mouth. Tim flicked his tongue at my pulsing cockhead, his eyes alive with anticipation as he closed his hand around my throbbing shaft.

I closed my eyes as he jerked me off, the pleasure so intense it drowned out Darren's rising groans. In a minute or two, only my voice was heard, crying out as that ecstatic explosion detonated within my cock. I opened my eyes then, just in time to see my pent-up load burst onto Tim's pretty face, to see him close his eyes as creamy, white jizz splashed onto his forehead, nose and cheeks.

When my balls were finally drained, I wiped the last droplet of cum from my cockhead onto Tim's lower lip. Darren had gotten off, too, and was carefully pulling out of Tim's hammered hole. Cary sat in a corner chair, lazily playing with his sagging dick as he watched us on the bed.

And walking through the bedroom door was a fifth man.

"Oh, shit!" I said, leaping off the bed like it was flea infested. Darren likewise jumped away, yelping like a kicked puppy. Cary scrambled for his clothes, muttering something about not knowing Tim had a boyfriend.

The man raised his hand. "It's cool," he said, pulling off his shirt. He was a muscular, tattooed brute of a guy, ten years Tim's senior at least, but just as hot. A smile showed through his dark beard as he stared at Tim lying on the bed, sweaty and cum-soaked.

Tim smiled back. "Hey, baby."

The man unzipped his pants and stepped out of them. A formidable looking hard-on fought against the front of his white boxer briefs, though not for long. In seconds, the man stood naked at the foot of the bed, stroking his monster cock, admiring the mess we'd made of his lover.

Then he pounced, kissing Tim and roughly pulling off the jock strap. "Is Daddy's little slut ready for him?" the man asked between kisses, licking my splooge off his lover's face.

"Yes," Tim gasped, running his hands down the other man's broad back. "They got my hole all ready for Daddy's big dick. Fuck me now! I've got a big load saved up just for you."

Darren, Cary and I exchanged glances that wordlessly asked: *Should we leave?* But we stayed, not only because we wanted to watch Tim and his "daddy" fuck like enraged animals; because we knew we were supposed to. We were accessories in one couple's sexual game, and we had to see it through to the end.

Grinning slyly at Cary, I said, "I told you there was a catch."

Sex Riot

"Your ass looks good enough to eat in those shorts."

The voice was hotter than the moist Florida air that enveloped us. The man's words cut through the din of the crowd, burning their way into my ears and all the way down to my crotch.

We were all gathered before the well-lit entrance to the Weathersby Center, waiting to be let into "The Ultimate Circuit Event" the ads had promised. The ads also promised doors opened at 10:00 p.m., and we were an hour past that now. "Must've meant 10 Queer Central Time," someone said, a comment that was funnier when someone else made it thirty minutes earlier. A little past 11:00, one of the doors opened, and a bearish-looking guy stepped out, holding up his hands and announcing it would be a few more minutes. But the crowd didn't listen, surging forward only to have the heavy steel door slam in its collective face.

I was closer to the door now, and closer to men around me. My ass admirer was standing close enough I could tell he, like 95 percent of the guys here (including myself) wasn't wearing a shirt and, judging by the feel of his hard pecs pressing into my back, the guy spent more time in the gym than he did on the couch.

"I heard that," said a man standing inches in front of me. He was wearing a pair of tan cargo shorts stretched tight across his bubble butt and had a Phoenix tattooed across his broad, tan back. He looked over his shoulder at me and smiled. "Looks like he heard it, too," the man said to the ass admirer, indicating me, "the way he's blushing."

I'm ordinarily a jeans-and-T-shirt kind of guy, but tonight I wore a pair of tiny white shorts that barely covered my ass and weren't any more modest up front. I'd only agreed to wear them because my boyfriend Liam had a matching pair; with him by my side I'd feel less like an idiot. But we broke up two weeks before the event, and now I wore the shorts out of spite. Malice did little to temper my feelings of idiocy, however.

"Thanks," I drawled. "I feel like I'm in a Halloween costume."

The man behind me brought a hand down on my ass so hard my right butt cheek stung. "Boo!"

I turned then. My ass admirer was a little older than I (I'm twenty-eight; I guessed he was over thirty), his predatory smile framed by an auburn goatee and mustache. The man's pecs weren't the only hardness I felt. His hands slid up to my hips, gripping me there as he pushed his own hips forward, the firm mound of his hard cock pressing against the groove of my ass. Two of his fingers on his left hand dipped beneath the waistband of my shorts. "They keep us out here much longer, I won't be able to wait. Just eat that hot ass right here."

I sprouted a hard-on so rapidly, so suddenly, I half-expected to hear my cock go *"Ping!"* It might as well have. My ass admirer thrust his hips forward again, more forcefully this time, propelling me against the Phoenix flying up the back of the man in front of me. "Feels like he wouldn't have a problem with that," Mr. Phoenix chuckled, once again looking over his shoulder at me. He brought a hand back, blindly seeking my crotch.

"Oh, yeah," said Mr. Phoenix, his fingers roughly mapping the stretched contours of the front of my shorts, "he wants it *bad*."

I thought maybe we should introduce ourselves, and started to say I liked to know the names of my molesters. But before I could say anything the man behind me had an entire hand down my shorts. His fingers traced my ass-crack, his middle digit quickly finding my hole. As the tip of his finger wiggled against my ass-lips the man's deep, raspy voice told me, in excruciating detail, how he'd give me a rimjob so spectacular I'd come three times before he was through. His explicit erotic promises had me so horny I barely realized he'd pulled my shorts down in back, exposing my ass to the warm, night air.

Mr. Phoenix had turned, introducing me to his front side, Mr. Six-Pack. My nipples were stiff, brown peaks and Mr. Phoenix Six-Pack tweaked them casually. "You two are getting me so hot," he said. "Wanna unzip my pants and see?"

I wanna!

Unzipping wasn't really necessary to see the evidence. He wasn't wearing any underwear, his hard-on pushing the front of his cargo shorts out at a 45-degree angle, the top of that tent pole nudging the swollen, sopping bulge in my shorts. His offer was too good to pass up, however, and I pulled his zipper down, catching his boner as it poked its way outside.

My fingers curled around Mr. Phoenix Six-Pack's cock. My thumb and forefinger couldn't meet. "That's pretty hot," I said. He leaned in and nibbled on my earlobe, telling me between nibbles to go ahead and suck his dick.

My ass man had slipped a moistened index finger up my hole and whispered in my other ear that after he finished eating my ass he'd fuck me so hard I'd come three more times.

Several guys nearby laughed, and another guy said, "Get a room!" Someone else told him to shut the fuck up. Mr. Phoenix Six-Pack pressed his mouth to mine, pushing his tongue inside, and then the world outside didn't exist.

I began to sink, my face gliding down the smooth, ripped torso of the man standing in front of me. "*Whoa-nelly!*" whooped a guy with a heavy Southern accent. More laughter.

My mouth connected with Mr. Phoenix Six Pack's cock. The voices in the crowd became a distant burbling, drowned out by my slurping of the stranger's fat dick. I took that cock down my throat, Mr. Phoenix Six-Pack thrusting his hips forward to make sure I swallowed every inch of it. The space around me shrank as the other men closed in to see the show. Ordinarily I'd be self-conscious; the few times past boyfriends initiated sex in public I never enjoyed it, too busy looking over my shoulder for a passer-by or cop. But this time the onlookers only heightened my excitement. Already I was so horny I thought I might have the first of my six promised orgasms before my ass admirer ever got down to business.

The ass man wasn't going to let that happen, however. My worship of my buff acquaintance's cock was interrupted by the sudden lifting of my body, my admirer, with the help from a few onlookers, hoisting me ass-over-head, stripping my shorts completely off in the process. My thighs, secured by his hands, rested on my butt man's shoulders, and his face was wedged in between. He nuzzled my ass-crack, his hot breath caressing my asshole and making my sphincter pulse. My ass admirer grunted, pushing his face deep into the crevasse of my butt, his coarse facial hair prickly against my freshly shaved trench.

Hanging from his shoulders like I was, my face dangled before my ass admirer's denim-encased crotch, his hard cock looking as it were about to break through the fabric. I reached for the zipper, eager – no, *desperate* – to free the monster struggling in those jeans. But the forceful, wet invasion of my ass man's tongue held me in spasms of pleasure. All I could do was grab his thickly muscled thighs and hold on, moaning and gasping, rubbing my dick against his chest and my face against his crotch as his tongue stabbed my chute.

Others around us were not so impeded. A slender young man dressed in olive green cargo shorts, with dark curly hair and full lips, knelt before my ass man's crotch and freed his hard-on. It sprung forward, its sticky head smacking my right cheek. The curly haired young guy immediately seized it, pulling it to his mouth. I'd only a moment to appreciate its size and shape – not as thick as Mr. Phoenix Six-Pack's, but an impressive length – before it disappeared between those luxurious lips.

My ass admirer groaned as the mystery mouth worked on his dick, his voice vibrating within my splayed ass and heightening the sensation. I attempted tease the base of the ass man's shaft with my tongue, often making contact with curly's face. My cocksucking friend pulled the boner out of his mouth and guided it towards mine, glossing my lips with the spit-coated head. I wrapped my mouth around the dripping dick, the throbbing man-meat muffling my cries as my ass man shoved his tongue up my chute with renewed fury.

All around us other cocks popped free. From the corner of my eye, I could see the curly haired guy had moved on to Mr. Phoenix Six-Pack's dong, sucking it in regular, rhythmic gulps, and to my left another weeping cock nudged my face.

I'd been close to coming for the past ten minutes and couldn't fight it any longer. I rolled my hips, humping the ass man's face while jacking myself off against his chest, now nice and slick with my pre-cum. Pulling my mouth away from the man's cock, I breathlessly announced I was going to come. A millisecond later, I shot my load, the hot jizz oozing between the man's pecs.

"Oh, yes!" the man roared, nearly dropping me on my head as he let go of my legs. Unseen hands helped me to the ground. Dizzy and disoriented in my post-orgasmic state – not to mention having been upside down for so long – it took me a moment to realize I was literally surrounded by hard-ons. Cut and uncut; fat and skinny; long and short: everywhere I looked was a cock in need of attention.

The curly-haired guy had taken hold of my ass admirer's cock, stroking the shaft while he licked the head like a lollipop. Mr. Phoenix Six-Pack pushed me forward, ordering me to "help out" the young cocksucker. The curly-haired guy's lips and mine met as we worked on the ass man's pole, our tongues touching as they snaked around the pulsing crown. Mr. Phoenix Six-Pack stepped in close enough to smack his juicy cock against our faces. One of the men – I couldn't tell if it was Phoenix Six-Pack or the ass man – groaned loudly. "Oh, yeah! Oh, oh, *oh shit!*"

Cum erupted from the ass man's dick, and my fellow pole smoker and I struggled to catch as much of the sharp-tasting cream in our mouths as we could. The curly-haired guy greedily closed his mouth over the head, catching the remainder of the man's load. I had to be content with licking the stray dribbles of jizz streaming down my ass admirer's throbbing shaft.

In our haste to gobble up the ass man's load the young man and I had forgotten about Mr. Phoenix Six-Pack. He reminded us of his presence in a big, sticky way, his copious load splattering our faces and catching in our hair. My mouth clamped down on the spewing dick before my curly-haired friend could act, swallowing the final blasts of cum.

This was only the beginning of what could only be described as a full-scale sex riot. All those hard cocks I'd seen earlier were getting the attention they needed. Some guys stroked each other; others were getting blown and some just beat off as they watched. A cute blond guy with angel wings strapped to his back and wearing skin-tight silver lamé pants, simultaneously worked on two thick dicks belonging to a pair of guys in shiny red vinyl shorts and red horns sprouting from their carefully styled hair. A bald, burly guy in a leather vest rimmed a hairy, beefy guy in chaps, who in turn fed his cock to a lanky twink wearing low-slung jeans and a baseball cap turned sideways.

I was wearing nothing but black boots and sperm samples. I scanned the pavement for my shorts, finding them beneath the shoe of someone standing a few feet behind my spent ass admirer. Before I could move to retrieve them, two hands hooked me from beneath my armpits and pulled me to my feet. Once standing, I tried to turn around to face the owner of those two hands, only to have his muscular arms encircle my chest and hold me in place. The coarse hair of the stranger's chest felt crinkly against my back. He pinched my nipples, but the sensation that got the blood flowing back into my recently satiated cock was the weight of his hard-on against the crack of my ass. Either this guy was teasing me with a very realistic dildo or he had a near-superhuman endowment. This cock was much bigger than Mr. Phoenix Six-Pack's, forcing my butt cheeks apart as the veiny shaft sank between them like an over-sized hotdog in a bun.

Sweat and pre-cum turned my ass-crack into a slick runway, enabling the well-hung stranger to pump his cock easily against me. He brought a hand to my face and dragged his fingers through the rivulets of jism oozing down my left cheek and across my lips. I took one of his fingertips inside my mouth and sucked on it, tasting the rich man-cream that glazed them. His lips brushed against my neck, making me shiver.

A glistening black guy with a broad, beautiful smile grabbed my swelling rod and pulled on it, telling me I was "a motherfuckin' hot dude." The black guy's hand was replaced by the warm wetness of someone's mouth. I looked down to see my cock disappear between the lips of an exotically handsome young man with longish blond hair. To my left I saw the curly-haired guy who'd helped me suck-off the ass man and Mr. Phoenix Six-Pack, held aloft by members of the crowd while a hot, olive-skinned bodybuilder ate his ass like a pig at a trough, the sight enough to fully restore my boner.

Two men – one a slender redhead; the other thickly built with wavy brown hair – each took hold of my legs and my own feet left the ground. I was in a seated position, my ass resting on the stranger's fantastic endowment. My hands reached behind me for support, but the horse-hung mystery man had me, his arms clamped around my chest.

My hands found purchase on his legs, gripping the tops of the man's strong thighs. God, how I wanted to get a good look at him! The blond guy's mouth moved lower, over my balls, loudly sucking on each cum-engorged orb, and then his face disappeared beneath me as his tongue sought out my asshole.

"Jesus!" the blond guy exclaimed, loud enough to be heard over the collective moans and groans of the crowd. He'd discovered what the man behind me was pushing against my ass-crack and wasted no time in manipulating that huge pole into his mouth and gulping it down. The feel of the mystery man's shaft sliding between my open butt cheeks and the blond guy's forehead pressing against my choad had my cock to leaving thick, slimy snail trails across my belly.

The thickly built guy removed one hand from my leg to retrieve something from the waistband of his hot pants. The outdoor lights reflected off the foil wrapper as he handed the square packet to the blond kneeling beneath me, and that was the only warning I got for what happened next.

Seconds after the blond got the mystery man's cock sheathed, I was crying out from the pleasurable agony of that enormous rod pushing into my spit-lubed hole. My body jerked and legs kicked, and the guys holding me up almost lost their grip. But I never protested. No, I wanted to feel every inch of that monster cock up my chute, even if it split me in two.

The closest the mystery man had gotten to actually speaking to me was letting out a satisfied groan as my ass swallowed his enormous dong down to the hilt. The blond guy stayed where he was, kneeling between my thighs to lick the mystery man's balls. Occasionally, I felt his tongue swab my stretched sphincter as he lapped at the inch or so of the mystery man's shaft that wasn't stuffed up my ass.

I reached for my drooling cock, hoping I could pace my strokes, so I didn't come too soon. But then the blond guy's face popped back into view, wet with sweat and spit, his eyes bleary with lust; he promptly took my throbbing dick down his throat. I thrust my hips, pushing my dick deep into the blond guy's hungry mouth and then dropping my ass down onto the mystery man's pole. The sensation was so intense, it blurred my vision, the carnal riot becoming an abstract tapestry of sex acts: guys lining up to take turns fucking a slim young man with a Mohawk; a spiky-haired circuit clone getting his chest splattered with cum as guys stood jacking off over him; and at my very feet, the black guy who'd played with my cock earlier was now sucking off the redhead who held one of my legs.

The mystery man was grunting loudly and fucking me harder. The blond guy pulled his mouth off my cock and pumped it with his fist. I threw my head back, gasping as the erotic sensations became thrillingly unbearable.

"Yessss!" said the blond guy as my cock erupted.

His arms squeezed my chest tighter, holding on for dear life as he came inside me, his thick shaft pulsing against my sphincter with each shot. I squeezed my ass-cheeks together, wanting to milk out every last drop of jizz from the mystery man's balls.

I didn't remember closing my eyes, but when I opened them, I immediately wished I hadn't. An acrid smoke wafted through the crowd, stinging eyes and burning lungs. I heard shouting in the distance, and saw panic sweep through the crowd. The cops had arrived.

The guys holding my legs dropped me and ran. The mystery man withdrew his dick and pulled his arms away from me, leaving me teetering off balance. I turned to get a look at him before he fled, but the only thing I saw was the cum-filled rubber he left on the pavement.

A man grabbed my hand. "This way!" he shouted, pulling me away from the advancing policemen and clouds of teargas. I followed, blindly.

According to news reports the next morning, the organizers of "The Ultimate Circuit Event" had perpetrated the ultimate swindle, absconding with all the money earlier in the day. There was mention of a "riot" and that "several arrests for lewd conduct" were made, but no one in the media called it what it was: an orgy.

I switched off the TV and said: "I know technically we were ripped off, but I feel I got more than my money's worth."

"Well, I still owe you five more orgasms," said Quinn, my ass admirer, as he pulled me down onto the bed beside him. "I don't have to check-out until tomorrow, so let's get started on settling that debt."

The Go-Between

There was much to admire about Jim: his handsome face, its only imperfection a crooked nose, and even that somehow made him more appealing; his thickly muscled arms; his solid pecs sprinkled with dark blond hair. But right now, I only admired him from the waist down, watching his hard-on quiver as he eased himself onto my cock.

He let out a small grunt as sat astride my hips, his balls touching down just below my navel. I clasped his muscular thighs and Jim rolled his hips, letting out another grunt. I looked up at his face then, and he was smiling.

His chute was warm, igniting red-hot sensations as it enveloped my throbbing cock. I undulated beneath him, pumping my dick deep inside that tight-yet-pliant tunnel. Jim squeezed his butt cheeks together, massaging my shaft with his ass muscles. The intense pleasure made me shudder.

"Easy," I gasped. "Want this to last awhile." *Wanting it to last forever.*

Jim didn't say anything, just kept rolling his hips and squeezing my cock with his ass muscles. Pre-cum flowed from his prick, collecting on my abdomen in a sticky puddle. I raked up some of his juice with my fingers and curled them around his pulsing boner, using his natural lubricant to stroke him. He spoke up then. "If you want this to last awhile you'd better stop what you're doing."

"Don't know if I can," I said, stroking his cock harder.

"Then I don't know if I can hold back."

Jim started rocking wildly atop me, his hips moving back and forth as he milked my cock, trying to make me come first. Two could play at that game. My fist throttled his drooling dong, the sensation making his body jerk.

We came almost simultaneously, Jim firing streamers of jism across my belly seconds before I got off. He leaned down and we kissed, our tongues probing each other's mouths as my cock pulsed inside Jim's quaking chute.

He looked over at the clock on my bedside table. "Shit, I gotta go."

"Aren't you the romantic," I chuckled as he climbed off me. Carefully, I pulled the cum-filled rubber off my cock. "Throw this away while you're in the bathroom."

"Now who's the romantic?" he said as he plucked the condom from my fingers.

I was still lying on the bed when Jim came out of the bathroom a few minutes later. "Aren't you going to clean up?" he asked as he stepped into his underwear.

"Yeah, in a few minutes," I said dreamily. "Just want to bask in the afterglow a bit longer."

"Shit, I wished I worked from home like you and didn't have to go back to that fucking office."

I smiled, remembering when we met a few months ago, when I was contracted by Jim's company to do some consulting work. "If you didn't work at that 'fucking office' we'd never have met."

Once he was dressed, Jim dipped a forefinger into one of the globs of jizz cooling on my abdomen and brought it to my mouth, glazing my lower lip with his residue; then a lingering kiss. The pornographically romantic gesture made my cock tingle with new life. A minute later, Jim was gone.

Less than five minutes after that sticky goodbye the doorbell rang – three times, in short succession, needing to be answered urgently.

I knew who it was. "It's open," I shouted from the bedroom.

Mitch was removing his tie as he entered the bedroom. Standing at the foot of my bed, he looked down at me – naked, sweaty, splattered with cum – with that shell-shocked expression of his. Like someone who'd endured such intense emotions for so long that he'd become emotionless.

"One of these days he's going to catch you," I said, smiling like this was all in fun.

Mitch dropped his button-down on the floor and pulled off his undershirt with the methodical indifference of someone about to undergo a doctor's examination. He was a wee-bit thicker around the waist than Jim, but still quite nice. He tilted his goateed chin upward. "That his load?" he asked.

"Yeah," I said. "He sat on my cock and came all over me. 'Fraid it was gonna dry up before he left."

He gave a subtle nod in acknowledgement as he stepped out of his black pants. The gray boxer briefs he wore showed off his hard-on in sharp relief, but Mitch only allowed me a microsecond to appreciate the sight before his underwear joined his other clothes on the floor. Now naked, Mitch knelt onto the mattress, between my ankles, and leaned forward onto his hands, his body hovering over my lower half. His eyes were directed at my spooge-frosted abs, and I could almost see him mentally recreating the heated nooner that had just taken place, picturing Jim shooting his load while riding my pole.

And I knew when his mental picture was complete because that's when Mitch pounced, his face hitting my gut just hard enough to make me cry out. He rubbed his face back and forth across sticky belly, lapping up Jim's residue like a last meal, occasionally giving me quick, sharp bites as he fed on what was left over. Nothing pornographically romantic about it – just obscenely piggy.

By the time Mitch's mouth had traveled up to my chest, my cock was again hard and throbbing.

Mitch raised his head, meeting my eyes. His face was deep red and glazed; his eyes burning with all the tortured emotions that had brought him here. "I always loved to eat his load," he hissed. "He'd sit on my chest and jack off into my mouth. You ever do that?"

I shook my head, though the idea made my dick twitch.

"Maybe you should suggest it sometime." Mitch was smiling maliciously now. "I'd love to see his reaction to that, wondering where you got the idea."

"Don't go there."

He kissed me then, a ferocious, tongue-stabbing, lip-stinging kiss. When he pulled his mouth away – my mouth felt sore, raw – he said: "I've already *been* there."

His mouth backtracked, starting with the right nipple, and then the left, biting the engorged nubs just a little too hard. From there, Mitch continued down in a jerky serpentine, licking and biting – especially biting – all the way to my crotch. He curled his hand around my shaft with surprising gentleness. He tenderly stroked me, giving my cock, glistening with lube used earlier, the slightest squeeze. Pre-cum bubbled up from my piss-slit. Mitch rubbed his thumb over the tip of my cockhead, coating the glans with my natural juices. I got another smile, this one softer than the one I got earlier. A few weeks back when we first met – more a confrontation than a meeting – he had said he couldn't fault Jim for his taste. "You've got a great cock," he'd said then, when he'd virtually blackmailed me into bed. That's what his smile communicated now: You've got a great cock.

Though he regarded my prick tenderly, Mitch gobbled it viciously, undeterred by the chemical taste of the lubricant that coated it.

"Oh – god*damn*!" I cried out, arching my back off the mattress, clasping a hand over the top of his head. My cock hit the back of his throat while his tongue mapped the swollen veins of the shaft. His thumb and forefinger made a ring around my scrotum, tightening his grip until he had my nutsac in a stranglehold. Then – *fuck*! – he pulled, just hard enough to bring moisture to my eyes and to my cock.

Mitch released my dick from his mouth, my hard-on snapping against my abdomen with spring-loaded force. My balls, however, remained captive, cuffed between Mitch's fingers. He raised my strangled balls, so I could see them, the sack so tightly drawn around them that my nuts looked like an overripe nectarine.. Mitch licked that peach while I, teetering on that quivering tightrope strung up between pleasure and pain, held my breath. Mitch's lips then suctioned onto one of my distended testicles, his vacuum-like mouth pulling me into a sensation so unbearable, so thrilling, I thought I might faint.

Only when Mitch let go was I able to breathe normally, and even then it took a while. I slowly released my white-knuckle grip of the sheets, drinking in desperate gulps of air as I looked at Mitch incredulously. I was torn between angrily accusing him of being a sadistic bastard and gratefully praising his technique. My cock, as usual, exhibited no such ambivalence: I swear it seemed to have grown in length and girth since Mitch had sucked on it.

He sat up on the bed, his butt resting on his ankles. His cock, too, seemed larger than it had earlier, a big, fat, fleshy club rising up between his muscular thighs. And I wanted to suck it, as much as I'd ever wanted to suck Jim's, if not more. Sitting up, I made a move toward Mitch, placing a hand on his thigh, my eyes asking – *begging* – for permission to take his dick into my mouth. All he offered me was that malicious smile, more of a dare than an invitation. That was good enough for me. I lowered my lips to his trembling meatpole.

I wanted to take his cock into my mouth a little bit at a time, savoring it inch by inch as it slid over my tongue. But Mitch wasn't going to allow me that luxury. Placing both hands on top of my skull, he pushed my face down into his crotch and thrust upward, shoving his dick deep into my throat, the sudden force of it making me gag. I coughed violently and saliva sprayed forcing its way out of my cock-stuffed mouth.

My hair is cut short, but it's long enough on top that Mitch was able to seize it in his fists and pull. Though the pain wasn't great, it made me whimper. And it excited me – I was sure I was dripping all over the sheets – the way Mitch was treating me like a worthless whore, force-feeding me his cock like it was all my mouth was good for.

Mitch plucked my head out of his lap with a sharp tug of my hair. His cock was covered with a bubbly varnish of my spit, drops of saliva hanging in the wiry hair of his balls. My face must have telegraphed how much I wanted his dick back in my mouth because Mitch said: "That was awesome, but I got other things in mind."

"Like *what?*"

Mitch said, "Get on your hands and knees."

I rolled over and pushed myself up, my ass in the air, my weight resting on my elbows. I closed my eyes and waited, my cock tingling in anticipation of those "other things" Mitch had in mind.

Then my eyes popped open. A surprised cry burst from my mouth as Mitch attacked my ass, his tongue forcing its way past my puckered sphincter, jabbing inside me. The smooth, sharp edges of his teeth pinched my knotted-up ass-ring, applying just enough pressure to make me tremble from pleasure – and fear that he might actually bite down hard, *chomp*! The fear, of course, only fed the pleasure, intensifying the ecstatic sensations rocketing through my body.

Rimming and eating ass are used synonymously, but my experiences with Jim and Mitch taught me there is a difference. *Rimming* is what I do to Jim, gently lapping at his rosebud, prodding the gathered pinkish-tan lips of his hole with the tip of my tongue. It's almost … sweet, if tonguing someone's asshole could actually be described that way. But Mitch *ate ass*, digging his tongue deep into the chute, using his fingers to pry my hole open, so he could dig in still deeper. He gnawed my ass-ring, he slobbered up and down my crack, he nipped at my taint – making wet, guttural grunts all the while. Mitch *devoured* ass.

He abruptly stopped his butt munching fury. I craned my head around, getting a peripheral view of Mitch over my shoulder. "Stay put," he said, and I dropped my head back between my shoulders. Looking down my torso, I saw my dick staring back at me, its single eye oozing juice; its red, engorged head visibly pulsing.

My body tensed reflexively when I heard the soft rip of the condom packet. As glorious as it feels fucking someone you lust for, it's nothing compared to the savagery of getting fucked by someone who holds you in utter contempt.

A squirt of lube later, and I felt the sheathed head of Mitch's cock pushing against my hole. My sphincter contracted like a sea anemone as he rubbed his dong against it, as if my butthole was trying to protect itself from the imminent invasion. But Mitch didn't enter me violently. He eased his cock into me with a firm-but-controlled push. I gnashed my teeth as his fat dick opened me up, though it wasn't really painful – quite the opposite, in fact. My body relaxed as Mitch's dick sank deeper into my chute, generating a warm tension at the bottom of my gut.

Then the thrusting started. This was also controlled, at first, and not out of concern for me. Mitch was just finding his rhythm. He was like a car changing gears: first gear was careful, methodical thrusting; second was more of the same, only harder and faster; at third gear, he was pumping my ass in forceful, plunging stabs; and when he kicked up to fourth ...

"Ahhhhh-unghhh-fuuuuuck!"

Mitch's body was hunched over mine, trapping a humid heat between my back and his chest. He was really hammering my ass now, pulling out two-thirds of the way, then – *wham!* – driving his meaty cock all the way inside with such force the bed bounced. Each time he drove his dick into me – *wham!* – I let out a deep, ragged moan that simultaneously begged him to stop and encouraged him to keep going.

His weight pressed down on my back and his legs were straddling my ass, leapfrog style. I could feel his hot breath against my right ear. Through gritted teeth he hissed: "Every time you fuck him, I'm going to fuck you twice as hard."

I'd heard the words before, and they had sounded threatening at one time, back when he was only the cuckolded lover who had his suspicions confirmed by a P.I. Now, at this stage of the game – and by now it was a game – the words were titillating.

"You – *unghh* – promise?"

Mitch slowed his pace slightly, reaching beneath me and grabbing my hard, throbbing, dripping cock. "I'm not Jim. I keep my word," he said with ironclad certainty. The implication that one day Jim would betray me, too, caused a sharp dip in my excitement. Anger rushed in to fill the void.

"You fucking ..."

Mitch stroked my dick, his hand joining the rhythm of his ramming. "Fucking what?"

But I couldn't fill in the blank, my mind ceding control over to my cock. My thoughts became a swirl of *oh, god, that feels so fucking good, shit, I'm gonna come any second* – communicated through the rising pitch of my frantic gasping, and then my erupting cock. Mitch kept on stroking, using my creamy load as lubricant, chuckling as my body jerked and bucked beneath him each time his hand caressed my cockhead, as sensitive as a raw nerve.

Once he'd milked every last drop of jism from my dick, Mitch put his energy into fucking me. He went from fourth gear into overdrive, plowing into me with all his might, a full-scale rectal assault. If I hadn't grabbed a pillow and buried my face in it I'm sure he would've driven my head through the wall with his violent fucking.

Mitch reared back and slammed his cock in to the hilt one final time. With his dick embedded in my chute, he came, a roar tearing out of his throat as he pumped out his hot spunk.

He pulled out, leaving my asshole feeling sore and squishy in his wake. It was a relief to have his cock out of my ass, yet deep in my chute, I felt empty.

I rolled onto my back to confront Mitch kneeling at the foot of my bed, drenched in sweat and breathing heavy. His eyes, cold and angry, bore down on me as he pulled the sagging rubber off his dick. The slimy latex sleeve was held up for my inspection, so I could see how Mitch had filled it to capacity. Then he threw it at me, the soggy rubber hitting me – *splat!* – on the side of my face.

"Happy now?" I asked, brushing the used condom off my left cheek like it was a bug.

Mitch climbed off the bed. "Yeah," he said. There was no satisfaction in his voice.

We didn't speak as Mitch got dressed, and I didn't move. I needed to take a shower in the worst way, but I always waited until after he left.

When he was dressed and ready to go, Mitch asked, as he always asked: "You'll call me, next time you and Jim get together?"

That private dick wasn't necessary now. I nodded, and Mitch started to leave. "Wait, there's something I've been wanting to ask you."

He stopped at the bedroom door. "Yes?"

"How come you and Jim just don't just break up if you know he's ... *seeing* me?"

Silence, then: "Because I love him."

He was gone before I could tell him Jim gave the same answer to that question.

Kept Men

"Here we are, boy: The beautiful Bay Manor Hotel. What'cha think?"

Chad surveyed their suite, with its pale colors and imitation Chippendale furniture. It was okay, but hardly the regal splendor the hotel's brochure promised. "It's all right," he told Lamar.

"*All right?* The place is a fucking palace!" the Texas millionaire exclaimed, sweeping his arm across the air as if showing off the fabulous prizes on a game show.

Chad shrugged and looked away. Looking at Lamar made him uncomfortable. He didn't like being reminded he was stuck with him. Lamar may have been hot at one time, Chad supposed, before his skin became leathery and his muscles had turned soft. The man did have a handsome face and a huge cock, but Chad was really more interested in the bulge in Lamar's wallet than the one in his crotch.

"How 'bout this bed?" Lamar said, sitting on the king-sized mattress, bouncing up and down. "Think we need to try it out."

Chad tried to keep from rolling his eyes. "Now?"

Lamar gave him a lecherous grin, stood and unzipped his Bermuda shorts. At fifty-four Lamar Chalmers got more hard-ons than a seventeen-year-old in a whorehouse, thanks to those goddamned blue pills. Chad forced himself to smile and walked over to the obnoxious millionaire, sinking to his knees in front of him. *This pays my rent*, he told himself as he guided Lamar's cock into his mouth.

# # # # #

Randolph Maxwell IV's convertible Beemer was a flaming red blur as he gunned it down the two-lane highway.

"Just another twenty miles, and we're there," he told Mark, grasping the young man's firm thigh.

Mark smiled. Randolph moved his hand further up his thigh. "We don't have to wait until we get to the hotel, you know."

In spite of himself, Mark felt a slight twinge in his crotch. He wasn't really attracted to Randolph; he looked okay, he guessed, even with his thinning, sandy hair and the few extra pounds around the middle. Yet except for sex, the two had nothing in common. Randolph would talk endlessly about the pressures of running an international electronics company, and Mark would nod periodically as if he understood what the hell he was talking about. Sometimes he'd initiate sex just to get Randolph to shut the fuck up.

Now Randolph was initiating it. Mark was leery. Sure there was no one else on the road, but it was in the middle of the afternoon. A truck could pass them and see everything. Besides, Randolph was driving way too fast. He didn't need the distraction.

Randolph guided Mark's hand to his crotch. He was hard. "C'mon," he urged. "No one will see."

Mark leaned down and undid Randolph Maxwell IV's fly, freeing his stiff dick. He sucked it vigorously, hoping Randolph got off quickly. Randolph began moaning, telling Mark he was the best cocksucker in the country. The car swerved onto the shoulder a few times. Mark sucked the wealthy businessman's dick at a faster pace.

The sound of an eighteen-wheeler's air horn blasted beside them. Mark heard the truck driver shout, "Faggots!"

He doubted Randolph heard; he was too busy shooting his load down Mark's throat.

#

Tony Ruscetti was a handsome man at forty-three, with the face of a movie star and the body of an athlete. Mario was attracted to him to moment he first saw him. Now he was afraid of him.

And, so was the Bay Manor Hotel's porter, now that Tony had locked the door behind him.

"I want to fuck you," Tony said calmly.

The bellboy, a cute young man with dark hair and wide eyes, offered a stuttering protest. "S-s-s-sir, I've gotta g-get back to the front desk. M-m-m-my boss would …?"

"I'll handle your boss," Tony said, standing inches away from the frightened bellboy, unbuttoning the front of his red jacket. "Right now I want to fuck you."

The porter remained silent. He'd already deduced that Tony was a very dangerous man.

Tony stripped the uniform off the bellboy's body, making comments as he tossed his clothes on the floor ("Beautiful chest." "Fat cock." "Nice ass.") Then Tony removed his clothes. Mario watched, not sure what was expected of him. Better to wait until Tony told him.

Once nude, Tony began fondling the nervous bellboy. He ordered him on his knees: "Ya' like Italian sausage?" he chuckled. "Go on, suck it."

The bellboy did as he was told, curling his tongue around the tip of Tony's hard dick then nearly gagging when Tony abruptly shoved it down his throat.

Tony turned to Mario. "What? You think we're putting on a show here? Get your ass outta those clothes an' get over here."

Mario stripped immediately and walked over to the two men.

"Eat my ass!" Tony demanded.

Mario knelt behind Tony, sliding his tongue between Tony's butt cheeks and lapping at his hairy asshole.

Tony tossed his head back, grunting as the scared hotel porter sucked his cock and Mario tongued his hole. Then he ordered the bellboy to get on the bed with his ass in the air. He promptly obeyed. Tony roughly shoved two fingers into the frightened man's chute. "Like to get fucked, boy?"

When the bellboy didn't respond, Tony shouted: "I said, *do you like to get fucked!*"

"Yes," the bellboy whimpered.

Tony smiled maliciously and told Mario to get him some lube. Mario got him the bottle out of his travel bag. Tony oiled up his cock then forced his cock into the bellboy's tight hole. The young man cried out, and Tony rammed his dick deeper into his ass.

Taking a chance, Mario did not wait for orders from Tony before climbing onto the bed, positioning himself in front of the porter and putting his cock to the whimpering man's lips. The bellboy opened his mouth, letting Mario slip his dick inside. Mario figured he'd take advantage of the situation because Tony sure as hell wasn't going to suck a dick. In the year Mario had been with the mobster, the only time he got off was with his hand or when Tony forced someone else to join them.

Tony grunted loudly, forcefully slamming into the hapless bellboy's ass. His body jerked a few times and then he was through. He pulled his dick, greasy and dripping cum, out of the bellboy's ass and forced him off the bed.

"Get on the floor. You," he said, motioning for Mario, "you so horny for his mouth, get over here and come on his face."

Mario stood over the bellhop jacking off furiously, wishing he could let the guy suck his dick a while longer, but figuring Tony wouldn't want that. In a few minutes his balls were tightening, his body shivering. Ribbons of hot jism rained down on the bellboy's young, wincing face.

Tony shoved the bellboy's clothes into his arms, stuffed a hundred dollar bill in his mouth and pushed him, naked, out the door, into the hall. "Thanks," he said, shutting the door.

# # # # #

Poolside at the Bay Manor Hotel, three young men sat next to one another in chaise longues. One, Chad, was tall and lean, with wavy blond hair. Another, Mark, was muscular and smooth, with brown hair that fell across his eyes. The third, Mario, was slightly below average height and an above average body, with a broad chest accented with a triangle of dark hair in the middle of his firm pecs.

"So, what brings you here?" Mark asked Chad.

"A polyester cowboy. You?" Chad asked Mark.

"A millionaire who can't afford a personality." The two young men turned to Mario. "You here with anyone?" Mark asked.

"Spring break for the mob," Mario said. "Only the psychotic motherfucker had to fly off to Vegas this morning. Got knees to break, I guess."

"Mine's passed out. Too much sun and Jack Daniels," Chad offered.

"Mine's spending his vacation on the phone, talking to corporate headquarters," said Mark.

"So yours is in Vegas?" Chad asked Mario, lowering his sunglasses and giving the Italian hunk a seductive stare.

"Won't be back until tomorrow morning," Mario said with a smile.

"Let's continue this in your room," Mark suggested, "while mine's still on the phone."

They followed Mario up to the suite he shared with Tony. Only the paintings on the walls distinguished it from the suites Chad and Mark shared with their respective paramours.

Chad ran his hands across Mario's chest, "Beautiful body," he whispered.

"Yours is pretty nice, too," Mario said, hooking an arm around Chad's torso, drawing him close. He tilted his head up and Chad gave him a deep, probing kiss. Chad's hands glided down Mario's back. A warm, tingling feeling radiated through Mario's body. He felt like a flower opening up to the sun. Tony wasn't much on kisses and caresses.

Chad's cock, semi-hard when he entered the suite, was rock hard now. He loved the feel of Mario's young, firm body against his own. It was a thrill that Lamar's millions could never give him.

Mark moved in behind Chad, squeezing his butt cheeks and planting small kisses between his shoulder blades. He reached around Chad's waist and grabbed his crotch, feeling his huge, hard cock caged within his tight boxcut. "Oh, yeah," Chad moaned.

Mark then felt Mario's crotch. His dick was rigid, also, the head peaking over the waistband of his Speedos. Mario groaned and stepped back to remove his skimpy swimsuit. Chad and Mark stripped as well. The three men were naked in seconds, their stiff rods jutting out into the air, demanding attention.

Chad was the first to take action. He knelt on the gray carpet and Mario and Mark shoved their cocks toward his beautiful face. He started with Mario, taking his thick, hard dick into his mouth.

Mario grunted, grinding his hips forward. "Suck my dick, man," he hissed. It was nice to give the commands for a change.

Then Chad moved his mouth over to Mark's uncut cock. Dewy drops of pre-cum oozed from it, coating the cockhead with a glistening sheen. Chad's tongue fluttered over the crown, licking up the pre-cum glaze. He slurped the juices that had collected in the folds of Mark's foreskin.

"Jesus, that feels so good," Mark panted.

Chad swallowed Mark's cock, taking it down his throat with ease. Lamar always liked getting deep-throated, and Mark was no different.

Mark groaned loudly, relishing the feel of Chad's warm, moist mouth closing in around this cock. Not wanting to be left out, Mario thrust his cock into Chad's face. Chad wrapped his hand around it, stroking it while he sucked Mark's dick. He then released Mark's cock from his mouth and gulped Mario's prick. Mario grasped Chad's head and began to fuck his mouth, moving his rigid rod back and forth across Chad's tongue.

Mark and Mario turned to one another and kissed. As their tongues slid into each other's mouths, Chad grabbed their dicks and swabbed his tongue over the crowns of their cocks. He opened his mouth wide and took both their pricks into his mouth simultaneously. Mark and Mario grunted in unison, the sensation of their dicks pressed together in Chad's mouth making their entire bodies quiver with pleasure.

The two men pulled out of Chad's hot mouth. "Let's get on the bed," Mario said gruffly.

They arranged themselves on the bed, with Chad lying on his back, Mario hovering over his face and Mark hunched over his crotch. Mark took Chad's fat, hard cock deep into his mouth. Chad twitched, Mark's mouth on his cock sending electric shocks through his entire body. Mario's dick muffled his moans.

Chad sucked Mario's cock ravenously, tracing the thick veins on the shaft with his tongue. Mario slid his drooling dick out of his mouth and batted Chad's face with it a few times. The young blond man licked and sucked the dark-haired stud's hairy, cum-swollen balls.

Mario turned around, putting his ass in Chad's face. "Eat my hole," he commanded, excited that he could use Tony's words on someone else.

Chad gently prodded the outer edges of Mario's hole with his tongue. He seldom gave Lamar rim jobs; Lamar was pretty much a suck-and-fuck kind of guy, and Chad had no interest in giving the wealthy Texan anything more than that unless he could get something out of it, like a Sak's shopping spree or a new car.

But this wasn't for money; this was out of genuine desire. Chad pushed his tongue deeper, forcing Mario's tight ass ring open. Mario gyrated his hips, riding Chad's mouth and stroking his dick. "Oh, yeah," he said under his breath. "I wanna fuck you."

Mario climbed off Chad's face, and Chad reluctantly pulled his aching cock out of Mark's mouth and turned over. Pressing his face into an overstuffed pillow, Chad raised his ass in the air.

Mario grabbed a bottle of lubricant from the nightstand and squeezed a generous glob of the clear liquid into his palm. After making his dick slick, he worked his slippery fingers inside Chad's waiting ass: first one, then two and then three. Chad's sphincter muscle stretched easily. He was ready for more.

Positioning himself behind Chad, Mario took hold of the base of his cock and carefully guided it in. He wasn't going to just shove it in like Tony did – the mobster always seemed hell-bent on making sure you couldn't sit down for a week after he fucked you. So Mario tried to be gentle.

Nevertheless, Chad let out a grunt as his hole was filled with Mario's thick cock. His ass muscles closed in around the hard flesh of Mario's rod, holding it inside. Mario fucked him in short, careful thrusts.

"Fuck me harder," Chad begged. Mario picked up his pace, slamming his prick deep into Chad's ass, his thighs slapping against Chad's firm butt cheeks.

Mark stood beside the bed pulling his cock, trying to figure how he could join in. Mario reached forward and grabbed his arm. "Get up here," he said.

On the bed, Mark stood astride Chad, his cock level with Mario's face.

"Let me get a taste of that uncut cock," Mario whispered, bringing his mouth to the other young man's cock. His tongue flitted around the crown of Mark's dick, prodding the foreskin bunched up around the head. Mark forced his cock deeper into Mario's mouth, the hot Italian sucking it until his balls tightened in their sack, ready to explode.

Mark didn't want to shoot his load just yet and tried to ride the growing feeling of ecstasy. But his cock had other ideas.

"I'm almost there," he groaned, his cock twitching in Mario's throat.

Mario released Mark's cock from his mouth. "Come all over my face," he said, his voice low and gruff.

Tony would shoot on his face, making it an act of debasement. "Filthy cocksucker," he'd snarl. But he *wanted* Mark's load all over him and he soon got it, Mark spewing his thick, milky jism onto Mario's high cheekbones and full lips.

"Oh, yeah," Mario sighed as the warm, viscous drops of cum rained down on his face.

Mark squeezed the last drop of spunk from his cock, rubbing his sticky cockhead across the fellow kept man's mouth. Mario's arousal ratcheted upward, spurring him to fuck Chad harder. No longer was he concerned with being gentle; all that mattered now was satisfying his lust. He forcefully pumped his prick into Chad's gut, making the slender blond to yelp like a dog. Mario gripped Chad's narrow, riding his ass like a rodeo cowboy. A few minutes later, he was digging his nails into Chad's tan flesh, crying out as he released a flood of cum into Chad's bowels.

His load shot, Mario let out a satisfied sigh and slowly slid his dick out of Chad's ass. Chad rolled over; his cock was throbbing. He started jacking off, but Mark stopped him, kneeling down and swallowing his rigid prick. The young blond's body convulsed and then froze as his cock fired off molten bullets of sweet-tasting man-juice. Mark swallowed it all, lapping up the final drop with a flick of his tongue.

The three men fell together in a heap, kissing, their hands gliding over each other's bodies. It was the first time any of them had truly enjoyed sex since hooking up with their respective keepers.

It was Mark who reminded them of their responsibilities to the men who paid for their lifestyles. "Guess I better see if my guy's off the phone," he said resignedly.

"Oh, yeah, them," Chad said, rolling his eyes. "This would be a great vacation if we weren't with *them*."

Mark hopped off the bed and put his swimsuit on. "You know, we don't have to be with them."

"You try breaking up with the mob," Mario said.

"Lamar's all I know how to do," Chad said dejectedly. "'Sides, you should see the condo he got me in Dallas."

Still, Mark had gotten them thinking.

When Mark got back to his suite, Randolph didn't even ask where he'd been. He immediately started babbling about his company's new product, in development for years, now ready for market.

"So, what is it?" Mark asked.

"I've got the paperwork here," Randolph said, pulling a large envelope from his briefcase. "It's a computer system so advanced it'll put us up there with Microsoft and Apple!"

Mark smiled. "Maybe we should celebrate," he said, walking toward Randolph.

"Great idea! Let's go out to dinner."

Mark put his hand on Randolph Maxwell IV's crotch and squeezed. "I'd rather eat in," he said.

# # # # #

"What time is it," Lamar groaned when Chad entered the room.

"'Bout four," Chad said, looking down at Lamar's flabby, sunburned body. He walked away from the bed and sat down on a chair on the opposite side of the suite. He'd barely settled in the chair when Lamar's cell phone sounded. The ring tone was a snippet from "I'm Too Sexy."

Lamar groaned as he rolled over to pick the phone up from the nightstand. Lamar became more animated and excited as his conversation progressed.

"Good news?" Chad asked when Lamar hung up, though honestly he couldn't give a shit.

"Great news! That buyout I'd been talkin' 'bout? It's going through! By the end of next week, Lamar Poultry will be the biggest in the business."

Chad raised his eyebrows. "That ain't chickenshit."

"Sure ain't," Lamar agreed.

Chad stood up and slipped off his swimsuit. "I'm going to take a shower. You're welcome to join me."

Lamar responded with a lecherous smile, but when he tried to stand up he winced from the pain of his sunburn. "I'll have to sit this one out, baby," he moaned, falling back onto the bed in a heap.

# # # # #

Tony returned early the next morning. He greeted Mario by shoving his hard dick in his face.

"Wake up and suck it." Tony didn't waste time with hellos.

Afterwards, while Tony was in the shower, Mario noticed a briefcase sitting on the table across the room. He hobbled over (Tony had fucked him more brutally than usual) to check it out. It was locked, but could be picked easily. Tony didn't like combination locks; "The only numbers I can remember have dollar signs in front of 'em," he had said.

When Mario got the case open, he found what he thought he'd find: cash. Lots of it.

My days of being Tony's whore may be coming to an end, he thought, shutting the case the moment he heard Tony turn the water off.

When Tony Vinceti Ruscetti and Mario returned to New Jersey, the gangster said he'd have to see "the boys." After Tony drove off in his Cadillac, Mario called a cab. About the time it was discovered the briefcase was a million dollars lighter, Mario was at the airport, boarding his flight.

When Lamar Poultry's buyout of another major poultry producer was announced, stocks in the company went through the roof. One investor, a Charles David Belew, also known as Chad, bought two-hundred shares three days before the buyout was announced. After share prices spiked, Chad sold. A stockbroker advised him to hold on to the shares, but Chad said he'd waited long enough. Besides, he had a plane to catch.

When Randolph Maxwell IV learned his new computer system was about to be put on the market by a competitor, he collapsed on the floor of his office, sobbing. Then he began systematically firing anyone who had access to the plans. The guilty party wasn't to be found at his offices, but by the time Randolph Maxwell IV realized who really sold him out, Mark's plane was at cruising altitude.

#####

The three young men celebrated on a beach in Sitges, Spain. Mark popped the cork on bottle of champagne. "Anyone remember to bring glasses?" he asked, holding up the bottle.

"We don't need glasses," Chad said, stretching his naked body on a blanket spread out on the sand.

"I'll just drink it out of your ass," Mario said, pinching one of Chad's nipples.

Mark chuckled. Standing over Chad and Mario, he held the bottle up in the air and turned it upside down, the cold champagne splashing onto his chest and raining down on Chad and Mario.

They all burst out laughing. They were rich. They were free. And now they were horny.

The Author

JONATHAN ASCHE is the author of the erotic novels *Mindjacker* and *Moneyshots*, both published by STARbooks Press. His short stories have appeared in a variety of gay magazines, including *In Touch for Men*, *Mandate*, *Torso*, *Men*, *Inches*, *Playguy* and *Honcho*; and in the erotic anthologies *Friction 3*, *Three the Hard Way*, *Manhandled*, *Buttmen 2* and *3*, *Best Gay Erotica 2004, 2005, 2007* and *2011*, *Hot Gay Erotica*, *His Underwear*, *Rough Trade* and *Muscle Men*. Asche lives in Atlanta, Georgia, with his husband, Tomé.